1978

D1590867

Peace,

B. P. Reiter

# The Saturday Night Knife & Gun Club

J. B. Lippincott Company
Philadelphia and New York

# The Saturday Night Knife & Gun Club

B. P. Reiter, M.D.

*This book is a work of fiction,
and any resemblance
between the characters and real persons,
living or dead, is coincidental.
The institutions, as well, do not exist.*

U.S. Library of Congress Cataloging in Publication Data

Reiter, B      P        birth date
    The Saturday night knife & gun club.
    I.  Title.
PZ4.R379Sat  [PS3568.E525]      813'.5'4      76-51437
ISBN-0-397-01141-5

for my parents, Sylvia and Max

"Interns, Residents and Fellows comprise the House Staff of a hospital. The members of the House Staff have obligated themselves by contract to assist in providing professional care for the indigent sick of New York City. In return they receive education and experience."

—*General Rules Governing House Staff*

# The Saturday Night Knife & Gun Club

# The E.R.

GYPSY WAS SITTING on the edge of his bed, sucking on his water pipe in the dark. He had his headphones on and he was lost in the Grateful Dead. Some soft knocking began, which he didn't hear at all. The knocking got a little louder. After a while Gypsy lifted the earphones off his head and squinted at the door. His eyes were red.

"Who's there?" he croaked.

The knocking stopped for a moment and then started again, still not very loud, but rapid and urgent.

"Ah, shit," Gypsy said. He dropped his earphones onto the bed and turned on a light. Then he picked his way across the room and opened the door. There was a short, wide cop standing right in front of it, wearing a blue helmet with a plastic visor and a black bulletproof vest. He was holding a shotgun.

"I don't want to scare you," the cop said, "but we'd like to look around your apartment."

Gypsy stared at the shotgun. "Absolutely, man. Come right in."

The short cop with the cannon marched into the apartment, followed by five or six other policemen who had been standing behind him in the little hallway. Gypsy's apartment was stuffed with laundry, guitars, amplifiers, and a lot of cardboard boxes filled with things like his dishes. There was no room for a half-dozen policemen, and somebody knocked over the water pipe. "Heh, heh," Gypsy said, stamping ineffectually on the cinders, "water pipe." He

[11]

was trying to remember the name of his father's lawyer.

Nobody was paying any attention to him. One of the cops was peering out the window. The short one with the bullet-proof vest had put the shotgun down next to Gypsy's electric guitar, and he was scribbling on a little pad.

Gypsy wondered if there was something new in his dope.

"Is the apartment underneath you laid out the same as yours?" the cop with the vest on asked him.

"What?" Gypsy said. "Uh, yeah. I guess."

The cop flipped down his visor, picked up the shotgun, and marched back out into the hall. The rest of the policemen had clustered themselves in front of the window. "Can we get out on the fire escape through here?" one of them asked.

"Oh, sure. Let me unlock the gate." Gypsy had installed a steel gate over the window right after his TV was stolen. He had also replaced the television set, and chained the new TV to the bed—his bed was too big to fit either through the window or into the elevator. There was a combination lock on the gate, and Gypsy was too stoned to work the combination.

"Jesus," Gypsy said to himself. He dragged a big card-board box over to the window and hoisted himself up on it. From the top of the box he had a better look at the lock, and this time he managed to open it. He swung the gate out of the way and raised the window. By then the cops had become disgusted and gone up to the roof to climb down from there. A couple of them, with unlit flashlights, were crawling around on the fire escape.

"Uh," Gypsy said, "I got the window open. What's going on?"

One of the policemen was trying to maneuver another shotgun down the narrow metal steps. His partner had a walkie-talkie. "Hello?" he said into it. "Hello? Is anybody there?"

[12]

Gypsy stared at him. "Don't you have a code or something?" he asked dubiously.

"Hello, hello," the cop repeated, shaking the walkie-talkie. "Is anybody there or not?"

"Augie, for Christ's sake!" the one with the shotgun hissed from below. "Shut up before he hears you."

"Fuck," Augie swore. "This goddam machine won't work." He looked at Gypsy. "Go tell the officers in the hall not to shoot. Tell them there's two officers out here on the fire escape."

"Sure," Gypsy said. "What's going on?"

"Some idiot's trying to murder the lady downstairs. Didn't you hear anything?"

"Well, no. Actually, I was kind of busy. How do you know she's getting murdered?"

"He let her call her psychiatrist."

"Oh," Gypsy said. He climbed down from the cardboard box, padded over to the door, and pulled it open. He looked outside. There were even more cops in the hall now, and a row of them were crouching along the stairs with their pistols drawn. They were all gazing intently downstairs.

"Excuse me," Gypsy said, "but there's two policemen out on the fire escape and they said not to shoot because they're out there."

"We know, we know." A cop at the top of the stairs waved his pistol at Gypsy. "Get back in your apartment if there's any shooting." Gypsy retreated back inside. He walked across the room to the window and clambered up onto the box again. He stuck his head out, slowly. "What's happening?" he whispered.

"Shut up," the cop with the shotgun ordered. "Get away from the window if there's any shooting."

"Oh, boy," Gypsy said to himself and climbed off the box. He went and stood in the center of the room for a minute, looking back and forth from the door to the window. He

[13]

lived in a one-room apartment. "Shooting?" he said out loud. "Holy shit." He sat down on the edge of his bed. Then he started thinking about people setting off shotguns one floor underneath his ass. In an old wooden building. "Fuck this," he said and got up. He walked into the bathroom, took a pint bottle of sloe gin out of the medicine cabinet, and sat down in the cast-iron bathtub. He was a coward.

The shower had a small leak. He sat there and watched the water drip onto his shoes. Suddenly there was a lot of shouting. "Put your hands on your head, put your hands on your head! Get out in the open!"

"Don't shoot! I got no gun. Don't shoot!"

"Don't shoot is right," Gypsy muttered; "the floor is too thin." There was a lot more shouting, from downstairs, from out in the hall, from everywhere. Then it grew quiet. Gypsy stepped out of the bathtub and peered through the bathroom doorway. The cop named Augie was crawling in off the fire escape. "It's okay, we got him."

"Congratulations," Gypsy said, looking around cautiously for more people with guns. "Is he crazy or something?" The policeman was staring at Gypsy's feet. "Hey," the cop said suddenly, "you know your shoes are all wet?"

The one with the shotgun lowered himself in through the window. "We got him," he announced also. "He slit her throat."

"Oh, my God," Gypsy exclaimed.

Gypsy was about six foot one. He had a tremendous moustache, blond hair down to his shoulders, a crumbling 1961 Fiat, and a wonderful old motorcycle. He was a lapsed Jew who liked medicine, rock and roll, girls, and dope. He had returned to New York only the day before, after sitting on a beach in Samoa for seven weeks. Before that, he had been sitting in medical school for four years. He was anxious to begin his internship, although he had no fantasies about saving humanity, or stamping out disease, or any crap like that. It had just always seemed to him that there were very few jobs around that meant anything. If all the advertising men in the world disappeared one day, nobody's life would be any worse. How important really, Gypsy had asked himself, was the guy who invented feminine-hygiene spray? Or some divorce lawyer? Or the mayor of Pittsburgh? Medicine seemed important, and worthwhile. It seemed to be a profession that might actually make a difference in someone's life besides his own. And rock and roll, of course, was out, because he was tone-deaf. Gypsy had not been much of a medical student. His medical school had been filled with compulsive overachievers from some of the best colleges in the country, and Gypsy had been an underachiever at one of the worst colleges in the country. But he had a good heart, he liked people, and everybody said he had tremendous potential. He wasn't so sure about his potential, but he was certain that he was going to be much better at taking care of patients than he'd been at memorizing eighteen-hundred-page medical textbooks. Gypsy had hated medical school, and immediately after his farcical graduation in May he left for the West Coast, and from there, he'd split to Samoa. His new Chief of Medicine had decreed that he would start his internship on July first with the only three weeks of vacation that he was going to get all year, so Gypsy had spent the past two months bumming around the islands. Except for the bizarre timing of his vacation, the year looked very exciting: a little more than two months in the Emergency Room, followed by a series of three-month rotations on the private service, the Intensive Care Unit, and then, finally, the wards.

\*      \*      \*

[15]

It was now late July, he was back in New York, and he was ready, at last, to begin taking care of people. Gypsy grabbed his black bag, which was one-third filled with medical stuff and two-thirds with spark plugs for his motorcycle, and ran downstairs.

The hallway and the stairs were almost free of policemen, because most of them had jammed themselves into the apartment beneath Gypsy's.

"Excuse me, please," Gypsy said, trying to get in. "I'm a doctor." The police, of whom there were about twenty in the one-room apartment, made way for the doctor.

Gypsy's downstairs neighbor, a nice and inoffensive lady, was stretched out on the floor partly covered with a raincoat. She was, as far as Gypsy could tell, otherwise naked. She was also cut up some around the face and head. Her throat was certainly not slit, but she was quite hysterical. "Now, miss," a young-looking cop was saying to her in an amateur D.A. tone of voice, "did the alleged perpetrator attempt to assault you?"

"You stupid damn people!" she hollered. "Why didn't you get here before? He wanted to rape me! He tried to kill me—he tried to murder me!"

"Excuse me," Gypsy interrupted, kneeling down next to her, "can I see if you're all right?"

She looked up at him. "Get away from me!" she yelled. "Didn't you hear me screaming? He was murdering me! Didn't you hear me? Didn't you hear me?"

"Well, you see, I had my headphones on," Gypsy explained apologetically. "I really couldn't hear too much. Uh, look, I just want to be sure you're okay . . ."

"Get away from me!" she shrieked again, banging her fists on the floor. "Get away from me, get away from me!"

Gypsy sighed and stood up. "Why don't you take her to the hospital," he suggested. "She's not bleeding much or anything."

[16]

"We already sent for an ambulance," another one of the policemen said. "It'll be here any minute. What's your address, doc?"

"I live right here. I mean, upstairs. Why?"

"We're gonna have to subpoena you, probably. You're a witness."

"Oh," Gypsy said. "To what? She won't let me touch her."

"Don't worry, doc. It ain't gonna come to court for three years anyway."

"Oh. Well, whatever you say," Gypsy agreed amiably.

There was a commotion at the door, and then several of the policemen were shoved aside by a little Spanish guy lugging a huge stretcher. He was wearing a dirty white uniform with "Manhattan County Hosp." stitched on the arm. He pushed his way across the tiny apartment, dragging the stretcher, and stopped when he saw Gypsy's neighbor lying on the floor under the raincoat. "Out of the way," he shouted, "heart attack!"

"Nah," the D.A. cop corrected him, "she was allegedly assaulted."

"Heart attack, it's a heart attack all right," the ambulance driver argued. "I know what I'm talking about."

"Excuse me," Gypsy said, "she hasn't had a heart attack. She just needs to have her lacerations sutured." The ambulance driver glared at him. "Who the hell are you?"

"He's a doctor," the cop pointed out. Gypsy smiled proudly. "That's right. I'm going to start my internship tomorrow." He gestured at the insignia on the man's uniform. "At your hospital, as a matter of fact."

"Oh, yeah?" the ambulance driver said to him. "Hot shit." He turned, less solicitous now, to Gypsy's neighbor. "Get up on the stretcher, lady. You gotta go to the hospital."

She looked over at him. "I want to see my psychiatrist."

[17]

"Yeah, sure. You can call him up when you get to the hospital. Now get on the stretcher, will you?"

"I want my psychiatrist!" she screamed. "I want my psychiatrist!"

The little ambulance driver jumped. "Hey, lady, take it easy. We got plenty of psychiatrists at the hospital."

"Get away from me, all of you! I want to see my psychiatrist!"

"Be reasonable, miss," the D.A. cop said, bending over her, "we're attempting to assist you." She grabbed his nightstick from his belt and flung it at the ambulance driver, who leaped to one side, cursing. The nightstick sailed across the room and crashed into the television set, shattering the picture tube.

"Stop it, you nut-fuck!" the ambulance driver shouted at her.

"Excuse me, please," Gypsy said. He picked up his black bag and left. When he got back upstairs to his own apartment, he found the cop with the shotgun poking around the water pipe. "Hey," the cop asked when Gypsy walked in, "what do you smoke in this?"

"You were wrong; he didn't cut her throat," Gypsy said. "I smoke dope in that."

"Yeah? What kind of answer is that?"

The other cop took the first one by the elbow. "Gus," he said, "what do you care? Let's go."

"Wait a minute, for Christ's sake," the one with the shotgun insisted. "I think he was smoking drugs. We can bust him!"

"Gus, stop it," Augie told his partner. "I don't see any dope around here, and we don't have a warrant, and besides, the doc did us a big favor when we were climbing down the fire escape. What do you want from him?" He led Gus toward the door.

[18]

"Ahh, you're lousing up a great chance," Gus complained unhappily on the way out. "I think there's drugs all over the place."

Eight hours later, Gypsy picked up his medical-school-issue black bag again and drove to his new hospital on Ninety-second Street for the first time. Once he got there, the guard refused to let him into the hospital parking lot because he had no parking sticker. He spent the next thirty minutes driving up Third Avenue and down Lexington Avenue looking for a place to park. He finally gave up and parked the car next to the Emergency Room entrance, way over at the side, where he wasn't blocking anything. Gypsy left a big sign on his windshield:

DOCTOR WORKING
IN
EMERGENCY ROOM

Then he took a deep breath, walked through the wide doors of the Emergency Room, and started being an intern.

As soon as he stepped inside he was engulfed. Everywhere he looked, there were people arguing, shouting, bleeding, and throwing up. "Jesus," Gypsy said, and started to pick his way through the carnage. He became hopelessly lost almost immediately.

The Emergency Room was not merely a room; it was the entire ground floor of the hospital—a labyrinth of examining and treatment rooms, all interconnected by gaping doors that had been built wide enough to push stretchers and litters through. The walls were lined from one end to the other with a huge array of equipment, dressings, medicines, and intravenous bottles, reflecting whatever special type of disaster each particular area of the E.R. was used for.

Gypsy clutched his black bag and tried to figure out what

[19]

he was supposed to do. He walked into several of the rooms to offer to go to work, and each time he wound up directly in somebody's way and got yelled at. Finally he found a room that had a whole crowd of people in white uniforms congregated in it, and he imagined that someone there must know where he was supposed to go. He walked up to the cluster of people and tapped one of them on the shoulder. "Excuse me, I think I'm looking for Dr. Allen Gallberg."

"Hold him!" the doctor yelled. "Hold the son of a bitch!"

"Pardon me?" Gypsy said.

At that moment the body that was at the center of the crowd got a leg free, and with one tremendous kick swept two aides and a nurse all the way across the treatment room. "I kill you!" the patient screamed. "I kill all you fucking doctors!" He had a long, plastic naso-gastric tube hanging out of his nose, and he was prodigiously drunk.

"Jesus," Gypsy said again.

This time the doctor he was standing behind noticed him. "Don't just stand there, you asshole," the doctor shouted at him. "Grab his goddam leg!"

Gypsy dropped his black bag and hastily took hold of the patient's leg. He was still on the outer fringe of the circle of people surrounding the patient and he couldn't see what was happening. There was the sound of an I.V. bottle smashing, and then another upheaval radiated outward from the region of the patient. The doctor in front of Gypsy yelped in pain and went down. Once this doctor hit the floor, there was nothing between Gypsy and the patient except the patient's leg. The drunk suddenly jerked his leg free again and kicked Gypsy really hard right in the head. Gypsy went down.

The injured doctor crawled past Gypsy and over to the door. "Security!" the doctor yelled into the corridor. "Security! Help, security!" Gypsy got to his feet, feeling very

[20]

dizzy, and picked up his black bag. He stepped over the fallen physician, who grabbed him by the pants and said, "Christ, get the fucking guards, will you?"

"Okay," Gypsy said, holding his head. He walked down to the far end of the hallway where there was a knot of big hospital guards arguing with each other.

"Ahh, fuck you, man," one of them was saying. "I went last time. You go."

"Stick it up your ass."

"Excuse me," Gypsy said. "There's some trouble in one of the treatment rooms back there. I think they need the security guards."

"Yeah, sure, doc," one of the other guards answered. "In a minute." He turned back to the argument.

"You go get the fucking coffee," the first guard said. "Why should I get the coffee every goddam time?"

"What the fuck do you want?" the second one responded. "You know I got a bad back."

"Bad back?" the first one yelled. "All you gotta do is carry five lousy cups of coffee! You lazy fuck!"

Gypsy's head was swimming. He needed air, and he walked out of the E.R. through a set of big swinging doors. The doors opened onto a concrete courtyard that served as docking space for the hospital's ambulances. Gypsy waited in the courtyard until his head began to clear a little. While he was standing there, a steady procession of ambulances pulled up: every couple of minutes another casualty was trundled off an ambulance and into the Emergency Room. It was like the Berlin Airlift.

After ten minutes Gypsy's ears were still ringing, but he walked back into the E.R. to try again. He wandered down another corridor, jammed with people lying on stretchers and propped up in wheelchairs, and picked out what he thought was a likely-looking room. It turned out to be a

[21]

treatment room also. There was a bum dressed in a moldering collection of rags lying on the treatment table, and a nurse and an aide were peeling off the newspapers wrapped around his feet. The bum's feet, once they were uncovered, were revealed to be a dull red instead of the caked-dirt black Gypsy had expected. It took him a second to realize what he was looking at—raw red flesh. The skin had come off with the newspapers.

Gypsy swallowed a couple of times. The smell hit him, and he thought there was a fair chance he was going to throw up. He backed out of the treatment room and escaped to the ambulance dock again. He did some more deep breathing. Then he returned to the Emergency Room for another attempt.

He stopped a nurse who was racing by and asked for Dr. Gallberg's office.

"Who?"

"Dr. Gallberg," Gypsy repeated. "Dr. Allen Gallberg."

"Oh, the schmuck." She pointed him down a different corridor. This time he found a door with a little sign that read, "A. Gallberg, M.D.—Acting Director, Emergency Room." He went inside.

There were two other guys already sitting there waiting, each one with a black bag like Gypsy's in his lap. One of them, who had freckles and a red crew cut, was very healthy-looking and introduced himself as Otto Dlugeffesh. He said it was easier just to call him Kid Otto. The other one said his name was Vittorio Mazzoli. He looked pretty miserable already. Kid Otto launched eagerly back into a speech he was making about how important it was to bring your whites into the laundry room on the right day, or you'd never see them again. Gypsy smiled and tuned him out. He wasn't very interested in his uniforms. He began speculating to himself about how soon he'd be able to go looking for nurses.

An exceptional burst of shrieking from out beyond the door brought Gypsy's thoughts back. Kid Otto was still talking: "Besides, I'm going to like working here. I drove in at five-thirty this morning and I jogged around the reservoir in the Park." Very clever, Gypsy thought. You keep on doing that and they'll drag you in here with a knife sticking out of your ear.

Vittorio shook his head sadly. "I don't think my dog likes this apartment I got very much. I lived in a house with a nice backyard in medical school. He's a big dog, you know?"

Gypsy was about to ask him what kind of dog he had when a bum wearing an eye-patch walked into the room, looked the three of them over contemptuously, and flipped the wet stump of a cigarette onto the floor.

"I'm Dr. Gallberg," the bum announced.

Kid Otto chuckled nervously and folded his big hands over his black bag. The black bag almost disappeared from view. Gypsy looked in Vittorio's direction. Vittorio shrugged.

"Okay," the decrepit-looking doctor told them, "listen. I'm just as unhappy having you guys working here as you are to be here. More unhappy. The thing is, you're going to work so goddam hard you won't even know what day it is. You'll be through with this rotation before you know what hit you. You're getting off easy, anyway—you're supposed to be here for three months. Another thing, I don't want to hear about any trouble between you and the nurses. Whatever it is, you're wrong and they're right. You understand that? We can get new interns a lot easier than we can get goddam nurses.

"Oh, yeah, one more thing. These bums are the scum of the earth. Watch yourselves. One of you guys gets stabbed or something, the other two have to cover his shifts."

The doctor-bum left. "This isn't a very friendly place," Vittorio said.

[23]

"I'd like to meet that guy in the parking lot some night," was Kid Otto's contribution. "I'll break his ass." All in all, it was not exactly what Gypsy had expected.

Gallberg reappeared in the doorway. "Well? What the hell are you waiting for?" The three of them scrambled to their feet and followed Gallberg out into the corridor. He deposited each of them in a separate treatment room. Gypsy sat down at the small desk near the door of his room and opened up his black bag. A few spark plugs fell out, bounced onto the floor, and then rolled under the desk. Gypsy got down on his hands and knees and crawled under the desk after them. Dr. Gallberg walked by again in the corridor, stopped, and looked into Gypsy's room.

"Are you still on vacation or something?" he said to Gypsy. "What the hell are you doing in there?"

"No," Gypsy answered, "I'm..."

Gallberg was gone. He came back a moment later, stopped in the doorway once more, and glanced impatiently behind him. "Hurry up, will you—move your ass, pops." An old man hobbled up to the door and stood there wheezing. "In here," Gallberg said. "This guy'll take care of you." He walked off looking angry.

"Come in, sir," Gypsy said, getting up off the floor. "Please sit down." The old man walked slowly into the room and lowered himself painfully into the little metal folding chair in front of the desk.

Gypsy smiled at him. "Yes, sir, what seems to be the trouble?"

"Bad heart. Legs is all swole up."

Gypsy began to take a medical history from the patient. How long had he had heart trouble? Did his parents have any heart diseases? His grandparents? Did he have high blood pressure? Diabetes? Had he ever had a heart attack? A stroke? Fainting spells? Had he had rheumatic fever when he was a child? Scarlet fever? Had his mother had German measles? Were his parents alive? What did they die of? Did he know what his grandparents died of? Did he have any brothers and sisters? Did any of them have heart trouble? Diabetes? High blood pressure? Did he get short of breath? When? How short of breath? How many flights of stairs could he climb? How many blocks could he walk? How many blocks could he walk on a windy day? How many pillows did he need to sleep on? Did he ever wake up in the middle of the night short of breath? Did he get pains in his chest? And on and on.

The old man was describing the second heart attack that his fifth brother, who lived in Georgia, had had when Gallberg stalked into the room again.

"What the hell are you doing now?"

"Taking a history," Gypsy said, with a startled expression.

"Jesus Christ! Come out here with me a minute, God damn it." He turned on his heel and walked out of the room. Gypsy excused himself and walked out after him. Gallberg was already down at the end of the corridor, standing in the doorway to the waiting room with his hands on his hips. Gypsy caught up to him.

"Okay, look at this." Gallberg gestured at the waiting room with an abrupt nod of his head.

Gypsy looked. The waiting room was packed to the bursting point with patients. There were people lined up on benches, people sitting in wheelchairs, people strapped onto stretchers, and people milling around in front of the registration desk. There were people sitting on the floor. There were people crying, sleeping, throwing up, and nodding out. There were a lot of bloody heads and bloody shirts.

"Look at that," Gallberg repeated. "And these aren't even the sick ones. These are the ones who won't die if they have to wait five hours. Now what the hell were you doing back there?"

"I was taking a history," Gypsy explained once more. "Do

you have time to take histories and do physical exams around here?"

"A history? You were in there three-quarters of an hour with that old putz! Listen, two minutes for a history, two minutes for your physical, and that's it. Most of these bastards got nothing wrong with them anyway."

"Uh-uh," Gypsy said, shaking his head. "I can't do a good history and physical exam in four minutes."

"Tough," Gallberg said. "Where do you think you are, the Mayo Clinic? This is a city hospital emergency room. We're the receiving hospital for everything in Manhattan east of Fifth Avenue. Do you know how many goddam people that is?"

Gypsy shook his head again. "That's no excuse for bad medicine."

"Bad medicine? You snotnose, we do the best medicine in New York. And we do it fast. And we don't have time to fuck around with people who got no business being here. This is an emergency room!" He terminated the lesson and was back in the treatment room in a few quick strides. This time Gypsy kept up with him.

"All right, grandpop, what's wrong with you?" Gallberg said brusquely to the old man, who was still sitting in front of the desk.

"I got a bad heart. My legs is all swole up again."

"You come to clinic?" The old man nodded. "You take digitalis?" He nodded again. "Water pills?"

"Can't. I run out of water pills two weeks ago."

Gallberg scribbled something on a prescription and ripped it off the pad. "Here. Come back to Cardiology Clinic next week. Make an appointment out front." He stuck his head into the corridor. "Next patient," he yelled, and left.

"Okay," Gypsy said to himself, "I can do it his way and

[26]

practice good medicine, too." A tall, smooth-looking guy, unmistakably a pimp in his lavender satin jumpsuit and big gaudy hat, sauntered through the door and stopped.

"Come in," Gypsy said politely. "Have a seat, please."

"Shit," the patient said, standing there. "You the slowest doctor in the world. How come it take so long to get waited on here?"

"I'm sorry," Gypsy apologized. "I had some trouble with the last patient. Can I help you?"

"You bet your ass. You can give me some methadone."

"Oh." Gypsy was taken a little aback. "Well, I can't do that. I mean, we don't have any methadone in the Emergency Room. I think you have to go to the Detoxification Program upstairs for that. But I can find out for you."

"Forget it, man. They know me in the Program. Just let me have some Demerol, huh?"

"Demerol? What do you need Demerol for?"

The pimp walked casually over to Gypsy's desk and sat down in front of it. Then he opened the zipper on his jumpsuit and took out a big black .45 automatic. He held the gun between his legs and pointed it up at Gypsy's head. "You going to give me the Demerol?" he asked. "Or should I blow your fucking head off?"

"I'm going to give you the Demerol," Gypsy said, and raised his arms high in the air.

"Put your fucking hands down," the pimp snarled at him. "Be cool, man!"

Gypsy was cool. He unlocked the medication cabinet and found a bottle of Demerol. He unscrewed the cap. "How many do you want?"

The pimp rolled his eyes in disbelief and grabbed the bottle of little white tablets away from him. "How many I want?" he parodied. "Two or three pills be fine, man." He stuck the gun back in his jumpsuit, shaking his head wonderingly. "How many I want! Where you been all your life, boy?" He headed for the door, and then stopped halfway out into the hallway. "Don't you say nothing about this, you hear? Or I'll come back and kill you, man!" Gypsy nodded.

The pimp turned and ran. Gypsy immediately sprinted out into the hallway, and spotted him running for the exit. He raced after him.

"Holdup!" he yelled. "Holdup! Holdup! Drug addict!" Yelling "drug addict" in the Emergency Room was like yelling "faggot" at the Empire Baths, but Gypsy didn't know that yet. A couple of the hospital guards, from a careful distance, watched the thief run through the waiting room and tear out the door. They didn't move. Gypsy chased along behind him, yelling "Come on, come on, holdup!" as he passed the guards. They looked at him like he was crazy.

Out in the street, he found a police car double-parked, with two policemen sitting in it drinking coffee. "Hey," Gypsy asked breathlessly, "did you see a guy run out of here with a gun? He just stole a bottle of Demerol!"

The cop on the driver's side took a swallow of his coffee. "Say, doc, can my wife get a dose from me?" he asked. "You know, if I been fooling around?"

"What?" Gypsy said. "Did you see where that guy went?"

"What guy?"

"The pimp in the fancy suit," Gypsy said excitedly. "He just held me up with a gun in the Emergency Room! He came out right through this door!"

"I didn't see nothing." The cop glanced at his partner. "You see anybody?" The other cop frowned and shook his head, and went on drinking his coffee. There was no sign of the pimp on the street. Gypsy muttered something about civil servants and walked back into the E.R. He met Dr. Gallberg coming the other way.

[28]

"I just heard you run down the hall screaming," Gallberg said, looking at him oddly. "What's the matter with you?"

"Somebody held me up." Gypsy no longer sounded very surprised. "He took a whole bottle of Demerol. I was chasing him."

"Well, that was very smart," Gallberg said sarcastically. "Do you want to get killed?"

"But he took the whole goddam bottle. There's four, five hundred tabs of Demerol in that bottle."

"So?" Gallberg said with a nasty look. "What do you care? He'll be here again in a couple of hours, when he overdoses. You can ask him for the pills back. Anyway, you got patients waiting for you. What are you wasting time out in the street for?"

Gypsy returned to the treatment room. There was a little girl, maybe twelve years old, sitting in the chair in front of his desk. "Hello," he said, sitting down himself. "I'm sorry I kept you waiting. What seems to be the problem?"

"I need some birth-control pills," the little girl said.

"Birth-control pills? For who?"

"For my grandmother," she said. "Who do you think, for who? For me."

"For you? What for?"

The girl stared at him like he was an idiot. "What do you think for? So I won't get knocked up, for God's sake!"

"You mean you're, uh, sexually active?" Gypsy asked the child.

"How old are you?" she said to him.

"Never mind. I don't think I can give you birth-control pills."

"Why the fuck not? I been using my sister's for two years."

"That's your sister's fault, not mine. Look, you shouldn't be using pills at all. You're going to mess your body up."

[29]

"Oh, no?" she said. "You want me to get pregnant and get an abortion someplace and die?"

Gypsy thought about that. "I don't know what to do with you," he said honestly.

"Just give me the fucking pills."

"Look, birth-control pills can be very dangerous. I can't just write out a prescription. You have to have an examination first and everything."

"You mean a pelvic?" she asked. "Sure." She stood up, unbuttoned her jeans, and took them off and dropped them on the desk. Then she walked across the room to the examining table. She took her panties off, climbed up on the table, and without being told put her feet in the stirrups and spread her legs. "Let's go," she told him.

Gypsy walked over and pulled the curtains closed around the examining table. He started to hunt in the drawers for a pediatric speculum. The best he could do was a disposable plastic speculum that at least wouldn't be as cold as the metal ones. "Just relax," he instructed, putting on gloves and inserting the device.

"I am relaxed," she replied from the other end of the table. "What's your name?"

"Gypsy." He had been worried for nothing; she had a hole like a tunnel. She also had a yellow-green discharge, vaginitis, and she smelled.

"Hey, Gypsy," she said, smiling at him, "you're not that bad-looking. How would you like to stick it in?"

"You're too relaxed," Gypsy mumbled, busying himself taking cervical swabs for gonorrhea smears. He finished that, did a digital exam, and threw his gloves away. He started writing out labels for the smears. The girl climbed down from the table and put her clothes back on.

"Okay," Gypsy said, handing her a pile of forms, "you have to take these upstairs and get some blood tests."

[30]

"What about my pills?"

"I'm not going to give you any pills yet. You've got an infection. But I'm going to send you to the clinic, and they'll decide what to give you so you don't get pregnant. Okay?"

She smiled at him again. Gypsy couldn't figure out which clinic to send her to. He went looking for advice, and found Allen Gallberg arguing over the telephone with somebody at a nursing home about a patient they wanted to transfer.

Gypsy excused himself and interrupted. "Dr. Gallberg, I've got a little girl with a hot cervix back there who wants birth-control pills. Should I send her to G.Y.N. Clinic or to Pediatric Clinic?"

Gallberg looked up. "What the hell do I care where you send her?" he said without bothering to cover the receiver. "I don't give a shit if you take her home with you. And you'd better start doing some goddam work." He returned to his argument.

Gypsy went back to the treatment room. He decided to send the girl to both clinics. She collected all the forms, appointment slips, and prescriptions he made out for her, and grinned at him before she left. "Thanks, doc. You know, you're all right. Why don't you give me a call sometime?"

"I'll think about it," Gypsy said. "Take care."

He went on working. Around the middle of the day he tried to get away for lunch. He made a mistake, though, and walked through the waiting room on the way out. He found so many patients collected there, and they looked at his white coat so accusingly, that he turned around and went back to work instead.

Gypsy tried hard. He accelerated his pace, trying to keep up with the pressure from the waiting room, but it didn't do him very much good. Every time he stole a look at the packed waiting area, there seemed to be more people lined up than the time before. It was amazing; he couldn't understand

[31]

where they were all coming from. He saw an absolutely un-broken stream of patients: people with strokes, people with heart attacks, people with colds, and people with urinary-tract infections. People with pneumonia. People with syph-ilis, people with gonorrhea, people with crabs and with lice and with every other exotic kind of wildlife living on them. And he saw a lot of people who were merely old, or lonely, or just crazy, and only wanted somebody to talk to.

By suppertime Gypsy was starving. He decided at about seven o'clock that he had to go and feed himself or he wasn't going to be able to last through the night. He finished with the patient he was seeing and left through the ambulance entrance, feeling guilty, but much too hungry to care about it. Just as he got outside, three ambulances pulled in all at once, and the crews started unloading the results of a gi-gantic traffic accident on the F.D.R. Drive. Gypsy returned to the Emergency Room. He passed Vittorio in the corridor; his fellow intern was coming back from eating dinner. Vic looked grim nonetheless. "Well, how are you doing?" Vit-torio asked.

"Holy shit," Gypsy said. "Holy shit."

Gypsy continued working, on through the evening. Later at night he started seeing the transfers show up—the prod-ucts of the nursing homes. Wretched human beings on stretchers with notes pinned to their clothes, which said things like "Eighty-five-year-old female. Found disoriented and dehydrated. Please admit."

In the middle of the night, when he had not had anything to eat in almost twenty hours, Gypsy got dizzy again. He left his treatment room and walked outside to the ambu-lance dock. The activity was slower out there by then, and a couple of the drivers were standing around in the court-yard, talking. Gypsy sat down on the ground with his back against the building, and put his head between his knees.

[32]

Someone came over to him. "Hey, doc, you okay?"

Gypsy looked up. "Yeah," he said, "sure. I just didn't have any time to eat all day. We're awful busy in there."

The man who was talking to him, a very big ambulance driver, shook his head. "Some of you doctors got no sense. How you going to help anybody if you can't even stand up? You got to take care of yourself, man. Nobody else going to—not around here."

Gypsy nodded ruefully. "You're right; I know. There's just so much fucking work to do; I can't keep up with everything."

"What you worried for, man? You ain't supposed to run the whole place by yourself. You think those junkies gonna give a shit that you breaking your ass for them? Wait a minute." He disappeared briefly into one of the ambulances, and came back with a container of coffee and a half-eaten piece of fried chicken. "Here," he offered.

"Oh, thanks, no," Gypsy protested. "I can't take your dinner."

"Dinner, shit." The ambulance driver laughed. "That's just a little dessert, man. Go on. You want to starve?"

Gypsy devoured the chicken. "Wow," he said when he was done, wiping his mouth with the back of his hand, "you saved my life. My name's Gypsy."

"Jim MacKinley. Glad to know you, man."

Gypsy returned once again to the struggle. Somehow he made it through his first shift in the Emergency Room, although one of the patients did steal his hundred-and-fifty-dollar ophthalmoscope set out of his black bag. Eventually somebody told him he could go home. He was afraid to guess what time it was, but the sun was coming up when he got outside. His car was gone.

Gypsy walked over to the guard standing at the gate. "Ex-

[33]

cuse me," he said, "but I think my car is stolen. An old black Fiat—it was parked over there near the E.R."

"Nope," the guard informed him, "wasn't stolen. The cops towed it away."

"Towed it away? What are you talking about? I was right inside the Emergency Room! Didn't they see my sign? Didn't you say anything?"

"I don't know nothing about no sign," the guard said dourly.

Gypsy sighed and went back into the hospital to look for a pay phone. Five or six dimes later he got the right division of the police department, and some functional illiterate told him yes, they had his Fiat over at the police piers on the West Side.

He took one bus crosstown, another bus downtown, and found the appropriate pier. The cop who was in charge there wanted seventy-five dollars before he would give him his car back. "Seventy-five dollars?" Gypsy said. "I don't have seventy-five dollars on me."

"We'll take a check," the cop told him.

"Look, I came over here right from the hospital. I've been working in the Emergency Room since yesterday morning, and I don't have any checks with me."

"Too bad, doc," this servant of the people said to him.

Gypsy had about twelve hours left before he was due back at the Emergency Room, and what he wanted to do was go to sleep. "I tell you what," he decided out loud, "you keep the car. It's not worth seventy-five dollars."

"Cost you five dollars a day for storage if you don't pick it up now, doc," the cop let him know happily.

They had him.

"Ah, fuck you," Gypsy said under his breath, losing graciously.

"What?"

"Thank you. I said thank you, officer."

Gypsy took two buses back to the East Side, got his checkbook, took two more buses back to the West Side, and rescued.his car. He drove home, and went to McDonald's to eat something before he crashed. When his eyes started closing over the hamburgers he walked back to his apartment and fell down on the bed for a few hours.

The telephone woke him up. It was Kid Otto, and the place was mobbed with great cases, and where was he?

Gallberg had not been lying. The Emergency Room was staggeringly busy, and they did work their asses off. The shifts were rotated on some kind of insane schedule, so that sometimes they came to work in the morning, and sometimes they came to work in the middle of the night. There were times when Gypsy truly did not know what day it was. Within half a week he began to feel as if he'd been working there for ten years, and would go on working there forever. The Emergency Room dominated his life. It was his life. But the thing was, in spite of all the hours everybody was putting in, the patients always spent the bulk of their time sitting on their ass and waiting.

One of the reasons the Emergency Room was overburdened was that so many people were using it for casual purposes. It was designed to cope with acute emergencies, but a large number of the people who came strolling in were not emergencies at all. Not in the medical sense. No one minded patients coming in—that's what the Emergency Room was there for. But it took time for the staff to determine who had a cold, who just wanted some more pills, and who was really sick.

A lot of stray people sort of got deposited in the Emergency Room, and no one, ever, was sent home without seeing a doctor. Drunks wandered in off the street, and passed out. So the drunks had to be evaluated too. If they vomited all over the doctor, or woke up long enough to punch the doctor in the mouth, then that just involved a little more time. The police also dragged in their share of people for patching up—people who had gotten damaged somewhat while being taken into custody, say.

Homeless bums made the Emergency Room their home. Frequently. Repeatedly. One such bum was named Angelo. Angelo was a wino, and he was crazy, and periodically he would lie down in the street and wait for someone to call the police. The police would come, look at him, and call an ambulance. The ambulance would come, pick him up, and bring him to the Emergency Room. Gypsy would see Angelo two or three times a week, lying on a stretcher in the corridor with a filthy rag over his face. Angelo always brought his rag with him when he came to the Emergency Room. The first time Gypsy saw him, he removed the rag to look at the patient, and little white lice began to abandon Angelo and make the leap over to Gypsy. Gypsy went home early that day, to disinfect himself.

After a while, Gypsy got to know Angelo; he would walk over to the stretcher and speak to the rag from a respectful distance. "Angelo, this is Gypsy. Do you want to talk to the psychiatrist, Angelo?"

"Yeah, I think I want to talk to the psychiatrist" the answer would come up through the rag. Gypsy would get him deloused and send him off to see the shrink again.

Sometimes enterprising prisoners were brought over in handcuffs, to be X-rayed. The prisoners liked the hospital more than the jail, so they swallowed razor blades wrapped in tape. Then they went to the prison doctor and said, "I'm sick. I swallowed a razor blade." The prison doctor sent them to the Emergency Room, and they got an X-ray. The razor showed up because it was metal, the tape didn't, and

[36]

the prisoners were admitted. Then they had a nice rest in the hospital while everyone waited for them to shit out the razor. Depending on their bowels, they could have quite a long rest.

Some of the time the police came in without any prisoners at all: no broken heads, no razor blades, just embarrassed policemen. They ignored all the waiting patients, cornered some harassed doctor, and then shuffled their feet and said, "Uh, doc."

"Uh, doc," this one said to Gypsy in the middle of a hectic morning, "I need a shot."

Gypsy grinned wickedly. "A shot. Are you sick or something?" More foot-shuffling. More uh's and um's. Finally, "Yeah, I'm sick. I think I need a shot, you know?"

"No," Gypsy said. "What's wrong with you?"

"There's a drip. I got this drip." The policeman looked unhappy.

"A drip. Where? What's dripping?"

"Hey, look, stop this bullshit. You know where the drip is."

"Could be," Gypsy said unsympathetically. "But I ought to be sure, don't you think? Where is your drip? Is your ear dripping?"

"The drip is from my dick," the policeman mumbled.

"Your dick! You have a drip from your dick?"

"Jesus Christ! Not so loud, you schmuck. Are you crazy?" The policeman was looking a little wild, as if his wife was one of the bums who was watching.

"Officer," Gypsy asked, "you're sure about the drip? It isn't your nose that's dripping?"

"My God, I know my nose from my dick."

"I see. Tell me, does it smell bad?"

"Terrible, it smells terrible."

"Does it mess up your underwear?"

[37]

"Yeah, schmuck. I got to keep changing my underpants all day long. What difference does that make?"

"Gypsy. My name is Gypsy. Does it burn when you urinate?"

"What the hell is this, a circus?" The policeman stood up and made a speech. "Jesus Christ, I got the clap. I need a shot of penicillin and I don't want everybody in this goddam place to know about it. Don't you have any real doctors here? Just gimme my lousy shot, will you!"

Gypsy sighed and made a counter-speech. "Listen, smart-ass, what do you know about bacteriology? What do you know about pharmacology? Do you know that treatment for gonorrhea is inadequate treatment for syphilis? Do you know that syphilis can rot your insides for years? Do you know that syphilis can make you blind, and insane, and paralyzed?"

Gypsy filled out some forms. "Look, take these upstairs to the V.D. Clinic, and somebody'll get a urethral smear and a VDRL on you." The policeman flinched. "A what? A urethra what?"

Gypsy smiled again. "A smear. To look at under the microscope. So we can see what kind of germs are living in your penis." The cop glowered at Gypsy as if he didn't know how much to believe anymore. "Does it hurt?" he asked.

"It's terrible," Gypsy assured him. "They take a long wire and heat it up with a Bunsen burner, and then they fish around in your penis with it until they catch something. You'll just have to bite on a bullet and bear it, I guess. You have a bullet, don't you?"

The policeman looked like he was ready to hit Gypsy in the head with his stick. He picked up his forms and walked away, talking to himself about socialized medicine.

The police were great friends of the interns—when they came into the Emergency Room looking for a cure for their drip. Gypsy was not an unkind person; during his first days in the E.R. he always dropped whatever he was doing when a policeman walked through the door, even if the cop just wanted diarrhea pills. But after he worked a few more thirty-six-hour shifts only to come out of the hospital and find that the police had towed away his car again, he realized that the concern was not entirely mutual. Nonetheless, whenever he had to park outside the E.R., he continued leaving the same big sign on his car:

DOCTOR WORKING
IN
EMERGENCY ROOM

It never helped. After he had dragged his ass back over to the tow-away piers on the West Side maybe a half-dozen times, he began to lose his affection for the police. Once they even ruined his transmission and broke off one of his shock absorbers, but they never touched the sign on his windshield. For this entertainment, Gypsy paid seventy-five dollars each time. He learned. "You want diarrhea pills, smiling hypocrite? Wait in line with everyone else who has diarrhea."

Kid Otto came bursting into the examining room Gypsy was using early one afternoon, and started shouting at him. "We're late, we're late," he yelled. "Quick, it's time for lunch!"

Gypsy finished the prescription he was filling out and signed it. He handed it to the patient, and told the man where to go to make a clinic appointment. Kid Otto looked at Gypsy like he was about to pick him up and carry him down to lunch, and Gypsy hurriedly got to his feet. "Okay, okay, I'm coming, man."

Kid Otto loped out of the room and Gypsy trotted after

[39]

him. "Christ, where the hell is Vic?" Kid Otto asked, sounding very exasperated, when Gypsy caught up with him at the end of the corridor.

"I don't know," Gypsy said, laughing. "I haven't seen him for at least ten minutes. You think he's dead?"

"What are you laughing about?" Kid Otto demanded. "This is serious, Gypsy. It's five to one. Do you want to miss lunch?"

"Jesus, it's only food," Gypsy muttered. "They're not giving out blow jobs down there."

"Food is very important. If you don't eat lunch you won't have enough energy to run your body the rest of the day. That's very unhealthy for you."

Gypsy looked at the ceiling. "Who told you that? Did you go to medical school ever, Otto?"

"Where the fuck is Vittorio?" Kid Otto yelled, by way of a reply. Vic came out of the staff men's room. "What are you screaming about?" he said calmly to Kid Otto.

"Where the fuck have you been? Don't you know what time it is? It's almost one o'clock!" Kid Otto spun around without waiting for Vittorio's answer and raced off. Gypsy and Vic followed him, exchanging comic looks, and they all ran down to the house-staff cafeteria in the basement of the hospital. They made it just in time. Right after they received their slop, the kitchen people closed the line. The three of them sat down at a table next to the railing that guarded the serving counter, and examined their food.

Kid Otto looked at his plate. There was a small clump of dried-out tuna fish on it, along with one piece of lettuce and a broken cracker. "This is ridiculous. I'm not going to eat this shit."

"You better eat your lunch," Vittorio said, picking up his piece of lettuce. "We have to be back upstairs soon."

A girl in hospital whites hurried along the railing, looking at her watch, and stopped in front of one of the ladies behind the counter. "I guess I'm too late for lunch, huh?"

The slop-lady was putting tin covers over the serving trays. She didn't even look up.

The girl tried again. "Excuse me," she asked politely, "is it too late to get something to eat, please?"

The slop-lady banged down one of her tin covers. "You doctors never learn, do you?" she said loudly. "You must be pretty stupid or something. It's after one o'clock—we don't serve any food after one o'clock. How many times do we have to tell you that?"

The girl lit a cigarette, coughing a little bit. "I'm sorry," she apologized. "I know I'm late, but it's only a couple of minutes after one. I was admitting yesterday, and I was up all night, and we just got finished with rounds. And I didn't have any time to eat dinner last night. Couldn't I get a little tuna fish?"

"We don't serve nothing after one o'clock."

The girl looked resigned. "All right, all right. Just let me have a cup of coffee, please."

"No coffee," the slop-lady intoned. "No coffee, no tuna fish, no nothing after one o'clock. Don't you hear okay?"

The girl had a brief coughing fit. When she recovered, she sounded incredulous. "For Christ's sake, you mean you can't even give me a cup of coffee?"

"There's no more coffee left," the slop-lady said to her. "Now leave me alone, will you? We're closed."

Gypsy shook his head. "What's the matter with these people? Are we the bad guys or something?"

"I don't think we should let them get away with that shit," Kid Otto protested angrily.

"I think you should eat your lunch," Vittorio said. "We have to be back soon." Kid Otto and Gypsy looked at each

[41]

other and stood up. They walked around behind the serving counter and confronted the slop-lady.

"Why don't you give that doctor a cup of coffee?" Gypsy suggested in a reasonable tone of voice.

"Who the hell do you boys think you are?" the slop-lady yelled. "I said there's no more goddam coffee left! And get out from behind this counter before I call the guards." Gypsy walked past her to the big coffee urn and turned the handle; a stream of coffee immediately started pouring out onto the floor. He stuck a cup under the cascading coffee and handed it over the counter to the girl.

"What the hell are you doing?" the slop-lady shouted. "Shut that coffee off, it's running all over the floor!"

Kid Otto backed up and planted himself between the coffee urn and the frantic slop-lady. He was standing in a spreading pool of coffee, grinning. The slop-lady tried to get by him but he was at least a foot and a half taller than she was, and a lot stronger. "Lady," he told her, "you're a fucking liar—and a son of a bitch in the bargain."

"Come on, man," Gypsy said, "let's go have lunch. I think we made our point."

Kid Otto nodded agreeably and, still grinning, followed Gypsy out to their table. "Be careful there," he yelled at the slop-lady, "somebody spilled a whole lot of coffee on the floor. Don't break your ass or anything."

They sat down again with Vittorio, and the girl with the coffee joined them. She lit another cigarette. "Thanks," she said, chuckling and coughing some. "I can't ever manage to get here on time. They used to give me a little coffee, at least. I think you really made a mess for that poor lady."

Kid Otto laughed, and shook a little shower of coffee off one of his big shoes. "Yeah, well that lady better watch her ass. She got my shoes wet."

Vittorio didn't look amused. "You guys are still children," he informed them.

[42]

The girl took a sip of her coffee. "My name's Irene."

"Are you an intern?" Gypsy asked, automatically interested in any new female.

"God forbid; once was enough. I'm a first-year resident. Are all three of you interns?"

"I am," Vittorio said. "These two are just along for laughs."

Irene sounded puzzled. "How come I've never run into you before?"

"We got screwed," Kid Otto said sorrowfully. "They gave the three of us July off."

Irene coughed in appreciation. "Wow, you mean you've got to do the whole rest of the year without a break? You really did get screwed."

"That's not all," Kid Otto went on. "When I start my residency next year, nobody's going to let me take any goddam time off right at the beginning again. I might have to break my ass for two straight years without a vacation."

"Poor baby," Vittorio commiserated, finishing his tuna fish.

"Where are you guys working?"

"The Emergency Room," Gypsy answered. "What about you?"

"I," she said ruefully, "am running a ward. God help me."

"What's it like on the wards?"

"What's it like? Well, you know all those bums in D.T.'s that you send up from the E.R. tied to a stretcher? We have to untie them and try to fix them up."

Gypsy looked at her. "Irene, the bums are people too."

Irene stubbed out her cigarette. "Believe me, I know," she said. "I've been doing this longer than you. When I started out last year, I decided I was going to practice medicine my way. I wasn't going to get cynical, and I wasn't going to get fed up with the city hospitals, and I wasn't going to get de-

[43]

humanized. And you know, I don't think I did. At least, not yet. But it's a real struggle. I mean, it's a contest for survival some of the time in this place."

"I don't see why."

"Hah! I do, all right," Kid Otto proclaimed. "Look around that Emergency Room, Gypsy. It's them or us, man. It's just like Gallberg said, they're the scum of the earth."

"They're patients," Gypsy corrected him. "They're sick people."

"Of course they're patients," Irene acknowledged. "And we're supposed to take care of them. But nobody's helping us. And they're not the best patients in the world sometimes. Listen, Gypsy, where'd you go to medical school?"

"Fordham."

Irene smiled. "That's a very nice place. Very quiet. Tell me, how many of your patients were drug addicts?"

"One," Gypsy responded. "When I was in the third year."

She smiled again. "Do you want to know something? During my entire internship here, I had five patients who weren't drug addicts or chronic alcoholics, or both. Five patients, Gypsy."

"Okay, I know there's a lot of sociopaths running around. But somebody's got to take care of them when they get sick."

"Sure, somebody's got to. Only, they're not very easy to take care of. They don't want you to take care of them. They want your wallet. Or the battery in your car."

Vittorio allowed himself a small laugh. "I don't think any drug addict would want anything in Gypsy's car. Gypsy's got a Fiat from the Civil War."

"Yeah, well, I don't," Kid Otto told them. "I got a Stingray. One of those bums touches my car, and I'll break his fucking ass. I'm not kidding, man."

"Seriously," Irene said to Gypsy, "a lot of these people

will really try to hurt you if you give them the chance. What are you going to do?"

"I am serious," Kid Otto interjected again. "They're not going to hurt me. That's why it's good to stay in shape. I lift weights, I jog every day, and I eat good food at home. I'm as strong as a fucking ox."

"That's very nice," Gypsy said, sounding discouraged, "except that I didn't come here for a body-building course. I came to learn medicine and be a doctor. When do I do that?"

"The thing is just to have a little balance, I think," Vittorio said reflectively. "You come to work, you see the patients, you read how much you can, and you try to do your best. You can't make yourself crazy for this." Vittorio seemed so rational, and sober, and grown up, that he made Gypsy smile for a moment. "Vic, what about sex? Can I take time out to get laid?"

Kid Otto quickly answered that for him. "Boy, are you guys lucky you're not married. I hear these nurses fuck everything that moves. Shit, my wife would break my ass if I didn't come home when I was supposed to."

Vittorio frowned at him.

"You know, Otto," Gypsy said good-naturedly, "I'm surprised there's any asses left at all in your family."

Irene stood up. "Excuse me, but I better go back to work. There might not be anything left of my ward by now."

"Is it really that terrible upstairs?"

"Worse. Nice meeting you guys." She walked off, lighting another cigarette.

Vittorio got up also. "Let's go, huh? Gallberg's going to have a fit."

The three of them headed for the door. "I don't know," Gypsy said to no one in particular. "Why is everybody so pissed off around here? A hospital is for sick people, isn't it?" Vittorio had no further comments.

[45]

Kid Otto had made a detour. He had walked behind the counter again, and a big group of slop-ladies were glaring at him from a safe distance. With much banging of the tin covers, he sorted through the food and selected another piece of lettuce for himself. Then he turned on the coffee spigot, waved to the slop-ladies, and walked away.

A strange and fearful place, the Emergency Room, but more often strange than fearful. Infrequently, the E.R. would even grow quiet, at three or four o'clock in the morning, and if Gypsy had really had it by then, he would use one of the examining tables in the first room to go to sleep for a little while.

At a quarter to four one morning, Gypsy climbed up on an examining table, lay down on his back, and closed his eyes. At four o'clock someone woke him up. "You the doctor, sonny?"

Gypsy remained motionless on his back; for a second he thought he was having some sort of odd dream. He peered down the table past his feet. "I am," he said finally, rubbing his eyes. The woman he was talking to weighed probably three hundred pounds.

"Well, sonny, I need some pills."

Gypsy sat up on the end of the table. "Pills? What kind of pills?"

"I got an infection in my urine." The woman smiled at him.

Gypsy looked at the clock on the wall, and put his head in his hands. He sighed. "Ma'am, it's four o'clock in the morning. How long have you had this trouble?"

"Oh, about five years, I think."

"Do you go to the G.U. Clinic?" Gypsy asked.

"Yeah, I go to G.U. Clinic every three weeks," she answered. "I go next Friday."

"Next Friday," Gypsy repeated. "I see. What's the, uh, the problem right now, then? I mean, after all, it is the middle of the night."

"Well, I go to clinic every three weeks all right, but I just couldn't sleep tonight. And I'm out of pills."

"You couldn't sleep. Tell me, did you come by ambulance?"

The lady laughed, shaking all over. "Shit, no. I didn't call no ambulance. I called my son-in-law; he drove me down. That's why I got here so late—he lives in Brooklyn."

"Oh," Gypsy said. "He lives in Brooklyn."

"Yeah. Well, anyway, I couldn't sleep, and I need more pills."

Gypsy took the chart she was holding. Everyone got a chart in the Emergency Room, even at 4 A.M. The hospital was run by the city, and the city is a bureaucracy, and everyone got a chart. She had no fever. "Mrs. Brandon, you ought to have a urinalysis. And a clean-catch urine for culture, I guess. Do you know how to get a clean-catch urine specimen?"

Mrs. Brandon laughed again. "Nah, I always mess that up."

Gypsy sighed a second time and slid off the examining table. "All right," he said, "come on. I'll help you get a clean-catch."

A clean catch-urine sample is an interesting thing. It's much more fun than a regular old urinalysis. After all, anybody can piss in a little bottle, which is all you've got to do for a urinalysis. Now, a clean-catch is what you need when you're going to have your urine specimen sent for culture-and-sensitivity testing. The object is to find out what bacteria are infecting, say, the bladder in chronic cystitis. Well, for this the urine must be uncontaminated by any extraneous bacteria. If it is contaminated, then the doctor no longer has any idea which bacteria are actually causing the infection, and the test is worthless.

Okay. Except that there are bacteria living everywhere. On your hands. In the air. And certainly all over your crotch. The clean-catch is supposed to minimize any contact the urine makes with anything in between your bladder and the sterile jar you piss in. So the first thing you've got to do is take a bunch of little cotton balls and a bottle of antiseptic, and carefully clean off your pissing equipment. Once that's done, incidentally, you've got to be very careful that nothing else touches your urethra, especially your hands. Then you take the small plastic funnel and jar out of their sterile wrapper, without touching the inside of the funnel. Finally, you start to piss, but not in the jar. (And you still can't use your hands.) The first part of the urinary stream is assumed to be contaminated by organisms it washed out of the lower urethra, so you pass it by. What you're supposed to accomplish is a "midstream catch," which is, indeed, something like trying to catch a long fly ball while you're running through a stream in the outfield with your pants down. But harder. Then you seal up the little jar, fast, again being very careful not to touch the inside of anything. You're allowed to use your hands for that.

Clean. Piss. Wait. Piss some more. Catch! Finish pissing. This is usually a pretty funny performance even by an agile male patient, who at least has a penis to aim with. For a three-hundred-pound female patient, it was going to be very interesting.

"Sonny," the woman pointed out, "I weigh three hundred and twenty-seven pounds, and like you said, it's four o'clock in the morning. If we gotta go through all that clean-catching bullshit, you're gonna lose your appetite for breakfast."

"Oh," Gypsy said again.

"Damn right. Now, you be a good boy, and just give me my pills. And Friday I'll go back to G.U. Clinic."

"Well," Gypsy said dubiously, "what kind of pills do they have you on?"

"I don't know."

"How long have you been taking them?"

"The pills? About six months, I guess."

"And you don't know what they are?"

"Nope." She smiled. "They never told me."

"Well, what do they look like?" Gypsy asked.

"I don't know. They're all gone."

"Yes, I know they're all gone," Gypsy said. "But I don't know what they are. I can't just give you pills; I have to know what pills you're taking."

"Yeah, well, I don't know what pills I'm taking."

He thought for a minute. "Look, I'm going to put you on tetracyclines, until you go back to clinic."

"No good. Tetracycline don't work."

"Oh. Well, I'm going to try Azo-Gantrisin, then."

"No good," she said again. "That makes my pee turn orange."

"Mrs. Brandon, it's *supposed* to make your pee turn orange. That's how it works."

"No," she said. "No good."

"Okay, okay; let's try Mandelamine."

"No good. Mandelamine makes me throw up."

"Furadantin," Gypsy suggested hopefully. "How about Furadantin?"

"I like the sound of that one," Mrs. Brandon said.

"You sure?" Gypsy asked. "You're not allergic to it, or anything?"

"Nope, I never even heard of it before."

"Wonderful," Gypsy exclaimed. He wrote a prescription

[49]

out and handed it to her. "Here you go, Mrs. Brandon. Be sure and come to clinic."

"You bet. Thank you very much, sonny. You take care now."

"Good night," Gypsy said, and climbed back onto the examining table. Then he saw that it was getting light outside once again, and he realized that he had to start the next day's work.

The essential link between the hospital and the rest of the borough of Manhattan was its ambulances. But there were only a limited number of ambulances and drivers, and an ambulance sent out to pick up a patient, whether sick or only hysterical, was totally occupied until that patient was brought into the hospital. Someone else could bleed to death in an automobile wreck in less time than that takes.

There were a lot of good reasons for calling an ambulance. These did not include finding out why your social worker didn't show up the week before, making a new clinic appointment for your grandmother, impressing the Welfare Bureau with how sick you were so they wouldn't make you get a job, or adding a little drama to some internecine family hysterics.

The hospital had a small ambulance driver named Rafael (the same one who had come to pick up Gypsy's allegedly assaulted downstairs neighbor) who could not go on an ambulance run without bringing a heart-attack victim back with him. Whatever he went out for, Rafael brought back somebody with a heart attack. He would come hurtling through the doors, rolling the stretcher in front of him and bawling "Heart attack, heart attack!" as loud as he was able to. It was very colorful, and it always made a lot of people converge on his patient from all over the Emergency Room.

One night Rafael went out on a run to 113th Street.

When he got there, what he found was a hysterical fourteen-year-old girl named Luz. Luz and her boyfriend had been having a fight, and he'd called her a whore or something. She had started running around the apartment and screaming, and wouldn't stop. Her family had decided they had a medical emergency to deal with, and they dealt with it by calling an ambulance.

When Rafael wheeled her into the Emergency Room, she was sitting up on the stretcher and screaming "I can't breathe, I can't breathe!" Rafael was yelling "Heart attack, heart attack!" They thundered toward Gypsy and almost ran him down. Rafael bounced the wheeled stretcher off a wall of the corridor and finally skidded it into the Cardiac Room—the only area in the E.R. specially set up to handle cardiovascular emergencies. A whole tribe of the girl's relatives poured into the Cardiac Room right behind Rafael, the stretcher, and Luz. Gypsy walked in after them.

"Gypsy, Gypsy, heart attack!" Rafael yelled at him as he came through the door.

There is a saying in medicine—If you hear hoofbeats, look for horses; don't look for zebras. Unusual things can always happen, but you look for what's common first, and then for what's rare. Adolescent girls don't have heart attacks very often.

Gypsy came over to the stretcher. One of the aides was pushing an electrocardiogram machine through the crowd. Gypsy raised his voice above the din: "All right," he said in a loud, firm command, "stop this bullshit. Put that EKG machine back." The room quieted noticeably. He turned to the girl sitting on the stretcher, who had shut up also. "Now," he asked, "what's wrong?"

As soon as he spoke to her in a friendly tone, the girl began screaming again. "I can't breathe, I can't breathe!" she yelled, banging her fists on the rails of the stretcher.

[51]

"Well, I don't know," Gypsy said quietly. "You breathe pretty good when you stop screaming."

The girl looked at him for a second, rolled her eyes back in her head, and with a loud moan fell flat on the stretcher. She stopped breathing. Gypsy was not impressed. He pulled up the girl's eyelid and checked her pupil.

"She's dying, she's dying," someone in the room cried. The rest of the family took up the chorus. The Cardiac Room quickly got noisier than it had been before, when Luz was doing the screaming. "Oh, my God, my baby's dead!" the girl's mother shouted. She collapsed onto the floor and started beating her head with her hands.

"Crap," Gypsy said. He broke open a vial of ammonia carbonate and let it soak into a gauze sponge. Then he took the gauze and clamped it over the girl's face, so that her mouth and her nose were both covered. He held it there hard.

The girl, of course, was not dead. She didn't move for about five seconds more, and then she took her first whiff of the ammonia. She ripped Gypsy's hand away from her face and leaped off the stretcher. "You cocksucker, get the fuck away from me."

"Ah," Gypsy said, "miraculous cure."

"Hey!" The girl's boyfriend spoke for the first time. "That's my woman. What you doing to her?" He pushed himself in between Gypsy and the girl and tried to look menacing.

Gypsy glanced wearily around the room, surveying the mob. He walked to the door, turned around, and stood in the doorway. "You know," he said, "you people are crapping around in an emergency cardiac-resuscitation room. We need to have this room free for patients who come in here very sick, patients who are dying. There's nothing wrong with any of you. Now you get the fuck out of this room."

The boyfriend marched over in front of Gypsy and waved his fist in Gypsy's face. "Listen, man . . ." he began.

Gypsy cut him off. "This is a hospital you're in. For sick people. You want to fight with somebody? Okay." Gypsy walked out of the room and called, "Security!" A couple of hospital guards appeared, looking put-upon. "Would you please clear the Cardiac Room," Gypsy said to them. They reluctantly went to work, and ten minutes later the Cardiac Room was finally available again for cardiac emergencies.

Gypsy left to get some coffee. The guards had moved Luz and all of her relatives out to the waiting room, and Gypsy found them gathered there on his way back from the coffee machine. Luz was sitting imperiously in the middle of one of the benches; her mother, two of her sisters, and the boyfriend were gathered around her in a circle—fanning her. Everyone stared hatefully at Gypsy.

He took a sip of his coffee. "Okay, look, I'm sorry I lost my temper back there. The thing is, when you come storming in here from an ambulance like that, our staff thinks somebody's really sick. It messes everything up for us. Do you understand?"

"My baby was sick!" the girl's mother said to him spitefully.

"No," Gypsy said reasonably, "she wasn't sick. She was just very upset. And so you got upset—that's understandable. And maybe she needed to see a doctor. But you have to realize . . ."

"Sure she needs the doctor," one of the sisters interrupted. "Didn't you see her screaming, man?"

Gypsy pressed on. "You have to realize that this is a very busy emergency room, a very busy hospital. We have to take care of thousands of people here. It's very, very important that we keep our ambulances free for seriously injured people. We don't have that many ambulances to begin with. And the room you were in is a special room for

[53]

heart-attack patients—it's the only room we've got like that."

"She could have been having a heart attack," another sister objected. "How do you know? Didn't you hear that guy yelling it was a heart attack?"

"I know because I'm a doctor," Gypsy said, "and he's not. Now, listen, she's all right. She's going to be fine. But you see, when you do something like this, it's the same as turning in a false alarm to the firehouse. It's very dangerous. Somebody else's house can burn down while the fire engines are out on a false alarm."

He got a lot of sullen looks.

"I want you to promise me you won't ever call an ambulance again," he continued, "unless you really need one. Okay?" Nobody answered him.

Gypsy gave them a friendly parting smile and left the waiting room. "I'm not gonna walk all the way home," Luz announced as he reached the examining rooms. "I want to go home in an ambulance."

Odd problems walk into the Emergency Room in the middle of the night, and some of them are not covered in medical school. One Friday night Gypsy was sitting at the little desk in front of the examining tables. Vittorio was trying to ask him serious questions, and Gypsy was not in a serious mood.

"Cut it out, Gypsy," Vic said, "you go into medicine to be a doctor. I mean, what did you expect?"

Gypsy smiled. "You know that old doctor on 'Gunsmoke'? He comes over in the middle of the show, looks at some cowboy all shot full of holes, and he says, 'He's dead, all right.' And then somebody buys him a drink. It seemed like a pretty good life."

Vittorio shook his head. "How did you ever get through medical school?"

[54]

"By the skin of my ass," Gypsy said. "I think they just decided, after four years it was somebody else's turn to put up with me."

"Gypsy, for real, what ever made you go to medical school in the first place?"

Gypsy scratched the back of his neck. "Vic, who knows? I figured, I don't know—I figured I'd get more girls, I guess. Why does anybody do anything? What about you?"

Vittorio grinned. "I'm Italian. A young Italian doctor is the prince of the neighborhood. I'm a bigger deal than the gangsters on my block."

At this point in the conversation a radio-car cop, whose head Gypsy had recently sewed up, walked in. Behind him came a tall, gray-haired, middle-aged man. Gypsy was wondering what was going on as he got up; the gray-haired man was overdressed for this emergency room. He had on his own shoes, socks, pants, a shirt, everything. He wasn't handcuffed, so he hadn't done anything too terrible. And he wasn't bleeding, so nothing much had been done to him. He wasn't a girl, either, so he hadn't been raped.

Vittorio had already left to find something more interesting to become involved in. Gypsy walked over to the pair and spoke to the patrolman. "Hi, Morris. What are you bringing me?"

"Hello, Gypsy," the cop answered. "Did Willie get here yet?"

"No, I haven't seen Willie. Isn't he out in the car?"

The cop sat down heavily, in the chair for patients next to the desk. "Gypsy, I don't know where Willie is, and I don't know where the squad car is."

Gypsy looked at him. "Morris, you mean you lost your partner and your radio car, and it isn't even Saturday night?"

"No. I mean I walked here from Sixty-third and Park with

this guy, and Willie drove the car. That's why I don't know where Willie is."

"Morris," Gypsy said, "why did you walk all the way from Sixty-third Street? Wouldn't Willie let you ride in the car any more? Maybe you have bad breath, Morris."

"Oh, shut up. We had to walk because the guy is afraid to sit down." Morris got out of the chair and moved to one of the examining tables in the far corner of the room. "Come here," he said to Gypsy in an urgent, low voice.

Gypsy dutifully followed him into the corner. "What are you whispering about, Morris? Do you have the clap again?"

"Gypsy, would you shut up and listen, please? I don't know what the hell to write in my report!"

"I know," Gypsy laughed. "You have the clap."

"I have a pervert," the cop answered. "This guy is a regular pervert! Him and his boyfriend call nine-one-one and they say that they need some help. So me and Willie drive over, and we go upstairs to this fancy apartment, and we find these two perverts."

Gypsy laughed again. "Ahh, come on, Morris. What have you got against rich queers?"

"Gypsy, will you listen to me?" Morris whispered fiercely, as if he was uttering some necessary piece of blasphemy but didn't want to be heard doing it. "These two guys were playing games, see, and the other one pushed a vibrator up this one's ass, and then they couldn't get it out. That's why he wouldn't sit down in the car, and that's why I had to walk here from Sixty-third Street." Morris glared like he was describing some kind of disgusting insect.

Gypsy looked back and forth a few times, from Morris to the dignified-appearing patient, who was now standing at the desk. Then he walked over to the man, cleared his throat, and said "Sir, what's wrong with you?"

"Doctor, wouldn't you know it, there's a vibrator caught in my behind."

[56]

"Oh," Gypsy said. "I see." He thought about that for a while. "Look, you wouldn't bullshit me, would you?"

"Heavens, no. I wouldn't have interrupted a perfectly lovely evening otherwise. And I certainly wouldn't have come to a place like this without an excellent reason."

"Yeah," Gypsy agreed, "of course not. Well, you've got a good reason, all right. Come on; let's see if I can find it." He led the man back to one of the examining tables and closed the curtains around them. "Drop your pants," he instructed, "lie down on the table on your side, and pull your knees up."

"Don't be naughty, now," the man cautioned as he climbed up on the examining table.

"Drop dead," Gypsy said under his breath. He lit a cigar, something he often did before performing a rectal exam in the Emergency Room. It was just aesthetic self-defense. Then he put on a disposable rubber glove and squirted Surgilube lubricant onto his index finger. Gypsy fished around with his gloved finger, and an amazed look appeared on his face.

"So? Was I lying?" Morris asked when Gypsy came out from behind the curtains.

Gypsy drew the rubber glove off slowly and dropped it into the garbage. "Morris," he said, "I think he has a vibrator stuck in his ass."

"Ha! I told you, didn't I?" Morris took out his black report book and started writing. "Vibrator . . . in . . . ass," he recited laboriously as he wrote. He scribbled a few more things down and snapped the book shut.

"Gypsy, he's gotta be admitted, right?"

Gypsy worked on his cigar, looking troubled. "I guess so, yeah. I can't get the damn thing out."

"Fine," the cop answered, heading toward the door, "that's fine. I'm finished with him then. I have to look for Willie."

"Good night, Morris," Gypsy called after the retreating blue figure. "Thanks for the present."

"Any time, Gypsy," Morris's voice echoed faintly from beyond the door, "any time."

Gypsy sighed and walked into the examining room next door to request help. "Vic," he said resignedly, "I got a problem. There's a queer back there with a vibrator stuck up his ass, and I can't get it out."

Vittorio looked at him peculiarly for a long moment. "Gypsy," he said finally, "you wouldn't bullshit me?"

"That's the same thing I said. Go see for yourself." They returned to the first room together, and Vic disappeared through the curtains. A short while later the curtains opened again, and Vic dropped a second rubber glove into the garbage.

"Well?" Gypsy said.

"You were right," Vittorio confessed. "He has a vibrator up his ass."

Gypsy chewed on the cigar. "Now what?"

"I don't know. I can feel it, but I can't pull it out. I think it must have turned sideways."

"All right, let's send him for some X-rays." Thirty minutes later the man came back from Radiology, holding his X-ray report. Gypsy read the report:

*Abdomen, supine and upright.*
*Pelvis, A-P.*

Films demonstrate normal osseous structures. No organomegaly. Intestinal gas pattern unremarkable. No abnormal masses or calcifications seen. A cylindrical density measuring approximately 4 centimeters x 20 centimeters is projected over the lower pelvis, in the midline, perhaps representing a foreign body. Please repeat if clinically indicated.

"What does it say, Gypsy?" Vic asked.

"It says he has a vibrator up his ass."

The two interns looked at each other. "Vic, what are we going to do with this guy?"

"You're supposed to be the smart one," Vittorio said. "What do I know?"

"Ahh, shit on you, man." Gypsy reviewed the situation silently, working his cigar around in his mouth and waiting for inspiration. None came. He looked reflectively at the patient—who was waiting hopefully, in front of the examining table.

More cigar smoke. Then, "I got an idea! Vittorio, I got an idea." Gypsy stood up, looking relieved and pleased with himself. He walked over to the telephone and dialed the page operator: "Hello. Would you please page Dr. Jack Schwartz for the Emergency Room? Thank you." He hung up. Then he went back and pulled the curtains shut around the patient and the examining table. Vittorio and Gypsy looked at each other again, and burst out laughing.

Fifteen minutes after the page, Dr. Jack Schwartz walked into the Emergency Room. He was short, dark, ugly, and nasty. He was also the obstetrics-and-gynecology resident on consults.

"Jesus Christ," Schwartz said as soon as he walked through the door. "Can't you guys do anything yourselves? I'm busy as hell upstairs, and every time some broad needs a pelvic down here, you come crying to me."

This was nonsense, of course. The obstetrical service was very slow, and Schwartz had hardly any deliveries at all to perform. He simply didn't like to move himself anywhere. He didn't like women much, either, and he particularly didn't like the raunchy atmosphere of the Emergency Room.

Gypsy was smiling. He handed the man's chart to the O.B.-G.Y.N. resident and pointed toward the examining table, which still had the curtains pulled closed around it. Schwartz stepped through the curtains, carrying the chart.

He stopped dead as soon as he saw his patient. Silence. He was apparently checking the name on the chart. "Excuse me," he said, "I was looking for someone named Leslie."

"Well, that's me," the patient replied. Further confused conversation followed, with Schwartz's voice growing louder and higher-pitched as he became more and more indignant.

"A what?" he was saying incredulously. "A vibrator? You mean with batteries and everything?" Leslie confirmed the nature of the vibrator. Poor Schwartz's middle-class sensibilities were being outraged.

Schwartz reappeared, shouting. "You bastards," he yelled at Gypsy and Vittorio and the Emergency Room in general, shaking his finger up and down. "You scum bags!" Vittorio and Gypsy were trying to look serious and professional, but they were both cracking up.

"Schwartz, Schwartz, listen," Gypsy said, "we need you, we . . ." He was laughing too hard to go on.

The gynecology resident threw the chart on the desk and marched toward the door, with his face turning dark red. "God damn you," he spluttered. "A queer. A lousy fucking queer."

Gypsy was entirely out of control; he was laughing so hard he had to sit down. Vittorio was almost crying. "Schwartz," he managed to choke out, "don't leave us—think of the patient."

"You can do it, Jack." Gypsy had regained his power of speech. "It's those long fingers you have. And all that experience looking up into those ladies. Just reach up there and grab it for us."

Schwartz stopped momentarily on his way out the door. "I'm going to report you guys" was his parting advice. "The both of you."

"Get fucked, man," Gypsy said cheerfully. "Thanks for the help."

The two interns sat there laughing fitfully for a few minutes more, wiping their eyes occasionally. Gypsy's sides hurt. "Vic," Gypsy said finally, "what am I going to do for him? He's still got the vibrator up his ass."

"I can't help you, Gypsy; he's your patient. I tried. Look, what the hell, at least the thing's not on."

Gypsy thought it over. "Well, I guess we should admit him to Surgery," he decided out loud. "Maybe they'll have to open him up to get the goddam thing out." He reached for the phone and called the surgical ward that was due for the next male admission. "Dr. Giardia, please." He waited a little while.

"Vince? This is Gypsy. I've got an interesting admission for you. You better come down here; you're not going to believe this one." Surgeons are very practical people. Vince Giardia admitted Leslie to his ward and gave him an enormous dose of magnesium sulfate.

The next morning Leslie shit out the vibrator and went home.

Gypsy discovered the elephant graveyard.
Elephant which?
Let's say you're really lucky for a long time. For your whole life. You don't get born with some fatal congenital defect. You don't get leukemia when you're ten years old. You don't get an osteogenic sarcoma when you're twenty-five. In spite of all the crap in the air and three million cigarettes, you don't get a bronchogenic carcinoma. Your brain manufactures no brain tumor.

You don't get shot to death in a whorehouse. No one mugs you on the Seventh Avenue I.R.T. and gratuitously slits your throat. Nobody breaks into your apartment, ties you to your bed, and sets the bed on fire. You never get run over by a garbage truck.

Congratulations.

The prize is—you get old.

You can't hear any more. You can't see. You can't walk without toppling over onto your head. Your teeth fall out. You shit in your pants. And your friends are all dead. Very nice.

Well, how about a nursing home for you, grandpop? That's not so easy. Full-time nursing-home care is very, very expensive. Nursing homes may not nurse too much, but they make a lot of money. The city hospital is free. It's much easier for your family just to ship you over to the elephant graveyard. By ambulance.

A particularly good season for elephant is right before a holiday weekend. People want to take off for the long weekend, and they've just about had it with grandpop anyhow. It's a bad time to be old.

Gypsy met Miss Brown and her elephant, also named Brown, the Wednesday before Labor Day weekend. "My mother, she sick," Miss Brown had announced.

Her mother was not sick. But she was ninety-three years old. She weighed 288 pounds. She was totally blind, and she was incontinent. And she was senile. She had been this way for years, though, and basically, none of the many things wrong with her needed medical treatment. She hadn't had a stroke, or a heart attack, or a gastrointestinal bleed. She didn't have pneumonia or bronchitis, or anything else, really. Her chest X-ray was normal. Her blood count and blood chemistries were normal. Nothing that was wrong with her could be treated, or made any better, or in any way alleviated in a hospital. What she needed was somebody to take care of her all day long, because the only thing really wrong with her was that she was ninety-three. And it was almost Labor Day weekend, and her daughter had had it.

"Listen, *I'm* sick," the daughter said to Gypsy. "I got a bad heart, and rheumatism, and asthma, and I can't take care of her no more. You got to admit her to the hospital."

Gypsy felt for her. He truly did. "Miss Brown," he told her gently, "your mother is a very elderly lady . . ."

"Elderly?" she interjected. "Elderly? Boy, she ninety-three. She older than Moses."

"Well, yes," Gypsy agreed. "I know. But you see, she's not sick. I mean, she doesn't have a disease or anything, something we can treat here."

"She ain't sick?" Miss Brown looked at Gypsy like he was an idiot. "She ain't sick? Blind old lady, weigh three hundred pounds, and shit in the bed, and she ain't sick? You crazy, man!"

"She only weighs two eighty-eight, actually," he said miserably. "And I realize how difficult it must be for you to take care of her. But you see, this isn't a nursing home. It's an overcrowded general hospital, and we can only admit people who are sick. People who need some kind of treatment for something. Your mother isn't sick, Miss Brown. All the lab tests, the X-rays, everything—everything's okay. Two different doctors have examined her, and there's no medical reason for her to be in the hospital. All we could do for her here is put her in a bed and feed her. Now, she is your mother, and what she needs is someone to kind of take care of her."

"You take care of her," Miss Brown yelled. "I ain't. She a sick old whale, and she shit in the bed. In the bed, man, she shit in the bed! I can't take no more of that, man—I'm sick, I tell you."

"I understand there's a problem," Gypsy said quietly, "but your mother really just isn't sick. There's nothing at all that we can do for her in the hospital that can't be done better at home. She's just old."

"Don't jive me, man. You damn right she's old. So am I. And I ain't taking care of her no more."

Gypsy didn't know what to do. This kind of thing was

hateful for him. "Miss Brown," he repeated, "I'm sorry, we're not going to admit your mother to the hospital. She doesn't need to be in a hospital. If she needed hospitalization, we wouldn't stand here arguing with you, we'd put her in the hospital. But she just doesn't need to be in a hospital."

Miss Brown finally agreed. She picked up her coat, and prepared to take her elephant home with her again. No elephant graveyard this time. On the way out, however, she was saying, "She gonna kill me, man. She gonna kill me. It's her or me."

Gypsy walked over to the window and looked at the street glumly. He hated being the villain. And he liked old people, or at least he felt sorry for them. He wasn't lying, though; it was like a zoo upstairs. The wards were always bursting with patients. All by themselves the overdosed drug addicts and the chronic alcoholics with bilateral pneumonias would have kept the wards overflowing. Not to mention the heart attacks, strokes, intestinal obstructions, and plain ordinary cracked heads that presented themselves in the Emergency Room.

It was simply not fair to anybody to admit a patient who did not need some kind of urgent treatment for something. Every hospital bed occupied solely because a family decided to abdicate meant one less hospital bed available for somebody who was genuinely sick. The capacity of a bed is one. Of course, no one who needs to be in the hospital is ever actually turned away, no matter how crowded the hospital becomes. There is supposed to be no such thing as a filled city hospital; they simply line beds up in the hallways. But what happens then is that all the facilities must be stretched even more, and the staff's finite time has to be divided among more and more patients. There were only so many hours in the day, and after a point, everyone got short-changed.

And in a way, Gypsy was actually trying to protect poor old Mrs. Brown. He knew a sad truth—that old, helpless people with nothing acutely wrong with them can end up worse off in the hospital than they were at home. Not nearly as bad off as in a nursing home, but in trouble anyhow. There just weren't enough staff to feed them, and change them, and get them out of bed and up into a chair. There were too many sicker people. Obligingly, they lay there in bed, staring at the ceiling, getting dehydrated, and acquiring bed sores that didn't heal.

But once individuals in Miss Brown's frame of mind decided an aging relative had turned into an elephant, they didn't give a damn about any of this. The overwhelming patient census on the wards was perhaps not their responsibility, but their own flesh and blood ought to have meant something to them. It didn't.

Miss Brown came back the next day with her elephant, wiser and more determined. She simply delivered her mother to the Emergency Room and beat it, just in time for the Labor Day weekend. She turned her mother into a ninety-three-year-old foundling, deposited her in the elephant graveyard, and vanished. The registration sheet that she quietly filled out before fleeing made Gypsy sick. Under "Name" she had written "Unknown Female." The following line, "Address," was left blank, along with everything else on the form except "Nearest Relative," which said bluntly "None."

Her mother spent that afternoon sleeping in a wheelchair in the Emergency Room. She spent the next four months on a Female Medicine ward, while a series of social workers tried to find a nursing home to maneuver her into. Finally she just got old enough, and died.

# The Saturday Night
# Knife & Gun Club

SINCE PEOPLE GOT SICK at night as often as they did during the day, the Emergency Room was always open. Someone, therefore, always had to be working there. The aides, the nurses, and almost everyone else in the Emergency Room worked eight-hour shifts. When their eight hours were up, they left, and a new shift came to work. It was not reasonable, after all, to expect anyone to actually want to work twenty, or thirty, or forty hours at a time. Even obsessive-compulsive doctors don't enjoy that kind of thing. So something strange happened to the Emergency Room at night: some of the doctors got tired and went home too.

During the day, there were all kinds of doctors around. There were interns, of course, as well as residents and fellows and attending physicians—a staff with increasing amounts of experience. If some intern had a problem with a patient, there were plenty of people right there he could ask to help him. As it grew later in the day, though, layers of expertise were gradually stripped away, starting from the top and working down. The attendings went home first, and by two or three o'clock in the morning a lot of other people had joined them. At this hour, even the remarkably well staffed emergency rooms of the city hospitals got a little short of doctors. Which meant that the burden of working really crushing hours was assigned to the house staff.

However, the more senior residents and fellows on the house staff were assuming supervisory roles; their responsibilities paralleled the specialization they were undergoing in their training. This was not unreasonable, since medicine had become so vast and protean a field that it was no longer possible for anyone, whatever his intellect, to remain a Renaissance man. There was too much knowledge to be absorbed for any doctor to become a competent and complete generalist; everyone was forced to specialize. Whom did that leave, then, to run around the Emergency Room all night? The least specialized, and most junior doctor: the intern, who never had to sleep. Principally because there was no one under him he could turn to and say, "You take care of it; I'm going home now." Since no one else wanted to do this work, it was assigned to the interns and renamed a "learning experience." Shit rolls downhill.

It is true that many of the people who wander into the Emergency Room at night are well within the competence of the intern to treat. There is nothing at all wrong with some of them, and a lot of the others simply got drunk, fell down, and cut their head open. An intern can sew them up again more or less as well as anyone else can. People who are obviously very sick are no problem either; they get admitted to the hospital right away, and once that happens, at least two more doctors are going to see them as soon as they hit their ward.

The difficulty was one of judgment; the intern had to decide who needed sewing up, who needed to be admitted, and who needed to go home and sleep it off. One of the hardest things in medicine can be deciding what is serious and what isn't. Sometimes it takes a lot of experience to be able to pick out the people who are sicker than they seem, and to realize that a lot of sound and fury and blood doesn't always herald a genuine medical catastrophe.

Whatever the difficulties, the situation at the city hospitals was still much better than things were on the outside. There may only have been an intern or a resident in a city

[67]

hospital emergency room, but most of the time he was at least no dummy, and there were always a lot of people somewhere nearby whom he could ask for help. The "emergency rooms" in some of the proprietary hospitals could be staffed by almost anybody except a veterinarian. Frequently, foreign-trained physicians who hadn't been able to qualify for a state license yet were used as the warm bodies. Whatever else they knew, often they didn't know much English. Or the doctor might be a moonlighting psychiatry resident from some residency program with a light on-call schedule, whose chief interest was sleeping all night.

But even at Manhattan County, there were sometimes fuck-ups. Arthur Nerd, a runty and terrified little intern, fucked up one night in the Emergency Room. A man about forty, with a long history of asthma, came in complaining that his breathing had been very tight. He had tried taking more of his usual asthma pills, but he had only gotten worse. His pulse was a little fast, and Arthur took an electrocardiogram, which looked funny to him.

Actually, this patient was having a silent heart attack, and while Arthur was taking the EKG he had gone into ventricular tachycardia: his heart was one step away from quitting altogether. He had the great good sense to do this in an emergency room, and not at home while he was sleeping—in which case he would have just died. He had the bad sense to do it in front of Arthur Nerd. Arthur blocked. He knew something was wrong, but he didn't know what.

Arthur ran off about twenty-five feet of cardiogram trying to figure out what was going on, without any luck. Then he gathered up the tracings and carried them down to the holding room in the back of the E.R. He knocked on the door to the room. "Gypsy," he called softly, "wake up. It's Dr. Nerd." No answer.

Gypsy was sleeping in the holding room. His own shift had ended two hours before, but he couldn't go home.

There was a girl in his apartment who wouldn't leave. She thought that she owned him because she'd spent a couple of idle hours swallowing his semen. She was an idiot, and what Gypsy wanted was a girl who was beautiful, bright, sensitive, kind, and rich. With great legs. And so he was sleeping in the holding room in the back of the E.R.

Arthur walked into the room; Gypsy was snoring on the last bed in his underpants. Arthur cleared his throat. "Gypsy, wake up."

Gypsy twisted around in the bed without opening his eyes. "What?" he said woozily. "Who's there?"

"It's Dr. Nerd."

"Arthur, go away," he mumbled.

"Gypsy, listen," Arthur persisted. "Would you help me read a cardiogram? I think maybe I've got the leads on backwards or something."

Gypsy forced his eyes open and shut a couple of times. "Nerd," he said finally, "you got your head on backwards. Go away, huh? I'm tired, man."

Arthur started to whine. "Jesus, why doesn't anybody ever help me out? I can't read a cardiogram by myself."

"Okay, okay," Gypsy said, sighing. "Stop complaining. I'll help you read your cardiogram. Let me get dressed and I'll come out and look at it with you." He sat up on the edge of the bed and started rummaging around on the floor hunting for his socks. The socks were buried under the yards of EKG tracings that Arthur had brought in. Gypsy found one sock, and as he disentangled it from the coils of paper, he froze and stared at the cardiogram.

"Holy shit." He jumped up off the bed. "Holy shit!" He ran out of the room in his underpants, flinging the sock away. Arthur ran after him, trailing the cardiogram like a paper fire hose. "What's wrong," Arthur said, "what is it?"

They raced into the treatment room. The patient still had the EKG leads on his chest but they weren't picking up

[69]

much; he was turning blue. Gypsy ran over to the machine and grabbed the tracing—the man was now in ventricular fibrillation. Which is to say he was dying. Gypsy climbed on top of him and started to pump his chest. "Call a Code," he yelled at Nerd. "Call it, call it."

Arthur dropped the EKG tracings he was staring at and rushed over to the telephone on the wall. He dialed 9-9, the cardiac arrest number, and started screaming into the phone. "A Code! A Code!" he shouted. "Call a Code! Call a Code!" He stopped screaming a moment. "What?" he said. "What? What? Oh, yeah . . . the Emergency Room— it's in the Emergency Room. Call a Code in the Emergency Room!"

The page speakers along the corridors made a little static, and then started booming, "Code Nine-Nine, Adult Emergency Room. Code Nine-Nine, Adult Emergency Room."

Arthur was still clutching the telephone receiver and yelling "Call a Code! Call a Code!" into the dead connection. Gypsy looked at him with his mouth open. "Nerd, you schmuck, they're calling it already. Get over here."

Arthur dropped the telephone and scurried back to the patient, muttering "a Code, a Code" under his breath. Gypsy was pumping the man's chest and sweating.

"Nerd, Jesus Christ, bag the guy. Bag him!"

Arthur had been standing there talking to himself about a Code. He had forgotten that pounding on chests is not enough; somebody also has to breathe mechanically for people who have stopped breathing. When Gypsy shouted at him again, he made a little involuntary hop in the air and ran around to the supply table on the other side of the room. He started to dig wildly through it looking for an Ambu bag, haphazardly knocking instruments and bottles off the table. An I.V. bottle crashed to the floor and shattered.

Gypsy glared across the room from where he was working on top of the patient. He stopped his pumping for a second.

"Nerd," he thundered, "don't move! Don't touch anything else! Just stand there—just fucking stand there!"

Arthur stopped dropping things on the floor. The operator had been paging the Code for about a minute and a half, and the cardiac-resuscitation team responding to the Code now came swarming into the room, shunting Arthur off into the corner. Before another two minutes had gone by, the patient was intubated, several cutdowns had been started for I.V. lines, and he had been defibrillated back into a normal sinus rhythm. His heart was working again.

A nursing supervisor with a clipboard began going around and asking everybody, "What time did the Code start? I have to know exactly what time the Code started."

"I called the Code," Arthur said to her, coming out of the corner.

"Oh, fine." She raised her ball-point pen. "What time did you call it?"

"I don't know. Right after Gypsy dropped his sock and started yelling at me."

The patient was being hustled up to the Cardiac Care Unit. The Code had been successful. "Which one is Gypsy?" the nursing supervisor asked Arthur.

"That one. The one in his underpants."

Gypsy was slumped in a chair, breathing heavily. The nursing supervisor walked over to him. "Doctor?"

"What?" he said without looking up.

"I have to know what time the Code started, please."

"What time it started? I don't know, maybe about two A.M., something like that."

"No, you don't understand—I have to know *exactly* what time the Code started."

"Come on," Gypsy said wearily, "what do you want? There was a Code going on; I didn't have time to look at the clock."

"Well," she snapped at him, "that other doctor wouldn't

tell me either. He said I should ask you. Doesn't anybody know anything?"

"Excuse me, please, I'm going to bed." Gypsy got up and walked slowly back to the holding room. The nursing supervisor walked right behind him. She stopped just inside the doorway. "Come in," he said. "Make yourself at home." He crawled onto the bed and turned his back to her.

"Don't you be rude to me—I've been here for twenty-six years. Now why is it so much trouble for you to tell me exactly when the Code started?"

"Go away," Gypsy implored her with his face buried in the pillow, "please just go away."

"That's what's wrong with you interns," the nursing supervisor lectured him. "All you want to do is run around and give orders and yell at everybody. You don't understand anything about the team delivery of medical care. Haven't you ever heard of the concept of the health-care team?"

Gypsy rolled over and sat up again. His eyes were bloodshot with fatigue. "Lady," he said to her, "I don't know when the goddam Code started. I was sleeping; I was dead to the world. It's not even my shift, for God's sake—it's Arthur Nerd's shift! Go ask that schmuck Nerd!"

"Why are you being so resistant to the health-care-team concept? It's my job to find out exactly when the Code started, that's all. We have to have exact records of these things."

Gypsy reached under the bed and put his hand on one of his shoes. "I'm warning you, lady. You better get the fuck out of here."

She gasped. "Young man, I'm going to report you to the administrator for that." She clicked the ball-point pen open. "What's your name?"

Gypsy reared back and fired the shoe at her head. It caught her smack in the nose and propelled her backward

[72]

out into the hallway. She picked up her clipboard, holding her nose, and scrambled out of range.

Arthur Nerd appeared outside the room. "Gypsy, where'd you go?" he asked. "There's a nursing supervisor looking for you."

Gypsy reached down and grabbed the other shoe. "Nerd," he said with his teeth clenched, "if you're still standing there in three seconds, so help me I'm going to stick the defibrillator up your ass!"

Nerd ran.

The next night was an extremely busy one also. Gypsy was sneaking a moment in between patients to tell Kid Otto the story about the nursing supervisor.

"Too bad you let her get away," Kid Otto said. "Why didn't you break her ass?"

Gypsy couldn't answer that. "I guess I was just too tired, man." He smiled wanly. "All I could think about was going to sleep."

"Well, at least you saved him. And at least he was a regular patient. Look what we got here tonight." Kid Otto shook his head. What he meant was that the whole shift had been a festival of bums. Mugger-bums, rapist-bums, wino-bums, and drug addict-bums. Nights like this really depressed Gypsy.

A hulking young patient with his arm in a dirty sling stumbled into the room. He was pretty ripped on something.

"Uh-oh," Kid Otto said warily. "I'm through arguing with this one. I'll see you around." He crossed into the adjoining treatment room.

The patient weaved over to Gypsy. "Man," he announced, "I want some methadone."

"I'm sorry," Gypsy said. "We don't keep methadone in the Emergency Room."

"Don't give me no hard time, man. I'm tired of that bull-shit. I want some methadone, right now! You hear me?"

"Hey, look. I told you, we don't have any methadone down here. That's all handled in the Detoxification Program."

"Detoxification, my ass!" the patient yelled. "I said give me the fucking methadone!" He pulled his arm out of the sling. There was a big kitchen knife in his hand. "All right, you son of a bitch," he shouted, "where's the methadone at?"

Jim MacKinley, the ambulance driver, walked into the room. He had just finished delivering another load of bums to the E.R. when he'd heard the shouting from the treatment room. "Anything wrong, doc?"

"Watch it, Mac, he's got a knife," Gypsy said warningly.

"Stay out of this, man," the patient threatened. "I'll cut you—I ain't fucking around!"

MacKinley stopped in the middle of the room. He was a little shorter than the patient, but he had at least thirty pounds on him. "Who you gonna cut?"

The patient made a move toward him. "I told you to fuck off. Don't you hear good?"

MacKinley undid the bottom button on his shirt and lifted the shirt out of the way with his left hand. The butt of a revolver stuck out of his pants, and there was a big jack-knife hanging from his belt. He raised his right hand away from his side. "Get your ass out of here," he said ominously.

The patient pulled up short, and then started to edge toward the door.

"Get out!" MacKinley bellowed. "Get the fuck out of this hospital!" The patient complied, as best he could. He ran out through the door of the treatment room, tripping several times along the way, and headed for the exit. "Man," MacKinley yelled after him, "you bring that knife around here again and you a dead motherfucker!" He turned to Gypsy. "He ain't gonna bother you no more. All them junkies are jive-ass."

"You saved me a lot of time, Mac," Gypsy said, laughing. "I was going to reason with him. And what the hell are you doing with a gun, anyway?"

Jim MacKinley looked at him tolerantly. "Gypsy, where do you live?"

"East Fifty-seventh Street. Why?"

Mac seemed amused. "You ever been on a Hundred Fifty-seventh Street, Gypsy? In the middle of the night? In one of them dark little hallways? Shit! I tell you, man, I never shot anybody in my life, but if I ever got to, I wouldn't think twice about it. Somebody try to hurt me, man, better them than me.

"You know, it was the cops taught me about the blade. They said if you got to shoot somebody, you be sure to shoot him dead. Then you open the knife, wipe it clean, and put it in his hand. They call it a drop knife. Self-defense, man. Say, you want me to get you a piece?"

"No, thanks," Gypsy said quickly. "I'm a pacifist."

"Pacifist?" MacKinley hooted. "Around here? In this neighborhood? Man, you better stay inside the hospital after dark. You going to get your pacifist ass shot off."

Gypsy shrugged. He was always claiming to be a coward, but he still hadn't learned to think of patients as threats to his physical safety. "Mac, seriously, doesn't that kind of thing get to you sometimes? When you've got to pull a gun right in the damn E.R.?"

"What you mean?"

"All these people . . . they don't have to end up like this. I mean, they didn't get sick or anything. They're making themselves sick; they're killing themselves. It's a sin, Mac."

"Gypsy, I been working here a long time," MacKinley

[75]

said. "And I live in this neighborhood. Let me tell you something—these bums ain't worried they're gonna kill themself. They gonna kill you if you don't watch your ass. You a real nice guy, but that don't count for shit in this place. This like a war, man. You got to grow up."

"I'm a doctor, Mac," Gypsy reminded him, as if that vocation somehow exempted its followers from the realities of living. "I don't believe in wars."

MacKinley shook his head. "I hope you make it through the year, man. I hope you make it."

Some of Gypsy's bums were alcoholics. Some of them were heroin addicts, some of them were barbiturate addicts, and a lot were all three. As he'd said, they were all killing themselves slowly. Gypsy had met his first one when he was still an amateur at the Emergency Room game.

Four or five kids had come drunkenly into the treatment room, dragging a semiconscious boy along with them by the feet. He was a big one, about eighteen years old. They deposited him in a heap in front of Gypsy.

"He's sick," the spokesman for the group announced. "He had too much of that Puerto Rican rum to drink. Pump out his stomach, okay?" The spokesman delivered his little speech holding on to the front of Gypsy's desk, and listing to one side. He had had some Puerto Rican rum to drink himself.

"Wait a minute," Gypsy said, "how long has he been like this? Did he take any pills? Does he have epilepsy?"

"Nah," the spokesman answered, reeling back toward the door with his friends. "He does this every night. Too much rum, you know? Just pump out his stomach, man. His name's Hector."

Gypsy went over to the patient and started to examine him. His blood pressure was normal and he was breathing

[76]

okay. Gypsy shook him by the shoulders. "Hector? Hector, what did you take?"

Hector mumbled something and belched in his face. He certainly had drunk a lot of rum. Gypsy decided to put a naso-gastric tube down into Hector's stomach, to see if he could find any pills and to remove whatever stuff hadn't been absorbed yet. Passing an N.G. tube in an unconscious patient can be dangerous, because it can make him throw up, and he may aspirate what had been in his stomach into his lungs. Hector seemed awake enough not to aspirate, though, and Gypsy thought he had an intact gag reflex. He started to pass the naso-gastric tube through Hector's nose into his throat.

Hector's gag reflex was indeed intact, as it turned out. Gypsy got about six inches of tube down, and then Hector made a loud, choking noise and lurched up off the examining table. He staggered around in a drunken little dance in front of Gypsy and pulled the N.G. tube out of his nose. Then he threw up all over himself, and all over Gypsy.

Gypsy wiped the rum-scented vomit off the front of his shirt. "Just relax, Hector," he said reassuringly. "I'm trying to help you."

Hector spit out some residual vomit and punched him in the mouth. "Don't fuck with me, man!" he yelled. "Don't fuck with me. I know karate, man." He saw the guards coming and beat it through the door.

Gypsy got up off the floor slowly, rubbing his mouth with his hand. He had been sitting in yet some more of Hector's vomit, and the seat of his pants was wet and sticky. "I wouldn't think of it," he said to himself. "I wouldn't think of fucking with you."

Alcohol is a poison. Taken in large, chronic amounts it will kill anybody. But you couldn't tell the bums that. Gypsy saw Hector again the following Saturday night. He was com-

[77]

ing back from his dinner in the house-staff cafeteria in the basement, and he found Hector tied up in a wheelchair outside the Emergency Room. Hector was drunk once again, but Gypsy was considerably less enthusiastic than he'd been the last time. His mouth still hurt.

Damn, he thought, if the son of a bitch was bleeding he could go to Surgery. Emergency Room patients were seen initially by either medical or surgical house staff, depending on what appeared to be wrong with them. There was no blood on Hector, though, just a whole lot of spilled and dribbled rum. Gypsy approached the wheelchair unhappily, to see what kind of shape Hector was in this time. "Hector, what's wrong?"

Hector mumbled something and tried to kick him.

Gypsy backed away and went to get help. He returned a few minutes later with an annoyed-looking aide. "Now, Smitty," he said to the aide, "I've got to untie this guy so I can take vital signs on him."

"What for? He looks okay to me."

"Smitty, just get a grip on him, will you? I want to take his blood pressure at least."

Gypsy untied the restraints holding Hector's arms, and Smitty cautiously reached around from behind the wheelchair and grabbed a loose handful of Hector's shirt. Gypsy started to wrap a blood-pressure cuff around Hector's arm. As he pumped it up, Hector suddenly came awake.

"Hey, stop that shit!" he yelled, and ripped off the blood-pressure cuff.

"Whoo-ee!" the aide said, smelling trouble. He let go of Hector's shirt and ran.

Hector stood up uncertainly and tried to take a step toward Gypsy. His feet got tangled in the wheelchair and he slammed over forward, crashing face first onto the floor and knocking down the wheelchair. There was a cracking noise when he hit. He had knocked himself out. He had also split his lip wide open.

Gypsy tried to pick him up. There was blood smeared all over Hector's face, and his lower lip was dripping. "Oh, well," Gypsy decided, "what the fuck. At least he's bleeding now." Gypsy located a pair of guards, and together they picked Hector up and carried him into a neighboring surgical room. "Manuel," Gypsy told the surgical resident who was working there, "we got someone for you to put back together again. Watch out for this one. He's nasty when he wakes up." Manuel nodded acknowledgment, and Gypsy left.

Predictably, fifteen minutes later Gypsy heard a melee break out in the surgical treatment room. He went back next door. Hector was standing on the treatment table, his shirt caked with dried blood, and his face sewed up. He was making karate chops in the air and yelling, "Fuck you, man! Stay away from me. I know karate, man!"

Manuel was cowering in the corner, looking astounded. "I warned you," Gypsy said to him, and walked out into the corridor. He waved for the guards again.

Three big guards came strolling over and entered the surgical room. The sergeant, a pleasant, husky West Indian, stopped in front of the treatment table that Hector was perched on. Hector was still slashing the air and making karate grunts. "Say, man," the sergeant said quietly, and shook his nightstick under Hector's nose. "There's sick people here. Why don't you come down from there?" The sergeant smiled.

"Fuck you," Hector replied. "I know karate."

"Listen, friend," the sergeant explained, still smiling, "if you don't get down off of there, we're going to beat your head in." The two other guards advanced on the table. They weren't smiling at all. Hector took a long look around at the three nightsticks and climbed down from the treatment table. The guards led him away.

Gypsy helped Manuel pick his instruments up off the floor. Manuel was talking to himself in Spanish about going back to Arecibo.

One Friday Gypsy finished his shift at midnight, after an incredibly gruesome siege in the Emergency Room. There had been nine Codes, and they'd lost four patients in a single, awful, two-hour span during the afternoon. And then, for the rest of the evening, it seemed like every drug addict in New York was camped out in the waiting room, campaigning for methadone, Demerol, Valium, and Quāāludes. When Gypsy finally got done and walked out of the E.R., he was feeling more like the junkie Santa Claus than a doctor.

He hiked slowly south for about six blocks, hesitated a minute, and went over to East End Avenue. He walked into Carl Schurz Park; the park was somber and still, and matched his mood. When he came to the Finley Walk, he sat down, spent, on one of the stone benches. Gypsy stared at the river. The East River, particularly late at night, was one of his favorite places in the city. He found himself returning to it, most often all alone, whenever he needed solace. He watched some barges silently appear through Hell Gate and make a slow sweep around the foot of Ward's Island. The massed lights of the hospital loomed up to the left of them in the distance. Then the string of barges passed in front of him and continued their nighttime journey down the river. Gypsy sat there on the bench without moving, wrapped in his thoughts. He was trying to get answers—to questions he hardly even understood he was asking—from the endless, quiet flowing of the dark currents. But he got nothing.

One of the police cars that roamed through the long, narrow park at night, keeping Gracie Mansion and the Mayor well insulated from the rest of New York City, passed behind him. The car slowed to a crawl, stopped, and backed up. The policemen inside inspected Gypsy's huddled figure. They decided he was harmless and drove on. Gypsy hadn't even noticed them. He was extraordinarily depressed.

At 3 A.M. he stood up and walked out of the park. He was very tired, but he just didn't want to go home to his empty apartment. He turned and drifted back uptown. A few blocks from the hospital he came upon one of the all-night pizza places, and he stopped and went in. The only companionship he found was a hostile Puerto Rican counterman and a drunk sleeping on the floor in the corner. He bought a large pizza and fled out of the store with it. Then he walked over to Vittorio's place. Vic had the night off and he was almost certainly fast asleep, but Gypsy badly needed somebody to talk to. Or simply to be around.

He trudged up the stairs to Vic's apartment; the high-priced tenement that Vittorio lived in didn't have an elevator. Vittorio's dog heard him coming, and was waiting, sniffing and scratching behind the door, when Gypsy got there. Gypsy rang the bell a few times. He heard some stumbling around inside the apartment and then the sound of footsteps. Vittorio opened his door.

The Angel rushed out into the hall, waving his tail like mad and jumping up in the air. He thought it was time to play. Gypsy said hello to the dog. Vittorio's dog had turned out to be a monster white German shepherd. He liked to eat and shit, both in great quantities, and he didn't much like Vic's cramped studio apartment.

"Gypsy," Vittorio said, looking perhaps one-quarter awake and rubbing his eyes. "Gypsy, what the hell are you doing here in the middle of the night?"

Gypsy walked into the apartment, with The Angel following him and sniffing excitedly at the pizza box. "Hello, Vic. Did I wake you up? I'm sorry, man; I didn't feel like going home." He sat down at the little dinette table.

"You didn't feel like going home? Gypsy, what's wrong with you? It's three-thirty in the morning. Suppose I was sleeping with some girl?" Gypsy didn't say anything.

Vittorio sighed. He put a pot of coffee on the stove, and stuck the pizza in the oven. Vic's one-room apartment was no bigger than Gypsy's, but it was like a completely different world. His clothes were hung up in the closet. He kept his books in a bookcase, not lying strewn all over the floor. He had some nice new drapes covering the windows. There was even a painting on one wall—a real painting, not a centerfold from *Penthouse*. And there was a little wine rack in one corner of the room. Vic managed to keep his apartment, like his life, under much better control than Gypsy did. And while Gypsy had never paid Vittorio any visits at 3 A.M. before, he had eaten a lot of dinners there. Vic owned all the basic equipment for living that Gypsy could never be bothered to unpack—or, in some cases, even to collect. Like pots and plates and forks. They both favored spaghetti, beer, and pizza.

Vittorio Mazzoli was a fair-skinned intern from northern Italy by way of Staten Island. His sister was going to Buffalo Law School. Gypsy and Vic more or less hung out together, in what time they had to do any hanging out. They didn't see too much of Kid Otto away from the hospital, because he usually hustled himself back to his wife in Bay Shore as soon as he got off duty. She was a terrific piece of ass who had once been Miss Wyoming, and she had Kid Otto by the balls. Gypsy admired tremendously how good Vic was at deciding what was wrong with a patient, and most of the time deciding right. For his part, Vittorio thought Gypsy

[82]

was quite crazy, but he didn't care. He needed somebody with whom to alternate quick trips back to his apartment from the hospital, so that The Angel could go out to crap an adequate number of times when they were working all night.

Vic took the pizza out of the oven and carried it over to the table, trailed by his dog. "Well, what's wrong?" he asked, sitting down opposite Gypsy. Gypsy shrugged and halfheartedly picked up a slice of pizza. He handed it to The Angel; the dog finished it in two quick bites and thumped his tail for more.

"Gypsy, what's the matter with you? I told you to stop feeding him that crap!"

"What?" Gypsy said, with a blank look. "Oh, yeah, I'm sorry, Vic. I just forgot. I don't know where my mind is tonight." He glanced at the dog and shook his head negatively. "Sorry, Angel. Vittorio says no more for you." The big dog looked plaintively at Vic.

"All right, don't make me out to be the son of a bitch—he knows he's not supposed to have that stuff. Besides, he figured out how to get the door on the refrigerator open last week. He's been eating everything I buy, as soon as I leave for work. I don't understand how the damn dog can eat so much."

"Maybe he's still growing," Gypsy said dispiritedly. "I don't know."

"Oh, certainly. He's going to be six hundred pounds when he's full-grown. He already weighs more than I do."

Gypsy didn't smile. He picked up another piece of pizza, looked at it, and threw it back down onto the table. He stood up and started to pace back and forth.

"Gypsy, what's the matter?" Vittorio said with a note of impatience in his voice. "You must have woke me up for something. Has Gallberg been making trouble for you?"

[83]

Gypsy stopped pacing and looked at Vic unhappily. "No," he answered. "I can handle people telling me what to do—I just ignore them. Gallberg's an asshole, is all. It's that goddam Emergency Room. It was a slaughterhouse there today."

"Oh, well, look, what do you want? Everybody gets depressed in that place."

"You don't."

Vittorio laughed. "My reality testing is better than yours," he said, "because I don't smoke all that pot that you smoke. You're as bad as the drug addicts."

"You're an old man." Gypsy smiled faintly. "I'm just less inhibited than you are."

"You're crazy," Vittorio said matter-of-factly. "You should get along very well with all the other crazy people in the Emergency Room."

"That's exactly what else was bothering me," Gypsy exclaimed suddenly. "Everybody's crazy there! It's like a madhouse."

"True," Vic nodded. "I noticed. You should fit right in."

"Vic, that Emergency Room is just like an armed camp. Every other patient comes in packing a butcher knife or a gun or something."

"So? What did you expect in a city hospital?"

"Training," Gypsy shot back, starting to yell. "Experience. Knowledge. Beautiful nurses. You know what I got? I got held up twice. Right in the fucking E.R.! Those douche bags would shoot their grandmother for some goddam methadone!"

"Gypsy, stop screaming, would you? You're going to wake up the whole building. Besides," Vittorio joked, "I think that the junkies sort of sense a kinship with you. They don't have any reality testing, either."

Gypsy failed to laugh. He looked morose. "Ah, Vic, I

don't know. Maybe I should be in some other business. You know what Jim MacKinley said? He said I should get a gun. Can you imagine me carrying a gun around?"

"No," Vittorio admitted. "You'd shoot yourself in the foot, for sure."

Gypsy sat down again. "I'd shoot you in the ass, man. You think you know everything."

"I know when someone isn't worth wasting my time over, and that's more than you know. You want all those bums to act like regular patients. You expect them to cooperate with you!"

"They keep taking me by surprise," Gypsy said, shaking his head slowly. "This one little girl wanted me to fuck her while I was trying to do a pelvic on her."

"I told you," Vic said triumphantly. "They're attracted to you. Did you?"

"Did I what?"

"Did you get into her?"

"Come on, Vittorio. I think she had gonorrhea."

"Oh, too bad. You might have had a meaningful relationship with her, Gypsy."

"Doesn't all that shit bother you ever, Vic?"

"What shit? The crazy people?"

"Everything," Gypsy sighed. "That whole fucking place." He stood up and began pacing back and forth once more. "I just don't understand what I'm doing wrong, man. I work my ass off, and I don't accomplish a goddam thing. Nothing ever changes. There's always a mob of patients waiting when I get there, and there's always a mob waiting when I leave."

"Gypsy, all you can do is see one patient at a time. Nobody expects you to take care of everyone—there's other people working there besides you."

"Ahh, it's not just that, Vic. The whole goddam E.R. is such a mess. Half of the patients don't even belong there—

they belong in a psychiatric hospital or a jail or something. I never even find out what happens to the sick ones. And I never have enough time to spend with any of them—I'm too busy getting held up. It's like a fucking insane asylum!"

"Look, Gypsy, you can't handle all the problems in the hospital by yourself. All you're going to end up doing is killing yourself if you keep on trying. You see your patients and you do what you can. Anyway, you'll get the hang of it sooner or later. Things will improve."

"I don't know, Vic," Gypsy said. "I don't know."

The drug addicts consistently did the alcoholics one better. They were the real sweethearts.

It was not unusual for a junkie's heroin to cost, on the street, two hundred dollars a day. Every day. What this produced was vicious, driven crime, nothing like the random shooting and carving of alcohol. Gypsy was regularly horrified by the savage kind of crimes the junkies chose to commit. How could anyone grab an eighty-year-old man and strangle him by stuffing his skullcap down his throat? Easily, was the answer; eighty-year-old men are not very strong.

Endless relays of junkies also overdosed themselves, because the dealers selling heroin didn't care very much what they cut it with; pleasant things like strychnine were popular. Even without poisons, though, heroin is routinely cut so many times before it reaches the street that huge amounts must be injected in order to get off; when a batch comes along that's a little stronger than usual, the addict has no way of knowing of the new potency. He shoots up in his customary manner, and overdoses. Sometimes he just dies right there. If the O.D. is lucky, someone drags him into an emergency room.

Heroin made the addicts behave like animals, and occasionally the people who were supposed to be taking care of them got brutalized by their experiences. Dr. Gallberg, the nominal head of the Emergency Room staff, had this problem. He worked full time in the Emergency Room, and it was said he had been a nice enough man when he first started. Unhappily, a few years of the same hostile, combative, and assaultive patients, overdosing over and over again, had changed him. The lasting symbol of the Emergency Room, for all the interns who were only passing through that strange place, was Allen Gallberg in his classic pose: bent over an O.D.'d junkie hunting for a usable vein, and slapping him in the face trying to arouse him, and all the while shouting fruitlessly, "What did you take? What did you take? Come on, you bum, what did you take?"

As for Gypsy, he had finally and painfully learned to watch himself with the junkies.

One unreasonably quiet September afternoon in the E.R., Gypsy was treated to the sight of a bunch of junkies carrying an O.D. in through the door. They were holding him off the floor, like an overturned turtle, by the arms and legs. His head was hanging down behind him, and his mouth was open. He looked bad. Gypsy dropped the comic book he was reading and ran to meet them.

"Up on the table," he shouted. "Put him up on the table." The salvage party unloaded their friend on the treatment table, heaving him onto it on his back. Then they stood around grinning and joking and looking pleased with themselves, as if they had rescued a drowning cat, say.

Gypsy checked him over fast. He felt for a carotid pulse in the neck; it was there, but it was very weak. The boy was hardly breathing at all. The pupils of his eyes were tiny dots. Gypsy didn't even try to get a blood pressure; he tore the O.D.'s shirt off and started yelling for Nalline.

Nalline is a fast-acting narcotic antagonist, especially useful for reversing the respiratory depression that heroin causes.

"Anderson! Miss Anderson!" he yelled. "I need some

[87]

Nalline fast!" Gypsy didn't look around to see if anyone was getting the Nalline ready; he was searching furiously along the boy's arms for a vein he could still use. There were hardly any good veins left. The constant shooting up that junkies do infects and scleroses their veins into hard, knotted cords that are no good to the junkie or to the doctor. This O.D. was very young; with his shirt off he looked like a skinny little child. Even so, almost all the veins in his arms were already scarred and useless. There were abscesses that were draining pus scattered over his forearms and the backs of his hands.

Gypsy now had tourniquets on both the boy's arms; he was attempting to make whatever veins were left come up. "What did he take?" he said urgently to the O.D.'s friends without interrupting his frantic search for a vein.

The little group stopped their jiving. "What you mean?" one of them responded angrily. "He's my brother, man. He don't take no drugs."

"Oh, sure. He got all these tracks on his arms by magic, right?"

"He don't take no drugs."

"Jesus Christ, what's the matter with you? Can't you see he's not breathing? Do you want him to die here? We have to know what he took!"

"My brother don't take no drugs, man! We just walking down the street, and all of a sudden he fall out, just like that."

"And stopped breathing," Gypsy added sarcastically.

"Yeah," the boy agreed, grinning. "Ain't that something."

"Terrific," Gypsy said, incensed. "You're a great help! Why don't you get the fuck out of here?"

At this, one of the medical students ran in, carrying a laryngoscope, endotracheal tubes, stylets, and a whole handful of plastic oral airways. He looked around wildly for some place to put all this crap down, couldn't find any, and dumped it all into the sink. Then he retrieved the laryngoscope, which looks like a flashlight with a metal tongue depressor sticking off the end. It is an L-shaped device used to insert a rubber endotracheal tube into a patient's windpipe, if the patient isn't breathing well on his own. The student started sorting through the pile of endotracheal tubes in the sink, trying to decide which size tube to use.

"Excuse me," Gypsy said to the medical student, "would you please get me some Nalline, quick."

"First I have to intubate this patient," the student told him self-assuredly.

"Please go get some Nalline," Gypsy repeated.

"Doctor, the most important thing that must be done with a comatose patient is to establish an adequate airway. Now, I'm going to intubate the patient first, and then . . ."

"Go get the fucking Nalline," Gypsy yelled at him, cutting him off, "or I'll kick your fucking ass in!"

The student dropped his equipment back into the sink and retreated out of the room. He passed Miss Anderson coming the other way, looking lost and carrying a little syringe of Nalline.

"Gypsy," she said uncertainly, "did you want the Nalline?"

"No, not me," Gypsy answered, grabbing the syringe. "Why would I need Nalline? I'm just making a TV show about medical students and drug addicts."

Miss Anderson stared at him. "You are?"

Gypsy managed to find one tiny vein in the boy's wrist that looked okay. He got a small, 22-gauge needle into the vein, and quickly injected five milligrams of Nalline intravenously. As soon as he finished making the injection, Gypsy skipped hurriedly around to the head of the table, behind the patient and out of harm's way. Just at this moment the

[89]

medical student came through the door again, looking sullen and defiant, and carrying another syringeful of Nalline. "Doctor," he announced formally, walking up to the foot of the table, "ten milligrams of Nalline."

"Get out of the way," Gypsy warned him.

The medical student arrived at the foot of the treatment table exactly as the first dose of Nalline started to work. The O.D., who had virtually stopped breathing altogether, began to breathe once more. He sat up on the table, scratching and looking around.

"Aha," Gypsy said. "Miraculous cure."

The patient was overcome with gratitude. "Where am I? What the fuck is this?" He looked down at himself and saw Gypsy's needle, still in his arm. Instantly he got wild. "You motherfuckers!" he screamed. "What the fuck are you doing to my veins?" He ripped the needle out of his arm and threw it on the floor. Then he climbed down off the treatment table and came face to face with the useless medical student, who was standing there pompously, holding his syringe of Nalline.

The newly resurrected patient took one look at the needle the student was holding and kicked him in the balls. Medical student and Nalline went flying. The patient ran for the door, calling everybody he passed motherfuckers.

Gypsy walked out from behind the treatment table and picked up the medical student. "I told you to get out of the way," he said. "Don't ever stand there like that after someone gives them their Nalline. If it doesn't work, then they O.D.'d on something else, like barbiturates, and you can see that in ten or fifteen seconds. If it does work, they usually wake up in a pretty bad mood."

"Oh." The medical student was now holding his crotch. "I see."

Miss Anderson reappeared, with a prescription. She looked around the room. "Did the overdose go home?"

"Yeah," Gypsy said. "Me and Harvey Cushing here cured him."

Miss Anderson shifted her gaze to the medical student, who was rubbing his crotch with a doleful expression on his face. "What's wrong with him?"

"He got a hernia picking up the Nalline he dropped."

"Wow, that's a shame." Miss Anderson remembered the prescription she was holding in her hand. "Gypsy, somebody's got to sign this prescription for all the Nalline. You know," she added, "I wish they wouldn't go home until we find out who they are. The prescriptions don't look good with 'unknown male' and 'unknown female' always written on them. The administrators hate that."

"Anderson, you're right," Gypsy confessed, signing the "unknown male" prescription. "From now on, I'm going to make all the overdoses tell me their name before I wake them up."

"Good," she nodded, walking away with her now legitimatized prescription, "that's a much better way to do it."

The Saturday Night Knife & Gun Club was what the Emergency Room staff called the episodic rape, battery, and murder that the surrounding community indulged in each weekend. The Club by no means restricted its activities exclusively to Saturday nights; there were people out massacring each other every night of the week. But the Saturday nights in the Emergency Room always seemed to be particularly terrible. The real madmen were loose on Saturday.

Gypsy was sitting patiently in the first medical room during one unusually peaceful Saturday night, although technically it was two-thirty Sunday morning. He was looking a little bored; after more than two months in the Emergency Room he figured he'd seen almost everything there was. Sitting with him, and doing most of the talking, were two men and a woman. Everyone except Gypsy was drunk.

[91]

Jim MacKinley stuck his head through the doorway. " 'Scuse me, please," he said to the drunks. "Say, Gypsy, there's seven drivers out here and nothing doing. I'm gonna take one of the ambulances and get some coffee and stuff. You want anything?"

Gypsy stood up and walked over to the doorway. He put on his long-suffering look and took the big ambulance driver by the elbow. "Mac," he said in a low voice, "do me a favor?"

"Sure, Gypsy, what you want?"

Gypsy's voice dropped further. "I'll go get the coffee," he whispered, motioning with his thumb at the three drunks. "You sit and listen to these charming people here."

MacKinley laughed. "No way, man. I just drive the wagon."

Gypsy laughed also. "Oh, well," he said, "I don't blame you. Come on, I'll walk you out." They fell into step together; Mac was chuckling under his breath. "Gypsy, you just don't want to listen to them drunk dudes in there no more."

"Who, me? I love it."

They walked through the wide swinging doors leading to the ambulance dock. Gypsy watched MacKinley climb into one of the high, square ambulances. "Take care, Mac," he shouted as the engine started. MacKinley smiled and then waved as he pulled out. The warning, of course, was not necessary.

Gypsy stared at the empty street after the ambulance turned the corner and headed uptown. Jim MacKinley was an unusual guy, he thought; a very tough and very fine man, and Gypsy believed he actually cared a great deal about the patients. It was raining lightly, and the neighborhood still looked quiet and peaceful.

He walked back into the Emergency Room and rejoined

the three drunks. It seemed like they hadn't even realized he had been gone. The lady drunk was telling a long and complicated story about her husband. She was so loaded that she would babble for a while, and then drift off and fall asleep in the chair. From what Gypsy could make out, she and her husband and her boyfriend had all been out drinking together, and she had decided to dump her husband at the hospital.

She floated close enough to a state of coherence to talk again. "Hey, what's your name, sweetheart?"

"Gypsy."

"Dr. Gypsy," she mumbled, "it's like this . . ." Her eyes glazed over then, and she stopped talking. She was too drunk to remember what it was like.

Suddenly she lurched up out of the chair, and after some fumbling, she got her skirt unhooked and dropped it onto the floor. She had blue underwear on. There was a profusion of bruises on her thighs.

"Look what he did to me, the bastard." She sprawled down into her chair again and started to sing to herself.

"Look what who did to you?" Gypsy asked.

She stopped singing, and surveyed him vacuously. "Oh, yeah," she said finally, "my husband, the bastard. We figured you could admit the bastard to the hospital, you know, and give him an examination and everything. Okay?"

"Lord," Gypsy said. "Lady, if your husband beats you up maybe you should talk to the police."

She didn't hear him. She had passed out.

He looked at this paragon of abused womanhood, flanked by her praetorian guard of drunken husband and drunken boyfriend. The two men were exceptionally well sedated with alcohol, and they were slouched down in little metal chairs on either side of their lady. All three of them were now snoring stuporously. Gypsy sat there along with them, and it occurred to him that he didn't even know which was the boyfriend and which was the husband.

A siren whined in the distance. Gypsy hardly noticed it. Sirens were not exactly unusual in this neighborhood; police sirens, fire-engine sirens, and automatic sirens blaringly announcing cars being stolen could be heard going by all night. But this siren didn't go by. It built rapidly to a piercing crescendo and came wailing into the ambulance dock. Flashing red lights flickered through the windows. Gypsy jumped up and ran toward the swinging doors. He hadn't heard any ambulances pull out since Mac left for coffee, and Mac never made a commotion with the siren and lights unless he had a real bad one in the back.

Gypsy rushed out into the ambulance dock. The whole courtyard was lit up with the eerie, flashing, red and yellow lights of the ambulance and two police cars. The police cars seemed to be filled with hysterical, screaming people. The back doors of the ambulance were kicked open from the inside before Gypsy could reach them. MacKinley jumped down from the ambulance. He hadn't even bothered with the stretcher; he was cradling a boy in his arms like a baby.

"Gypsy!" he yelled. "Gypsy, he's not breathing!"

Gypsy wheeled around and ran back to the swinging doors. He held them open for Mac, who raced into the Emergency Room carrying the boy.

"Put him in Surgery," Gypsy shouted, following after MacKinley. They ran into the first surgical room with the boy, and Mac laid him down on the treatment table. Gypsy and the surgical resident started ripping his clothes off. "I'm sorry, I'm sorry," Mac kept saying. "Gypsy, I'm sorry. I couldn't drive no faster."

A policeman appeared in the room. "He was stabbed, doc," the cop said breathlessly to Gypsy. "I think he got it in the chest." A woman and a lot of screaming people followed the policeman into the room. "Davey!" the woman shrieked when she saw him lying there. "Oh, Jesus, Davey!"

Gypsy didn't look up from what he was doing. "Get his family out of here, for God's sake!" he yelled to the guards.

They had the boy stripped. There was a small stab wound next to his sternum on the left side. He had no spontaneous respiration, no pulses, and the pupils of his eyes were wide and fixed. There was nothing left.

They Coded him anyway, more out of frustration than out of any hope of salvaging anything. Someone was pumping his chest. Gypsy intubated him and began bagging him. Some other people were starting cutdowns in both of his ankles.

A surgical resident, in desperation, tore open a thoractomy tray. He grabbed a scalpel and sliced open the boy's chest, right there in the Emergency Room. The whole mediastinum and the left pleural cavity were filled with blood. The left lung was lacerated and collapsed. The pericardial sac, around the heart, was filled with blood too, and there was a gaping tear through the myocardium, the heart muscle itself. They tried to sew up the hole; they injected epinephrine, and then calcium chloride, directly into the heart. Nothing. The boy's brain was already dead.

"All right," a chief surgical resident said finally. "That's it. The Code's finished."

Gypsy sat down in the corner. The whole thing had been hopeless from the start. All the magnificent emergency care available in a city hospital is useless when the patient gets there dead. This one was seventeen years old.

MacKinley came over to Gypsy. "I'm sorry," he said in a choked voice. He looked desolate. "I was going up Third Avenue . . . and there was this kid laying in the street, with all these people around him. . . . He was just laying there, Gypsy. I got him in the ambulance, but I seen right away he didn't look good. I got here as fast as I could. . . . Jesus Christ, I couldn't drive no faster . . . I'm sorry . . . I'm sorry." He was crying.

"Mac, stop it," Gypsy said quietly. "You didn't do anything wrong. He was dead before you picked him up."

Once it had ended, most of the people who had poured into the Emergency Room to help with the Code left and went back upstairs. One of the surgical residents returned to the E.R. from the direction of the waiting room. He motioned to Gypsy. "You the intern down here?" Gypsy nodded. "Well, you better go out there and tell his family," he said curtly. "Maybe you can get an autopsy consent."

Gypsy looked at him wide-eyed. "Jesus, I don't think I can do that, man."

The resident was already on his way to the door. He stopped and glanced at Gypsy without any sympathy. "That's part of your job, doctor. What do you think you're here for?" He walked out.

Gypsy hesitantly stepped through the other door and into the waiting room. The boy's family were clustered numbly around his mother. Gypsy walked up to them and bit his lip. "Uh . . . ," and he stopped. "I . . ." His voice cracked.

He swallowed dryly. "I have to tell you something," he began again, in a small voice. "Your son took a bad worse."

They all looked at him uncomprehendingly. "I mean," he said, floundering with the words, "your son took a bad turn for the worse."

"God, God," the mother shouted, "oh, my God, no!"

"I mean," Gypsy struggled on, "I mean, he . . . he passed away. He died."

"Davey, Davey!" She was screaming. "Oh, my God in heaven, Davey!" She flung herself on Gypsy and started to batter him in the face with her fists, screaming and crying. "You killed him! You killed him!" Some of the other people pulled her away.

Gypsy stood there, staring at his feet and feeling like a criminal. What are you supposed to say? Your seventeen-year-old son who was laughing and talking to you thirty minutes ago is dead now, I'm very sorry? In medical school Gypsy's disasters involved stuff like falling down drunk in front of the patient and his preceptor during Physical Diagnosis. He hadn't known anything about a thing like this. The intern always took care of it.

He went to McDonald's when he got off duty the next morning and bought his usual mound of hamburgers and french fries. But he couldn't eat. After a while he threw the whole tray into the garbage and walked out. He wandered over to the Central Park zoo and watched the seals swim around until closing time. Someone had to remind him to leave.

# The Private Service

WHEN GYPSY WAS STUMBLING his way through medical school, he was certain that the four years of torture would never end. And although a host of deans and department chairmen were constantly threatening to flunk him out, deep down inside he had a kind of mystical faith that they wouldn't really bounce him. He just expected to grow old and fade away, somewhere in microbiology. His friends, all of whom were also down there in the bottom tenth of the class and no intellectual giants themselves, kept reassuring him that four years was only four years. Small consolation.

Incredibly, one morning in May Gypsy found himself dressed up in a colorful academic gown, waiting in line to receive an M.D. He was filled with sloe gin. The line shuffled along, as Gypsy continued to sip from his pint bottle, chuckling over his imminent good fortune. He progressed to the foot of the stage and swayed drunkenly up the steps.

The hundred-year-old president of the university was propped up in the middle of the stage, getting his annual airing and handing out diplomas. Gypsy weaved over to the old gentleman and had a rolled-up diploma thrust into one hand. Then the president tried to shake his other hand, which was already occupied by the bottle of sloe gin. Gypsy and the hundred-year-old president each held one end of the bottle and pumped it up and down together a few times. The president let go. "Next," he croaked.

Gypsy stayed where he was. "Have a snort," he offered, holding out the bottle again.

"Keep moving, keep moving," one of the other fossil professors lined up on the stage whispered. Things were beginning to bunch up behind Gypsy.

"Have a drink," Gypsy insisted. "Don't you want to drink with me?"

The hundred-year-old president had no idea what was happening. He was running on permanent automatic pilot. Somebody handed him the next diploma, and he tried to give that one to Gypsy, too. Gypsy's hands were both full, one with his own diploma and the other with his sloe gin. "Heh, heh," he said, "I'll trade you, man. Let's have a party."

The guy behind him on the line poked him in the side. "Get the fuck out of the way, will you? My father's trying to take my picture."

Gypsy grinned and backed away, and fell off the front of the stage.

Medical school was over.

Like medical school, and like all the other ordeals of his delayed adolescence, the Emergency Room passed. Gypsy surfaced from the acid bath of the E.R. and found that he had learned almost nothing, except that the most important piece of equipment in an emergency room—when you could find them—was its detachment of hospital guards.

He also found that he had a whole new collection of assholes to deal with, because in October Gypsy got shipped over to St. Peter's Hospital, the voluntary hospital with which his program was affiliated, to put in his time on the private service. It was a pretty good private service. Since it was a teaching service, with interns, residents, and medical students, the private attendings had to be fairly sharp. Nonetheless, it was not a ward service, and that made a difference. The attendings on a city hospital-ward service are the senior, and chief, physicians on the ward. Their job is to oversee

[99]

the medical care of every patient on their ward, and to teach the house staff and the medical students. They are functioning in an academic role. The attendings on the private service were functioning in a different role. They were just what "private service" suggests—private doctors, physicians in private practice who had admitting privileges at this hospital. Since St. Peter's was not Elsewhere General Hospital, but was instead one of the teaching institutions of a large medical school, most of the people who held admitting privileges were of very high caliber. Some of them, in fact, were so good they were also attendings back on the wards. A few of them, including all the G.P.'s, were awful.

There is an outworn American institution—the family doctor. The G.P. Any English-speaking middle-aged male, so long as he has short hair and a Cadillac, qualifies as sacred family healer. Especially if he makes house calls, and has a lot of thick journals that have never been opened lining the walls of his office. People may resent their doctor's affluence (though not his working hours), and they may neglect to pay his bills, but they trust him, and they believe in what he says. No matter that he is a half-senile old crock of a general practitioner who had to go to Mexico to get into any medical school at all; no matter that he graduated forty years ago and hasn't read a textbook since; no matter that he thinks a platelet is a small dessert plate and that vitamin $B_{12}$ cures colds: he is Their Doctor. All the other doctors in the country are supposed to be medical robber barons, but this schmuck is Hippocrates reincarnate.

A lot of these G.P.'s blithely admitting patients to proprietary hospitals are doing frightening things, and getting paid for it. And even the G.P.'s at the affiliation hospital could fuck up anything. Gypsy, fresh from the Emergency Room, had barely finished adapting to homicidal patients with switchblades and guns. He wasn't ready for the culture

[100]

shock of the private service, and attendings with empty brainpans. An "emergency," for one thing, was defined a little peculiarly on this new rotation. Back in the pit Gypsy had just come from, an emergency meant that a patient was shot in the head. Here on the private service, it turned out to mean some patient didn't want to wait a week for a bed, so his G.P. had declared the elective admission to be, suddenly, an emergency. Patients were not often admitted to the private service because the police dragged them into the Emergency Room. They were admitted usually because their doctor said to them, "Look, you're sick. You've got to go to the hospital." The house staff had nothing to do with this decision, and ordinarily the private doctor was reasonably rational about it. Ordinarily.

Gypsy's very first admission was, sure enough, an emergency. The charge nurse on six paged him, and told him, "Doctor, you have an emergency admission in six-oh-three. A lady named Reilly."

"Six-oh-three," Gypsy repeated, "right. What's she got?"

"Dr. Braughtman sent her in with a diagnosis of shock."

"Oh, Jesus, I'll be right there." He ran for the elevator. The elevators were both motionless, with a penciled sign hanging between them that said, "Elevators Not Running."

"Christ, what's the matter with the elevators?" Gypsy shouted to a man in a hospital uniform who was sitting in front of the "Not Running" sign.

The gentleman turned down his portable radio. "Elevator man's on his coffee break."

"Well, who are you?"

"I'm the elevator starter."

"Okay, okay; start the elevator, quick, and take me up to six," Gypsy said urgently. "I have a patient up there in shock."

"Nope." The elevator starter shook his head. "Nobody's

allowed to run the elevator except the elevator man. Union rules. And he's on his coffee break."

"Get fucked," Gypsy told him. Then he took the stairs up six flights; they have a strong union, the elevator people. Gypsy reached the sixth floor and ran into Room 603. There was a fat lady sitting in the bed, eating Hershey Kisses out of a large cellophane bag.

"Mrs. Reilly?" he said,panting.

"Um?" she answered, with a big blob of chocolate in her mouth.

"Mrs. Reilly, how do you feel?"

She swallowed a couple of times, and belched. "Say," she asked, "how come I'm in a room with a black-and-white television?"

"What?"

"Dr. Braughtman said I could have a room with color television. Does that look like a color TV to you?" She pointed at the television set hanging from the ceiling; she was watching a hospital soap opera. In black and white.

Gypsy put his bulging doctor bag down and seated himself on the edge of the bed. "Mrs. Reilly," he said, trying to catch his breath, "I'm not in charge of the television."

"Too bad. It's ruining my whole day." She offered him a handful of Hershey Kisses.

Of course she wasn't in shock. Gypsy examined her anyway, assuming in his innocence that, for a hundred and fifty dollars a day, there must have been something wrong with her that she wanted fixed. He took her blood pressure and her pulse. He listened to her heart and her lungs. He felt her belly and banged on her back. He hit her in the knee with his rubber hammer. He flashed his little light in her ears, her eyes, and up her nose. He poked into all her holes. Everything was there that should have been there; nothing extra and nothing missing. And nothing wrong.

"Lady," he said finally, "I can't find anything wrong with you."

"Oh, of course not. Were you looking for something wrong?"

Gypsy was bewildered. "Well, uh, Dr. Braughtman said you were in shock. That's why he admitted you to the hospital, isn't it?"

"Oh, *that*." She made a deprecating gesture with her hand and laughed. "You should have said so. Of course I'm in shock; my house got robbed again last week. I was robbed once five years ago, and I was in shock then, too. I don't know what Great Neck is turning into. Whenever something like this happens I go into shock; it's really too much for me. I just need a nice quiet place to watch television for a couple of days. You know?"

Gypsy looked at her strangely. "Why don't you go to a hotel or something?" he said slowly.

"No, my health insurance would never pay for that."

He started packing up all his lights and hammers. "Mrs. Reilly," he requested, "would you excuse me, please? I think I have some other admissions to work up."

The next patient was in 547. Gypsy walked down one flight, left his footprint on a wet step, and got yelled at by the porter washing the stairs. Gypsy apologized and explained that the elevator man was probably still on his coffee break. The porter thought that was a poor excuse. Gypsy went to look for his patient.

He walked into the nursing station. "Hello," he said. "Do you have a Nachman here? Five forty-seven?"

"We sure do. The patient's on the floor already. That's an emergency admission, you know."

"Another one? What's the diagnosis?"

"It says 'Severe Cardiac Failure' on the admission card."

"All right," Gypsy said. "Which way is five forty-seven?"

"To your left, doctor. Ah, doctor?"

"Yes?"

"Are you the gypsy?"

Gypsy smiled. "That's my name," he admitted, not entirely without a trace of pride to his tone. He tossed his hair rather theatrically and walked out of the nursing station. Then he strutted confidently down the hall into 547; he thought he looked like Marcello Mastroianni playing a decadent doctor. The nurse thought he was just another intern who was a little crazy.

There was a scrawny old man in the room, and he was packing a suitcase. Gypsy put on his affected, mellow, doctor voice: "Mr. Nachman?"

The elderly, bony, frail-looking patient turned around. He was wearing long drawers, an undershirt, high black socks, and garters. He was holding an orange bathrobe. "So!" he said. "You! Stay away from me." He began to fold up the bathrobe, which had "Orlando Florida" stitched on the back in bright green.

"What?"

"You want I should drop dead in here, in this sweatbox?"

"What?" Gypsy said again.

The man finished folding his bathrobe, stuffed it in, and slammed the suitcase shut. He started hopping up and down on one leg, trying to get the other leg into his trousers. "No air conditioning! *Gevalt*, a room with no air conditioning! You want I should sleep out on the windowsill, maybe? What is this, a prison here?" He hopped into the bathroom, sat down on the toilet bowl, and got his other leg into his pants.

"Mr. Nachman," Gypsy said apologetically, "I'm sorry about the air conditioning, but you can't just go home. You're sick. You have, uh, congestive heart failure. Your doctor admitted you as an emergency."

Nachman waved a spindly finger at Gypsy. "Enough already with the heart failure. Enough already. The *momser* doctor should only get heart failure."

Gypsy spread his arms helplessly. "Mr. Nachman, I don't know what to tell you. This is an urgent medical problem you have."

Nachman had thrown his shirt on and he was heading for the door. "Enough with what you're going to tell me. I'll tell you something, boy doctor. Heart failure I can do without, maybe, but air conditioning I can't do without! When you got a room with an air conditioner, then you can fix the heart failure." He manhandled his suitcase out the door. "Some business you run here," he added, picking up the big leather suitcase bodily and marching toward the elevators.

Gypsy stood there for a moment, looking around the empty room.

A disturbance broke out almost immediately in the hallway. "Shit," Gypsy said to himself, "the poor guy has collapsed." He walked out of the room and stared in the direction of the nursing station. There was Nachman. He didn't look like a man in congestive heart failure. He had apparently finished paying his respects to the nursing staff, because everyone in the nursing station was gaping, dumbstruck, out through the glass partition. Across the corridor, Nachman was standing in front of the elevators, which of course weren't running. He was holding the suitcase over his head and banging on the elevator doors with it.

"Come up here! Come up here!" he was yelling. "You lazy goddam *schvartzes*, come up here with that goddam elevator!"

Gypsy approached the elevators. "Mr. Nachman, stop that. You're going to hurt yourself. You're a sick man, you know."

Nachman stopped banging and looked at Gypsy with his suitcase poised above his head. "You again? The boy doctor? With an earring yet!"

Gypsy fingered his earring. "You like it?" he asked. "A lot of old guys don't."

"I'll tell you what I like," Nachman answered him. "To maybe get the hell out of this place! Where's the goddam stairs?"

"Over there," Gypsy said, pointing. "But you shouldn't carry that big suitcase down those stairs. Your face is all red; you're a sick man, Mr. Nachman."

"Again with the sick business?" Nachman yelled. "Again? Twenty-five years I got heart failure, and now all of a sudden it's an emergency! I can't have an air conditioner, huh? You should all only get heart failure!" He lowered the suitcase and disappeared into the stairwell.

"Oh." Gypsy was mystified by the entire performance. "Thank you. Have a nice weekend yourself." He walked back to 547 and went inside to get his black bag. He picked the bag up, and then put it down again, and, saying, "Hospital, shit on you," he stretched out on the bed and closed his eyes.

There was a knock on the door. Gypsy opened his eyes and found a dietitian lady standing in the room. "Mr. Nachman? What would you like for breakfast tomorrow?"

Gypsy pointed to his black bag. "Nothing," he said. "I just work here." The lady left.

Gypsy sat up on the edge of the bed and sighed. He reached over to the telephone and dialed the Admitting Office. "Hello; this is the admitting intern."

"Oh, good," some clerk at the other end said. "We were looking for you."

"Me first. You know the emergency admission, Nachman? He went home."

"Doctor, you can't discharge that patient—he just got here. His attending is the only one who can discharge him."

"Okay," Gypsy agreed readily enough. "But I wouldn't try to collect any money from him if I was you."

There was a pause on the line. "What?" the clerk said finally.

"Nothing. Why were you looking for me?"

"Oh, yes, I almost forgot. You have another admission. An emergency."

"Of course," Gypsy said. "What other kind do you get here?"

"Schmedlitz," the clerk said.

"Schmedlitz? Schmedlitz who?"

"No, it's a patient of Dr. Schmedlitz," the clerk explained. "In room three thirteen."

"Three thirteen? Okay, what's this one got? Hiccoughs? Athlete's foot?"

"Dr. Schmedlitz phoned in. He said the patient has massive hematuria."

"Hematuria?" Gypsy said. "Massive hematuria? You mean somebody's really sick? God damn. Thank you." He hung up, ran out of the room, and raced down to the third floor.

He ran into the third-floor nursing station. "I'm the admitting intern. You have an emergency admission in three thirteen?"

One of the nurses nodded at him. "Yeah. Dr. Schmedlitz called the floor and left a message for you." She handed him a piece of paper. "I think this is what he said." The note read:

Sending in psychotic sixty-four-year-old man. Massive hematuria. Please evaluate.

"Okay," Gypsy said. "Get me a Foley catheter, and an

I.V. set, and a liter of D5/and W. And get me the G.U. resident in the house, please. Did anybody take vital signs on this guy yet?"

"They're taking them now."

"Good." Gypsy walked hurriedly over to room 313. Inside, he found a nurse taking the patient's blood pressure.

"All right, what are his vital signs?" he asked.

"They're pretty stable. Pulse is eighty-four and regular; blood pressure, one thirty over ninety."

"Great, he's not in shock yet. Let's make sure we keep him that way. I want to start an I.V. and get a Foley into him. Sir," he said, turning to the patient, "how long have you had blood in your urine?"

"He won't talk," the nurse said. "And he only understands Greek."

"Shit," Gypsy swore. He pointed at his own crotch. "Blood?" he said to the patient. "Lots of blood?" The man needed a shave. He patted his groin and grinned.

"Damn. You got the Foley?" Gypsy asked the nurse.

She handed him a catheterization tray. Gypsy opened the tray and put the sterile gloves on. Then he quickly cleaned off the man's penis with some alcohol sponges and greased the end of the Foley catheter with Surgilube. He took the catheter, which is a long, flexible rubber tube, and started threading it up the man's urethra.

"Aiiyiiiyiii!" the patient yelled.

"I'm sorry, sir," Gypsy told him. "But we have to know how much you're bleeding." Gypsy advanced the Foley into the man's bladder. Then he directed the loose end at the small plastic jar that came with the catheterization tray. He got a nice stream of clear yellow urine. He waited. No torrent of blood. In fact, no blood at all. Plain, ordinary piss.

"What the fuck? Now what's going on?" Gypsy pulled the catheter out and looked at the end that had just been swimming around in the patient's bladder. No blood; not even a drop. He tossed the catheter in the garbage pail, and then he carefully inspected the man's penis.

"Uh-uh," Gypsy said suddenly to the patient, "look what I found." He pointed at a meager little cut, about half an inch long, and twisted the guy's penis around on itself so he could see it, too. The minuscule wound wasn't even bleeding. "I don't believe it—is that the emergency?"

The man grinned at him again, and holding his thumb and first finger together, he jerked his hand up and down in the air.

"God damn it," Gypsy exclaimed, "that's it! That's really it." He walked into the bathroom, peeled off the rubber gloves, and threw them into the toilet. Then he started talking to the toilet. "What kind of place is this?" he asked. "Am I crazy or something? Is this what I went through medical school for?" The nurse was watching him talk to the toilet through the open bathroom door. The patient was holding his penis up by its tip and laughing.

"My God," Gypsy said. He walked out of the room and stalked toward the nursing station. His eyes were red. He met the charge nurse coming the other way. She was trundling an I.V. pole in front of her, and carrying an I.V. tray, a cutdown set, dextran—in effect a whole shock kit.

"Where are you going?" she demanded as Gypsy tramped past her. He stopped and turned around. There was a nasty expression on his face.

"Put all that crap back."

She gave him a what-does-the-stupid-intern-know stare. "Doctor," she said sarcastically, "if your patient has lost a significant amount of blood, don't you think he needs to have his intravascular volume replaced? Before he goes into shock?"

"Hah! Lost what blood? He didn't even lose his goddam

[109]

foreskin! Now put that crap away and get me this Schmedlitz's phone number."

She looked at Gypsy for a moment and decided not to say anything else. They marched back to the nursing station together and she handed him a file card with a telephone number on it. Gypsy dialed the number, and a lady flunky answered.

"Dr. Schmedlitz's office."

"I want to talk to Schmedlitz," Gypsy said menacingly. "This is the hospital."

A thick, peculiar accent came on the line. "*Ja?* Here is Schmedlitz."

"*Ja* yourself, you asshole."

"What? What?" Schmedlitz said indignantly. "Who is talking?"

"Gypsy is talking, you schmuck. Have you got any idea at all what the hell you're doing?"

"What? Who is going on here?"

"Certainly not you, moron," Gypsy said. "Tell me something, do you happen to know what's wrong with the man you just sent in to the hospital?"

"*Ach*, the man who is speaking only Greek. Yes?"

"Not quite, no. The man who is speaking only nothing. The man who is shaking his penis at us."

"So," Schmedlitz said, identifying the case. "The penis. *Ja, ja,* this man I am knowing, and sending I am to the hospital. Terrible hematuria he is having."

"Pigshit!"

"Doc-*tor*," Schmedlitz replied, accenting the second syllable, "my diagnosis you are questioning?"

"My God," Gypsy said, "are you blind? Did you do a urinalysis? Did you examine the patient?"

"No," Schmedlitz admitted promptly, "I am not examining the patient. For why I am making an examination?

The family is calling me, and saying terrible blood it is, in the u-*reen*. So I am sending him quick to the hospital, so."

"So your head is full of u-*reen*," Gypsy told him. "This guy is urinating nice, normal piss. Just piss. The only goddam blood he's losing is going to be when he pays your bill."

"Bleeding he is not?" Schmedlitz said slowly.

"No," Gypsy repeated, "bleeding he is not. He has a zipper bite. A tiny fucking zipper bite. He caught his prick in his zipper, and he has a little half-inch cut on it. And it isn't even bleeding! Let me ask you, Schmedlitz, do you think a zipper bite requires an emergency hospitalization? Do you realize this is costing that schmo a hundred and fifty dollars a day?"

"Doc-*tor*," Schmedlitz protested, "I am not knowing he is only bite in the penis by his zipper. The family is saying, terrible blood from the u-*reen* is coming."

"Oh, bullshit from your mouth is coming. The family? *The family*? Are you admitting the goddam family to the hospital? Schmedlitz, holy shit, why don't you examine your own patients?"

"Doc-*tor*, what I am to do? The family is calling me . . ."

"God knows what you're doing, Schmedlitz," Gypsy interrupted him. "Don't ask me. You certainly ain't practicing medicine. Tell me something else, will you? Do you have a license?"

"What?" Schmedlitz got hot again. "What you are saying? Forty-two years I am doc-*tor*, and never I am talking to like this by anyone!"

"Forty-two years, huh? What have you been doing for forty-two years—jerking off?" Gypsy hung up the telephone, and put his head down on the desk in front of him.

A minute later one of the other lines rang. The charge nurse picked it up and listened. Then she turned around in her chair and said to Gypsy, "Hey, what's-your-name, the

G.U. consult is calling about your emergency admission in three thirteen. He's on his way up to see the patient now, and he wants to know if they should get an operating room ready."

"God," Gypsy groaned, raising his head off the desk, "no! Look, tell him I'm sorry, but the whole thing is a mistake ... oh, yeah," he added, "and somebody put a Band-Aid on that imbecile's penis and send him home."

The charge nurse got off the phone. "Doctor," she reminded him innocently, "you can't discharge a private patient. Only his attending can discharge him."

"You're right, you're right," Gypsy said. "I'm sorry; I forgot. Just put a Band-Aid on his penis and do whatever you want with him."

"Doctor"—she finished showing him who was boss, smiling sweetly—"you have to write orders on the patient first."

"Fine, fine. Whatever you say." Gypsy took the order sheet out of the patient's chart and wrote:

Please put Band-Aid on penis. Thank you.


Since there was never anything very urgent to do on the private service, Gypsy began to amuse himself by playing games with the charlatans. Some of these fools were worse than others. Kevin Costello, for one, was an idiot who fancied himself a "G.I. specialist." He worked with the Abromovitz Gang. This bunch of crooks demonstrated nice rapport between the disciplines of Internal Medicine and Surgery. Dr. Costello was the front man; what he claimed to be was an internist. He would see patients who had wandered into his office for one reason or another, and find out that they had stomach pains.

"Oho," Costello would say, "you have to go into the hospital and have these pains in your stomach evaluated."

The patients would be admitted to the hospital, and Dr.

Costello would evaluate them. That is to say, he would have the radiologist evaluate them, by means of upper G.I. barium examinations. As soon as the exams were done, he would copy the radiologist's report into his note in the chart, and draw little diagrams demonstrating the minute ulcers that the radiologist had found. He was a good front man, and most of the people Costello brought in did indeed have peptic ulcer disease. Then he would walk into the patient's room in his three-piece suit and gravely show the patient his little diagrams. "I have finished my evaluation; you are suffering from peptic ulcer disease—that is why you have pains in your stomach. I am going to call in Dr. Tallman for consultation."

Which he did. Dr. Tallman was the gunman for the outfit—or in this case, the knife man. *His* fantasy was that he was a general surgeon. He would come in, also wearing a three-piece suit, feel the patient's belly a bit, and say, "I agree with Dr. Costello. You have peptic ulcer disease. We will do an operation and cure you." Which they would do. Except that, postoperatively, the patient always managed to get a wound infection. This was never actually a part of the holdup plan; the Abromovitz Gang just had a tendency to be a little sloppy in their work.

Dr. Tallman would return to the patient's room and say, "You have a wound infection. I am going to bring in Dr. Costello, the internist, again for consultation." So Dr. Costello would be called back in on the case.

With careful neutrality, Gypsy would watch the Abromovitz Gang work. After all, these patients did have peptic ulcer disease. But then Kevin Costello would come sidling up to him in the nursing station, fidgeting with the Consult sheet.

"Ahem," he would ask offhandedly, "uh, Gypsy, what's good for Klebsiella?"

"What?" Gypsy would say, straight-faced.

"My, uh, colleague, Dr. Tallman, has a patient with a wound infection—it's growing out Klebsiella. I, um, can't seem to remember which antibiotics Klebsiella is sensitive to." Pause. "What do you think I should put him on?"

This was the consultant talking.

Gypsy would play with him a little bit. "I don't know, Dr. Costello, I guess I'd stick with whatever the sensitivity report said the bug was sensitive to." Then he'd put his nose back in the chart he was studying and play mute. Of course the sensitivity report on the wound in question hadn't come up to the floor at that point. Even Costello could read.

"Well, uh, actually, Gypsy, I can't seem to find a sensitivity report. I don't think it's back yet." Costello would push the Consult sheet around in nervous little circles on the desk, trying to look reflective. He was reflecting that he had no idea what to write down.

"No sensitivity?" Gypsy would say distractedly. "Oh, well, why don't you just put him on, ah, what-do-you-call-it . . . you know."

"Right, right," would come the eager acquiescence from Costello, "that's it. It's on the tip of my tongue. Uh, uh . . ."

"Klebsiellacin," Gypsy would tell him blandly.

"Of course, of course, Klebsiellacin," Costello would say with relief, suddenly writing confidently in large, purposeful script across the Consult sheet. "Oh, yes, uh, Gypsy, what's the dosage for Klebsiellacin?"

"I forget, Dr. Costello; you better look it up." This would send Kevin Costello scurrying off ambitiously to look up the dosage of the new miracle drug. Five minutes later one of the other interns would come in laughing. "Hey, what's that asshole Costello talking about now? He's walking around asking everybody how much Klebsiellacin to give. There's no such thing as Klebsiellacin!"

Gypsy would be quiet.

\*　　\*　　\*

[114]

"Shit," Gypsy said out loud one morning, after he'd been marking time on the private service for a number of weeks. He had just taken the last pair of clean whites off his couch, which was where he kept his supply of them. This meant that he had to make an irksome trip to the house-staff laundry room at Manhattan County for more clean uniforms. He gathered up the huge pile of dirty whites from the other end of the couch and carried them downstairs with him. It was almost a shame, Gypsy reflected, even to be getting uniforms dirty on the slow, dull, gentlemanly private service. However, he stuffed them all into the already overburdened back seat of his Fiat, and after work that day he drove over from the voluntary to the city hospital. They had finally given him a sticker for the house-staff parking lot, once he no longer needed it since he was working at the affiliation hospital.

As he pulled into the parking lot, he saw Jim MacKinley crossing Third Avenue with Arthur Nerd. Nerd looked like a small white mushroom next to MacKinley. Gypsy parked the Fiat and collected all his uniforms from the back seat, and as he walked toward the gate Arthur's car came barreling past him. Nerd had all his windows rolled up and he looked even more scared than usual. Gypsy tried to wave and dropped a couple of pairs of white pants. He smiled anyway and yelled, "How's your ass, Arthur?" Nerd didn't even slow down as he went by him and roared out onto Third Avenue.

Gypsy tried to control the flapping uniforms with one hand and scoop up the pants from the ground with the other. MacKinley walked over and retrieved the trousers.

Gypsy grinned at him. "Thank you, Mac. How you been? What's happening?"

"My man," MacKinley said, grinning back. "You look like a ragpicker, Gypsy."

"I know, I know. I have to bring all my fucking uniforms

in; I think I let it go a little too long. What are you doing hanging out with Arthur Nerd?"

MacKinley laughed. "One of them junkies beat Dr. Nerd up in the parking lot last week. Now he won't go home by himself no more—I got to walk him far as his car."

Gypsy burst out laughing, too. "You're kidding! How come?"

"Who knows, man? Maybe Dr. Nerd wouldn't give him no methadone or something."

"You're probably right. What happened to Arthur? Did the guard rescue him?"

MacKinley laughed again. "No way—the jive guard went to get the police! You know that big resident, Dr. Di Bello? He come out and saved him. Dr. Nerd was scared shitless."

"My God," Gypsy said. "What a zoo."

They crossed the street back to the hospital together.

"Hey, take care, Mac. I've got to go to the laundry room."

"I got to go to work. Catch you later, man."

Gypsy trudged down to the house-staff laundry room in the basement. Anything that involved house staff always seemed to get relegated to the basement. On his way through the corridor he heard some fitful coughing, and when he turned the corner to the laundry room he found Irene standing at the end of a small line. She was balancing an impressive bundle of white skirts in both arms and trying to light a cigarette.

Gypsy put his own whites down on the floor and lit her cigarette for her.

"Thanks," she said. "How's life?"

"All right, I guess. I'm on the private service."

She shook her head sympathetically. "They've got some crew over there."

"You ain't kidding," Gypsy agreed. "How are you doing?"

"Oh, okay. I just hope today's my day at this damn laundry place. I always forget if I'm Tuesday or Thursday."

[116]

The guy in front of her left the window, muttering. Irene stepped up to the half-door and maneuvered her whites onto the little counter. The laundry man looked at the big pile suspiciously.

"Hello," she said. "I was wondering if I could exchange these skirts, please. They're not the right size."

"What's your laundry number?" the laundry man inquired immediately.

"Two-oh-six."

"Today's not your day. Thursday's your day."

"I'm sorry," Irene apologized contritely. "I forgot. Couldn't you make an exception, please? I need something to wear."

The gods must have been smiling. "Well, all right," the laundry man said without much enthusiasm. "What do you want?"

"I'd like to exchange these skirts, please. They're the wrong size, and they don't fit."

"What'd you say your number was?"

"Two-oh-six," Irene repeated.

He picked up the skirt on the top of the pile and peered under the hem. "That's what you got." He pointed at the skirt he was holding in his hand. "Two-oh-six, it says two-oh-six right here."

Irene took a deep drag on her cigarette. "Yes," she said, "I know it does. I didn't say I've got the wrong number. I said I've got the wrong size. They're too big." She took a skirt off the pile and held it up. It reached from her armpits down to the floor. "See?"

The laundry man examined the rest of the skirts, one at a time. "They're all clean," he said finally. "I can't take back clean uniforms. It's against the rules. They got to be dirty."

Irene threw her cigarette on the floor and ground it out under her heel. "What," she asked slowly, "would you like me to do? Wipe my ass with them?"

The laundry man looked very startled. "You know," he said after a moment, "you got some mouth for a little girl." Then he picked up the pile of skirts and disappeared into the back of the laundry room.

"Thank God," Irene said gratefully, and lit another cigarette.

There was a long wait. Finally the laundry man reappeared, carrying a new bundle of white skirts. He stacked them up on the counter. "I'm doing this special," he told Irene. "I'm not supposed to take any clean uniforms back."

'Thank you, sir. Thank you very much." Irene picked up the bundle, and then, with a knowing look, she put the skirts down once more. She examined the waistband on one of them, and quickly sifted through the others. She started to cough.

"You gave me the wrong size again," she said in a resigned voice. "They're all Extra-Large, just like the other ones. What good does that do me? Be reasonable. I'm five foot three. Does Extra-Large sound like my size?"

"Lady, what do you want from me? You said your number was two-oh-six, didn't you? Then I gotta give you two-oh-sixes. That's the rules. Why don't you make them shorter or something if they don't fit? Can't you sew?"

"Yes, I can sew," Irene snapped. "But I happen to be a doctor and I don't have the time to do any goddam alterations on any goddam skirts."

"Well, I gotta follow the rules," the laundry man insisted. "The best I can do, I can give you a form for a change in your laundry number. You fill that out, and you take it to . . ."

Irene had a coughing fit. "Forget it," she said when she recovered. "Just forget it." She picked up her pile of Extra-Large white skirts and walked off.

It wasn't Gypsy's day either, and he left with the same

pile of dirty whites he had arrived with. He caught up with Irene and they walked out together.

"Too bad," Gypsy said to her. "I thought you were going to win there for a while."

"Oh, I never win. This has been going on for a year and a half now, ever since I was an intern."

"I was wondering why you always wore such long skirts. Why don't you try to get a new laundry number, like that shithead said? Maybe it would work."

Irene smiled. "The last time I tried that they started giving me morgue attendant's uniforms. That makes a big hit, when you go up to the patient and it says 'Morgue Attendant' on your sleeve."

"Yeah, I bet." Gypsy laughed.

"Anyway, what do you think of the private service?"

"It's a big change from the E.R., all right."

"Like night and day." Irene nodded. "But at least you get a lot of time to read."

"Oh, sure," Gypsy agreed. "I've got a lot of free time to learn stuff. It's just—well, Jesus, I didn't know there were so many assholes around. Some of those damn G.P.'s don't know anything. I mean, forget about medicine, I don't think half of them are able to tie shoelaces. And they've all got big practices, too. Those guys really bother me, Irene."

"Yeah, I know what you mean. It's very depressing at first. You've just got to try to be better than they are," she said. "Well, keep the faith. I had enough for one day."

Gypsy was beginning to find the faith a little hard to keep.

Jacob Abromovitz was the other gunfighter with the Abromovitz Gang. Abromovitz was a night rider, and top dude of the gang. Gypsy found out about him one night in November when he was covering the Cardiac Care Unit. The C.C.U. was one of the few first-rate things about the

[119]

private service. It was, quite surprisingly, an altogether excellent Unit.

The on-call room for the Unit is right next door to the Unit itself; that way the intern is only fifteen seconds away from the patients, even when he's asleep. Gypsy was in the on-call room about 1:00 A.M., doing the part-time EKG technician, when the telephone rang. Gypsy didn't fuck around with the Unit; next door, perhaps, but that was something else. He snatched up the telephone while he was still inside the girl: "Yeah, what's wrong?"

"Gypsy, don't get excited," the nurse in the Unit said. "Nobody's gone bad."

"I was excited," Gypsy answered, feeling his erection shrink. "Not any more. What's up?"

"That's a bad joke, Gypsy. We're getting an admission. Post-op."

"Post-op? I thought we were a cardiac unit."

"Well, the patient may have had an infarct on the table," the nurse explained.

"An infarct on the table? In the middle of the night? What were they doing?"

"A diverting colostomy," the nurse said. "It's the Night Rider."

"The which?" What was left of Gypsy's erection disappeared. He sat up on the edge of the bed. "What are you talking about?"

"It's an Abromovitz Special."

"I don't know what you're talking about," Gypsy said. "Honest to God I don't." The part-time EKG technician climbed off the bed and sat down on the floor in front of him. She put his penis in her mouth. Gypsy got his erection back.

"Yeah, well, the Night Rider always operates at night," the nurse informed him casually, as if that explained every-

[120]

thing. "Anyway, it's not a big deal, Gypsy. It's just a colostomy, and the patient isn't even out of the Operating Room yet. Why don't you finish what you're doing first, and then you can come in here." She snickered.

"Ho-ho," Gypsy said sarcastically, "the C.C.U. nurse is a real wit." He hung up. The part-time EKG technician put her arms around his waist and took hold of his backside. Gypsy leaned back against the wall, but with a puzzled look on his face.

"You better hurry up," he requested. "Something funny's going on."

A short while after they finished, the phone rang again. The Night Rider was there with his patient.

"Don't go away," Gypsy said, getting his pants on. He walked next door to the Unit.

The oldest man Gypsy ever saw was lying in the end bed with a huge dressing over his abdomen. A thin, tired-looking man in a threadbare, shiny suit was sitting at the desk in front of the cardiac monitors, writing in a chart. He was almost completely bald, and the striking lack of hair made him look much older than he really was. He had combed the few hairs he had left all the way forward, from their origin at the back of his head, in a pathetic and futile attempt to improve his appearance.

"Who are these people?" Gypsy said to the nurse.

"Gypsy, this is Dr. Abromovitz. The old gentleman there is his patient. He just had a diverting colostomy performed, and he may have had an acute M.I."

Jacob Abromovitz and Gypsy looked at each other. Abromovitz took in Gypsy's flowing hair, and his earring, and his headband. "What are you supposed to be?" he asked snidely. "A wild Indian?"

"Dr. Abromovitz, until eight o'clock tomorrow morning

[121]

this is my Unit. What the hell do you think you're doing here?"

The nurse stepped between them, wearing a resigned expression. "Gypsy, come over here with me a minute, would you?" They walked into the corner, next to the old man's bed. The old man was looking at the ceiling, smiling and comprehending nothing.

"Say, listen, don't you know what this is all about yet?" The nurse seemed surprised. "What have you been doing all this time?"

"Minding my own business," Gypsy replied, "and trying to get laid. And I've got no idea what's going on here."

"Jesus," she said. "Look, what Abromovitz does is, he goes around to a bunch of nursing homes at night, see. He does colonoscopies on everybody he can find, and he gets thirty-five dollars a throw."

"Come on. In the nursing home? At night?"

"He does!" the nurse protested. "He's got a portable fiber-optic colonoscopy set, and he carries it around with him. Listen, it gets better. About once a month he finds somebody with a little polyp, and he does a polypectomy. You know—through the scope. Only, this time he perforated the colon. He had to whip the patient into the hospital to do his repair. Usually that doesn't happen."

Gypsy shook his head slowly. "But, my God," he said, "what for? Look at this poor old guy. He must be a hundred years old. He didn't know that he needed a polypectomy, and he doesn't know that he's had one now! He doesn't know anything! What's all this for?"

The nurse shrugged.

Jacob Abromovitz was a colon and rectal surgeon. He had been a bright child, and a bright young man, with no money. He broke his ass for four years in college, and for four more years in medical school. For the seven years after that, he really had no life of his own. All through a surgical internship, four years of a general surgery residency, and two more years of a colon and rectal surgery fellowship, all he did was work. He worked all day, every day, except that on alternate weeks he got Sunday off. He also worked all night, every other night. After seven years of this, he joined two other men in their surgical group practice, and of course became the junior man in the group. But nobody wants a junior man cutting on their colon, even if the junior man is almost middle-aged and three-quarters bald. So for a long time Abromovitz didn't get to do anything himself, except cover his partners' post-op patients. To do that, he went on call every night. It was a little too much. It had made him old and sick before his time. He quit the group and hooked up with Tallman and Costello.

Gypsy walked back to the surgeon sitting in front of the cardiac monitors. He watched the glowing tracings squiggle across the screens for a while. "Abromovitz," he said finally, "tell me something. Did you really have to do this guy tonight?"

The Night Rider looked up at him. "Of course I did; he had a perforated colon."

"Isn't that because you perforated it?" Gypsy asked.

"That's not the point," Abromovitz answered impatiently. "The point is that he had a polyp, and he needed a polypectomy."

Gypsy smiled a cold smile. "You don't think he could have gotten by with his polyp, huh? You really think he had to have the polyp removed in the middle of the night."

"Certainly." Abromovitz was becoming annoyed. "It's only a twenty-minute procedure. I wouldn't even have had to bring him into the hospital if he hadn't perforated."

"I know how long it takes to do a polypectomy," Gypsy told him. "What I'm wondering about is how you could possibly justify doing it to a patient like that."

Abromovitz swiveled his chair around to face the nurse.

"Is this the best we can do for house staff these days? Hippie freaks? When I was an intern I cut my hair and kept my mouth shut. Period."

"Let me ask you something else," Gypsy said quietly. "How much money do you get for this nonsense?"

Abromovitz jumped off the chair and turned purple. "That's not important," he yelled. "And it's none of your goddam business anyway! What's important is that I've improved the whole quality of this patient's life!"

Gypsy laughed out loud. "Improved the quality of his life? What are you talking about? Look at him, for God's sake! He's completely senile—he couldn't tell you what his own name is."

"Senility is no reason to suffer with treatable colonic disease," Abromovitz intoned. "The polyp might have become malignant at any time, if I hadn't found it."

"Become malignant?" Gypsy said incredulously. "Abromovitz, so what if it became malignant? Don't you think he could have lived out his life okay with a malignant polyp? What does he care if his polyp is malignant?" Gypsy walked back to the old man lying in the end bed, with the vacant eyes and the big white bandage around his abdomen.

"Look at this guy," he said pityingly. "You want to operate on him so bad, all right. Why don't you fix his cerebral atherosclerosis? Don't fuck around with his polyp, when he's got no brain left. Why don't you figure out how to give him his brain back?" There was no more hostility in Gypsy's voice, only resignation.

"I think you're crazy," Abromovitz said.

The nurse interrupted softly from across the room. "You want to know something, Gypsy?" She was rolling her pencil back and forth between her fingers and looked preoccupied. "The surgical fee for a polypectomy is nine hundred and fifty dollars."

"That's a standard fee!" the Night Rider immediately exploded. "I gave up half my life to learn to do this!"

Gypsy looked at him with renewed contempt. "Nine hundred and fifty dollars," he marveled. "Abromovitz, how do you live with yourself?"

"You think you're so special, you hippie?" the Night Rider yelled at him. "You think you're better than everybody else? Wait a few years. Wait until you start trying to pay off your loans. Wait until you have to pay for a nurse, and a technician, and a secretary, and the rent on your office. Wait until you've got to pay somebody just to sit there all day long and fill out insurance forms. Wait until you've got to pay a goddam fortune every year for your lousy malpractice insurance! Come back here when you've got three kids to support and preach to me about how much to charge!"

Gypsy went back to the on-call room to get another blow job.

"What was all that shouting?" the part-time EKG technician said to him as he was taking his pants off again. "What's happening out there?"

"Nothing," Gypsy said. "Just a bandit."

"Bandits? Real bandits? Where?"

"Right next door. In the C.C.U."

"Wow! Real bandits, in the hospital! I want to go see." She reached for her underwear.

"No, no," Gypsy said quickly, "I was only fooling. It's this surgeon, Abromovitz."

"Oh," she said, putting down her panty hose and looking disappointed. "Dr. Abromovitz. He's a nice man."

"He's a bandit, is what he is."

The part-time EKG technician looked at him accusingly. "You said there was no bandits."

"Forget it, I just meant he was a crook."

"He's a nice man," she repeated. "He has a very sad life."

"Yeah, I bet. He gets depressed making all that money in the middle of the night."

"Well, it's not his fault. He needs to make a lot of money."

"Why? Does he collect racehorses?"

"No, I don't think he has any racehorses," she said, sounding like she was attempting to remember if he did, "but his ex-wife gets twenty-five hundred dollars a month alimony."

Gypsy stared at her. "Twenty-five hundred dollars a month? Are you sure? That's thirty thousand dollars a year! He pays thirty thousand dollars a year just for alimony?"

"Yeah. I think he has to pay something for his kids, too."

"Holy shit," Gypsy said. "The guy is really screwed. How did you find out any of this?"

"He told me all about it one night when he came down here from the O.R. He said he wanted to run away to South America, but he was afraid he'd never see his kids again. He likes his kids."

"Jesus," Gypsy said reflectively. "What a lousy life. Why the hell was he killing himself all those years, then? He would have been better off if he was a garbage man."

"Well, I'm not sure," she ventured. "He doesn't look strong enough to carry big heavy garbage cans around."

Gypsy had sort of stopped listening to her. He was thinking about Abromovitz. "What am I doing here anyway?" he suddenly asked himself out loud.

"You're on call, aren't you?" the part-time EKG technician answered him, putting his penis back in her mouth again.

"Yeah, I guess so," Gypsy said. "I guess that's what I'm doing here."

Just before he was ready to come, he looked down at her

and asked another question: "Am I going to end up like that?"

She took his penis out of her mouth. "What?"

It was precisely the wrong moment for his penis to be waving around free in the air. Gypsy came right in her face.

"Jesus Christ, what'd you do that for!" she cried, and started hunting for some tissues. Gypsy said he was sorry and handed her the roll of toilet paper he was still carrying around in his black bag, a souvenir of the hay-fever season. She cleaned herself up. "What did you say before?" she asked then.

"Do you think—well, that I'm going to end up like that too? Like Abromovitz?"

"I don't know. I thought it depends on if your grandfather was bald or something."

Gypsy smiled sadly at her. "No," he said. "That's not what I meant."

After she left he stood in front of the window for an hour, staring down at the empty street. Once in a while a car would go by. At 4 A.M. he walked into the Unit and checked on vital signs. Everybody was okay, including the old man. Gypsy returned to the on-call room again and settled onto the bed, but he didn't take off his shoes or turn out the light. He knew he wasn't going to fall asleep.

# The Nurse
# Who Got Religion

A FEW BORING and tedious weeks later, Gypsy was sitting in the fourth-floor nursing station early in the morning, and having very little else to do, he was countermanding the orders on one of Dr. Sam Feldt's patients. He was trying to prevent a recurrent disaster from happening once again. This patient had fairly intractable congestive heart failure, but old G.P. Sam was afraid of digitalis. "Digitalis is dangerous in elderly people," he liked to say. Of course it was, but so was congestive heart failure. Sam figured, however, that nobody could blame him for a patient's heart failure, but that he might get blamed if the patient developed digitalis toxicity. So he wrote orders for puny—and hopelessly inadequate—doses of digitalis. Two days later, as the patient's blood levels of digitalis dropped, the poor patient would go into pulmonary edema. Most often at night. The house staff had to spend three hours fixing him up so he could breathe again, with morphine, and furosemide, and rotating tourniquets, and oxygen. The patient, of course, was constantly terrified. And sick. Naturally, the house staff rewrote saner digitalis orders after each of these episodes.

Sam got quite paranoid, though, about interns and residents rewriting his orders. Apparently this kind of clownlike stupidity was going on again, because Gypsy saw that some fairly reasonable digitalis orders on the patient had been crossed out. Printed in big red letters was:

NO ONE IS TO WRITE ANY ORDERS IN THIS CHART EXCEPT MYSELF.

Samuel Feldt, M.D.

[128]

Beneath the warning was a digitalis schedule that was going to have the hapless patient in pulmonary edema again by dinnertime.

"Ah, shit," Gypsy said to himself. He drew a neat line through the note from Feldt, and wrote:

Please disregard the above instructions.

Then he put down a realistic digitalis schedule. He handed the order sheet over to the floor coordinator when he was through, and started working on another chart.

The floor coordinator looked at the order sheet for a few minutes. She cleared her throat. "Uh, Gypsy, I don't know what to do with these orders."

"Don't tempt me, man, or I'll tell you. Just have the nurses pick them up, all right?"

"No," she said, "I can't." She frowned, trying hard to think. "Your orders say not to pick up Dr. Feldt's orders. But Dr. Feldt's orders say not to pick up anybody else's orders. Doesn't that mean we can't pick up any orders on this patient at all?"

Gypsy was composing a reply equal to such a question when a frantic medical student burst into the nursing station. "Gypsy," he shouted, "Gypsy, I need help, quick! A real bad G.I. bleeder just came in—a patient of Dr. Feldt's."

"Funny you should mention that name," Gypsy said, getting up.

"Come on, come on," the student urged. He rushed back out of the nursing station and went racing off down the hall.

Gypsy came trotting after him, laughing. "Hey, doc," he called to the student, "slow down. I'm getting too old for this kind of thing." That was not true; considering his lifestyle, Gypsy was in modestly good shape. He was just very lazy. At the rate he was moving he would probably have never caught up with the student, except that the boy went around a corner too fast and crashed into the gentleman emptying the garbage cans.

Gypsy picked him up. "I told you to slow down, didn't I? You should listen when I try to teach you something."

This medical student was a very official-looking one, even with garbage hanging from his eyeglasses. He had a lot of tubes and instruments sticking out of the pockets of his white coat. Gypsy brushed the student's clothes off for him, and the kid made an exasperated appeal: "Gypsy, I'm not fooling. The man's bleeding out."

Gypsy stopped what he was doing. "You got a sick one? Really?"

The student was desperate. "Yes, yes. The guy has bad rectal bleeding. He's a real pumper. ~~That's~~ *There's* blood all over the bed!"

"All right, let's go." Gypsy followed the student into one of the large, corner rooms. There was a man lying facedown on the bed, not moving. Except for his head and his shoulders, he was completely covered by a sheet.

There was also a nurse in the room. She was wearing a white pantsuit uniform, and she had long, burnished black hair. She was standing in front of the window with her back to the patient, looking outside. Gypsy got furious.

"Excuse me," he said loudly, "but could you tear yourself away from the view for a minute? There's apparently a patient here with massive gastrointestinal bleeding. Underneath that sheet there. Do you think you could get me some vital signs on him? Like a blood pressure, say, if you're not too busy?"

The nurse had turned away from the window at the beginning of this speech. She was no ordinary nurse; Gypsy recognized her immediately. She was a part-Malaysian, part-English piece of ass whom Gypsy had had his eye on for weeks. She came over to them and folded her arms in front of her.

[130]

"Fuck you," she told him. "Why don't you examine your patient, doctor? I don't think anyone else has bothered to yet, except for me."

With a sudden sinking feeling of *déjà vu*, he crossed the room to the bed and pulled the sheet back. There was no rectal bleeding. There was a cut on the patient's ass, and there were three little chromic stitches on the cut. The blood was all old and dried. Gypsy had made a terrible mistake; he had believed something a medical student had told him.

Gypsy turned around and rubbed the back of his neck. "Uh," he asked the student, "what happened to the rectal bleeding?"

"I have to go to a lecture," the medical student said, and left.

"Okay," Gypsy quietly addressed the nurse, "what is this?"

She shook her hair out of her eyes. "Well," she began, "the man got drunk at his office and fell down. Only, he had his bottle in his back pocket, and it broke, and he got cut in the ass." She went up to the wastebasket and retrieved part of a broken bottle of Hennessy cognac. "See?"

Gypsy walked over to her, and they inspected the broken bottle together. "That's good stuff," Gypsy noted.

"Oh, yeah; he's a lawyer. Anyway, his secretary got scared and called his wife, and his wife called Sam Feldt. Dr. Feldt sent him in as a G.I. bleeder; I guess it sounds better than a drunk who fell down. They sewed him up downstairs in the Outpatient Department," she continued, "but he was so drunk they shipped him up here to dry out. I told the charge nurse we had a new admission, and your student walked in and got hysterical. Anything else, doctor?"

"What's your name?"

"Karen," the nurse said. "Why?"

Gypsy shuffled his feet a little. "Look, Karen, I had no

[131]

business shouting at you. I was wrong—I'm sorry. Would you have dinner with me tonight?"

Karen laughed. "Why? Because you feel guilty for yelling at me? Or because you like my body?"

"Both," Gypsy admitted.

Karen fooled with her hair, thinking. "Okay," she said finally. "Write down your address. I'll meet you in front of your house about eight o'clock."

They had hamburgers for dinner. Then they took a walk to Carl Schurz Park, and watched the tugboats pulling barges down the East River. "Well," Karen said, smiling in the half-darkness, "that was a pretty elegant dinner."

"What's wrong?" Gypsy asked, looking hurt. "Don't you like McDonald's? I go there all the time for hamburgers."

She kissed him on the cheek. "I know; you told me. I was just kidding—I like hamburgers, too. But you can't eat hamburgers all the time, Gypsy; you'll get sick. You have to eat other things also."

"I do. I eat french fries, and chocolate milk shakes."

"You're going to get scurvy," Karen said. She held on to his hand, and they watched the river go by. It was very quiet. After a while, Karen shivered and squeezed his hand. "Gypsy, are you cold?"

"A little. You want my coat?"

"No," she said, "I want to go back."

Gypsy got up from the bench. "Okay. I'll walk you back to your car."

Karen stood up and put her arm through his. "Let's go to your house."

They strolled south, looking at the river. Where the John Finley Walk ends, there's a big stone stairway that goes right down to the edge of the water. A little concrete path starts at the bottom of the stairs. The two of them walked slowly along the path. Behind them, the cars whistled past

[132]

on the F.D.R. Drive. A couple of feet away, on the other side, the black currents of the nighttime East River were swirling by, almost without a sound. Further south, they could see the lights of the Fifty-ninth Street Bridge hanging over the river. They came to another set of stone steps, which led to one of the narrow footbridges over the Drive. Gypsy stopped when they were halfway across, and stared down at the lights of the cars rushing along underneath them. He was having a few laughs on the private service, and he was helping an occasional patient, and he was even learning a little medicine. But as the year dragged on, he was finding fewer and fewer things in either hospital that didn't end up making him depressed.

Karen watched him, wordlessly, for a long time. "Gypsy, what's wrong?" she said finally.

Gypsy sighed. "Oh, I don't know, Karen. A lot of things. Nothing's turning out this year like I expected it to. And I hate that damn private service—I'm not doing anything there."

"Hey," she said, laughing, "you've got it good at that place. What are you complaining about? We take all the shit from everybody."

"Really? I thought it was pretty easy for the nurses. You know, you have an eight-hour shift, and then you just go home when you're done."

"Well, yeah, we don't have to put in the hours that you guys do. But it's still a very frustrating place to work. Look, I spend half my time taking care of patients who aren't even sick, and the other half getting insulted by stupid G.P.'s who know less than I do. I didn't go to school for that."

Gypsy smiled at her. "You sound like me. That's what I'm always telling my friend Vic."

"At least the interns have some responsibility, Gypsy. You must get a little satisfaction out of that."

[133]

"Sure," he said. "I'm responsible for the color TV, according to my patients."

"You know something? Those people really like you. Your patients are glad you're there." Gypsy looked at her. He wasn't sure if she was making fun of him or not.

"I'm not kidding," she went on. "Kennedy talks about you all morning, after you guys make rounds."

"Oh, well, Kennedy; he's a prince. Kennedy likes everyone."

"Mrs. Feinberg, too," Karen insisted. "She's always saying Gypsy did this, and Gypsy said that, and isn't Gypsy wonderful. And she doesn't like anybody."

"That's the truth," he conceded. "Mrs. Feinberg hates the whole world. Why does she like me?"

"They all like you, Gypsy. You talk to them, and you crap around with, and you make them laugh. You don't realize how important that is. I wish I knew how to do that."

"Well," Gypsy said, "what you do is a lot more important than making them laugh. You're the one who has to be there with them all the time. Don't you like taking care of patients?"

"Not any more," she shook her head. "You want to know a secret? I'm quitting pretty soon."

"Honest? Is it hard to find jobs, for a nurse?"

"It's easy," Karen said. "But I'm not interested in another job. I've had it with nursing."

"You mean you're just going to give it all up? For good? What about nursing school and everything?"

Karen shrugged. "I made a mistake, I guess."

"Damn. I wouldn't ever have figured that; I thought you loved your work."

"I used to. Anyway, how do you know?"

"I've been watching you," Gypsy confessed. "I like to watch you bend over."

[134]

Karen poked him playfully. "You're as bad as the rest of them." She took his hand again. "Come on, let's go."

They walked over to Gypsy's building and got into the elevator. "Say," Gypsy asked on the way up, "what are you going to do if you quit?"

"Oh, I've got some plans," she said with a distant smile.

Outside his door, Gypsy started to fool with his keys. "Listen, Karen, it's a little messy in there. I mean, it's not really dirty, you know? It's just that I don't put things away. I don't want you to get freaked or anything."

"Gypsy," she said, "open the door."

He started to make another speech, stopped, and put his key in the lock. He swung the door open, and Karen followed him into his one-room home. Gypsy hadn't lied; everything that he owned except his Fiat and his motorcycle was piled up haphazardly in the room. Karen took her jacket off and draped it over some cardboard boxes. "What's in these cartons?" she asked.

"My dishes," Gypsy said.

"Your dishes?"

Gypsy opened one of the big cartons. He took out a dusty plate and held it up. "See?"

"What do you eat with?" she said, giving him a concerned look.

"Mainly I go down the block. For hamburgers."

"How come you never unpacked your dishes, Gypsy? I mean, you live here."

"Well, if I did that I'd just have to pack them up again, when I moved out."

Karen wandered through the room happily. "My God, it's like F. A. O. Schwarz in here."

"I know," Gypsy agreed. "I like toys."

She pointed at one of a number of piles of little blue boxes. "What's in all those little blue boxes?"

[135]

"Spark plugs," Gypsy said. "KLG F-eighties."

"But there's dozens of them. All over the place!"

"Yeah, I have a sick motorcycle. It needs a lot of spark plugs."

She looked around at the yo-yos, Tinkertoys, bubble blowers, and motorcycle parts. "Comic books!" she exclaimed, tripping over a pile of them. "Gypsy, do you really read comic books?"

"Sure," he said. "They're good for your soul. You want to see my coloring books?"

Karen laughed. "Do you have any crayons?" she asked. Then, "Never mind, I guess you've got crayons, too." She sat down on the bed, which was the only flat surface in the room that didn't have things stored on it. She lit a cigarette and scrutinized the apartment some more. There was a lot of stereo equipment, with speakers along one wall. A guitar amplifier was sitting in front of the bed, and Karen counted three guitars. It was hard to tell exactly, though, there was so much crap everywhere.

"You like music, don't you?"

"I like rock and roll," Gypsy said. "You want a Diet Dr. Pepper or something?"

"No, but I'd like an ashtray."

Gypsy went rummaging through the apartment for an ashtray, and Karen picked up an intravenous bottle from next to the bed. It had a little funnel covered with tinfoil and some tubes sticking out through a cork.

"Is this thing a water pipe?" Karen asked.

"Uh-huh," Gypsy said. "I made it myself."

"Do you have any dope?"

"Dope?" Gypsy repeated. He handed her the ashtray. "Oh, yeah, lots of dope."

"Let's get stoned."

They got stoned together. Actually, they weren't even

smoking very good dope. Gypsy had so many plastic bags and little bottles scattered around—all of them filled with grass—that he didn't know which stash was good and which was bad any more. By accident, he picked a stash of kind of average dope, but they smoked so much of it that they ended up very wasted anyhow.

Gypsy stood up, swayed back and forth some, and made it as far as the stereo. He started a big stack of the Rolling Stones playing, and turned on his blue and red lights. Then he made a slow circuit around the room shutting off the other lights. It seemed like hours went by before he got back to the bed.

Karen lit another cigarette, and dragged on it in slow motion. "Oh, wow," she said. Gypsy was quiet. He was lying on his back, getting off on the patterns the drifting smoke was making in the dim light. The Stones were doing "Wild Horses." Gypsy rolled over and smiled at Karen, and started tracing circles lightly on her stomach with his fingertips. He kissed her. She kissed him back and rubbed out her cigarette in the ashtray. Then she took his face between her hands. "Do you want to fuck?"

Gypsy looked at her stupidly. "Sure," he said.

She moved away from him and pulled her blouse off over her head. Then she half sat up, unhook'd her bra, and dropped it on the floor. She had small breasts, but it was too dark to say much about her nipples. She twisted out of her jeans. Then she put her head back, and using her heels to support her weight, she raised her hips and pulled her panty hose down to her knees. Gypsy managed to help her out of them.

He sat there smiling at her. She was a slender girl, with a tight, exciting body.

"Hey," she whispered, "get undressed."

Gypsy giggled a little from the dope. "Damn," he said,

"I forgot." He tried to unbutton his shirt. He didn't function as well, stoned, as she did. Even with Karen helping, it took him a long time to get rid of his clothes.

"Oh, fuck this," he muttered finally, when he was naked except for his socks, "I want to touch you." He left the socks on and lay down next to her on the bed. She stretched out her arms to him, and he shifted his body halfway over hers, hooking his leg across her thighs. Karen put her arms around his back and held him; he rubbed his mouth slowly against her lips and licked her face. "You're nice," she said. She kissed him and ran her tongue around the inside of his mouth. Gypsy sucked on her tongue.

They did this for a few minutes, but it seemed like they were playing with each other for a really long time because of the dope. Then Gypsy got up on his knees. He stroked Karen's face with one hand and took one of her breasts in his other hand. He squeezed it gently and then massaged it slowly with his palm. He felt her nipple standing straight up, and he reached for the other nipple. He rubbed this one back and forth between his fingertips. Karen drew a deep breath in and sighed.

Gypsy bent down over her and kissed her breasts. "You have a lovely body," he said.

She looked at him and smiled. "I think my tits are too small."

Gypsy woke up a couple of hours later. He tried to locate the water pipe and discovered he was too stoned, so he just sat there laughing to himself for a while. Then he crawled around Karen and slid down onto the floor. He found the dope and tried to roll a joint, but between the colored lights and his head, it wasn't easy. Karen came to also, and found him licking his fingers.

"Hi," she said, hanging her head off the edge of the bed

to watch him work. "What are you licking your fingers for?"

"Hello, Karen. I'm not licking my fingers. I'm licking the joint to make it stick together."

Karen laughed. "Gypsy, I don't see any joint."

Gypsy stopped licking and examined what he was doing. She was right; he had fucked it up completely. The dope had almost all trickled out of the joint he was trying to construct. He wasn't thinking very well, either; all he'd done was to go on adding more and more rolling paper in a muddled attempt to keep the joint intact. What he had ultimately produced was a damp little lump, made up of Zig Zag paper, spit, and not much dope. He looked at the lump.

"Fuck," he said.

Karen giggled and crawled off the bed. "Come on, we'll do it together." They tried again, sitting on the floor next to each other. With a certain amount of laughing and kissing, and half the package of Zig Zags, and a quarter of an ounce of dope, they created a single, multilayered, giant joint. It looked like a soggy cigar.

Gypsy held it up toward one of the blue lights and peered at it doubtfully. "What do you think?"

"I don't know," she said. "It's dripping. You shouldn't lick them so much."

Gypsy put his hand on her leg. "You're right," he agreed, grinning. "I shouldn't lick them so much; I'm wasting my talent. Let me lick you a little bit."

Karen laughed and crawled away. "Oh, no, you don't. Let's smoke it first."

"Heh, heh," Gypsy chuckled. "Okay, let's get high." Karen crawled back and arranged herself cross-legged on the floor in front of him. Gypsy handed her the slimy monster joint.

[139]

"You hold it," he said, "and I'll light it." He fished around and found the matches, and leaned over to light the joint. Then he got involved with gazing down at her crotch and forgot about the matches.

"Karen," he told her, "you have some beautiful body. I mean, lots of girls are exciting when they're undressed, but you're really nice to look at."

"Gypsy," she said, "light the joint."

"Oh, yeah, the joint." He put a match to it, and Karen took a cautious toke. Instantly her eyes bulged out and she pushed the joint at him frantically. Gypsy relieved her of it and watched her curiously. She was apparently fighting back a tremendous cough. Finally she exhaled a cloud of thick gray smoke.

"It's pretty hot, huh?"

"Whew," she said hoarsely, "it's a fucking dragon."

"Just take little hits," Gypsy encouraged her. "This is good for you." They worked on the gigantic joint, the two of them alternately coughing and choking, and then coming back to try again. They finished almost the entire thing, but at the end it was like trying to smoke a blowtorch. Gypsy carefully extinguished the mammoth roach.

"You want to do some coke?" Karen asked.

Gypsy shook his head. "I want to do you."

"We'll see." Karen languidly stretched her arms out over her head and leaned back until she was lying flat on the floor. Her ankles were still crossed in front of her and her knees were splayed apart. Gypsy was very stoned. He sat there feeling numb for a few minutes, staring between Karen's legs. Then he crawled over to her and separated her ankles. He put his head down and kissed her thigh.

"Stop."

"What?" Gypsy picked his head up so he could look past her waist.

[140]

She smiled at him. "Let's get up on the bed first."

"The bed? All the way up there? It's okay down here."

"Come on," Karen said, suddenly determined.

They tried to climb onto the bed together. It was only about eighteen inches off the floor but they were both really blown away. Karen got her shoulders up first, and then she just kept crawling forward on her face until she pulled the rest of herself up also. She finished flat on her stomach, giggling and exhausted. Gypsy made it up after her, eventually. "My God," he said, "why did we do that?"

Karen laughed into the mattress. She felt too stoned to get her head off the bed, and her voice came out muffled. "I think we smoked a pound of grass."

"Hey, you remember what we came up here for?" Moving around on the bed was a little tricky for him and Gypsy kept toppling over, but he finally managed to steady himself on his knees next to Karen. He climbed over her leg carefully, and wound up kneeling between the backs of her thighs, with Karen, still lying on her stomach, prone underneath him. Then he put his arm around her waist and reached down between her legs. She responded, spreading her thighs, and started to get wet again. She sighed softly. "Umm . . . that feels nice."

Gypsy leaned over and kissed the back of her neck. "Lift your hips up, honey."

"Oh, wow," she said sleepily, and did as he said. She kept her chest down on the bed and got to her knees, raising her hips in the air in order to bring her vagina up closer to him. Gypsy forced her legs a little further apart with his own knees and held her tighter. Then he tried to get into her rectum.

She jumped like he was using an old broomstick—with splinters. "Ow!" she yelled, twisting her ass around. "Stop it, stop it. Take it out!"

Gypsy stopped. "What's the matter? You have hemorrhoids or something?"

"That's the wrong hole! You're trying to put it in the wrong hole."

"It's a pretty good hole," Gypsy said, lifting her hips again. "Now come on, open up."

"Stop that! Gypsy, please, don't stick that thing up my ass. It's too big. It hurts!"

He let her go. "Really? It does?"

"Yes! It hurts a lot. Maybe . . . maybe if you used some Vaseline or something . . ."

"Vaseline?" Gypsy said. "Karen, I don't remember where the Vaseline is. I'm pretty stoned, you know? I mean, I don't even know where to look for any goddam Vaseline."

"Gypsy, please?"

Gypsy sighed and backed out from between her legs. He was way too stoned to cope with the problem; he looked around the room helplessly for Vaseline.

Next to one of the electric guitars there was a pile of spare parts for his motorcycle, and in the middle of the pile there was a big can that said, "Motorcycle Drive Chain Lubricant." Gypsy smiled and slowly made his way down from the bed. He crawled across the floor and pried the lid off the can. A strong odor of garage oil drifted up. He shrugged and climbed back on the bed with the big can.

Karen raised her ass in the air tentatively. "Gypsy, don't be mad at me. Do you still want to do it?"

"I'm not mad at you, I'm not mad at you. Just open up."

She raised her hips a little further and pressed her face against the pillow she was holding. "Did you get it, sweetheart?" Her voice was muffled once more. "Is that the Vaseline?"

"No, it's motorcycle grease," he answered. "Of course it's the Vaseline." He shrugged again, and stuck his penis into

[142]

the Motorcycle Drive Chain Lubricant. It came out of the can of dirty grease looking a little strange, but it felt okay. He crawled up behind her, pushing his greased penis in front of him, and put his arms around her. He held her breast with his left hand, and reached down between her legs with his right hand and stroked her. Then he slipped two fingers into her vagina.

"Gypsy, be careful," she whispered.

He tried to push his stiff, lubricated penis into her ass, and she tightened up again for a second. Then she relaxed, and this time it slid in easily.

Across the room the speakers were quivering, and Merry Clayton got into "Gimme Shelter."

The next time Gypsy woke up, something was climbing over his stomach. It turned out to be Karen. She went padding around the room picking up her underwear, silhouetted in the blue and red lights. She looked terrific each time she bent over, but Gypsy wasn't stoned any more. He felt like he was dead. Karen sat down on the edge of the bed and put her legs into her panty hose.

"What are you doing, Karen?"

"I have to get dressed," she said serenely.

"Oh," he said. "You mean now?"

"Yes. I have to go home."

"Oh. Sure." He turned over and buried his face back in his pillow. A minute later he sat up again. "What did you say?" he asked slowly.

"Gypsy, I have to go home now."

"Karen," he told her, "it's pitch black out there. It's the middle of the night. What are you talking about?"

"I have to go home now," she repeated a second time, matter-of-factly, as if that were a completely reasonable thing for her to have to do. "God wants me to."

[143]

Gypsy looked at her like she'd said she was going to piss out the window. He opened and closed his mouth, and swallowed. Finally he said, "Karen, I'm really tired, you know? I don't need this. Why don't you go to sleep?"

Karen continued putting her clothes on. "Sweetheart, you don't understand. I'm really glad I came over, and I'm glad we fucked and everything, but God wants me to go home now."

"God? God wants you to go home? Couldn't God wait until eight o'clock?"

"Gypsy, I don't have any choice about these things. I just know when God wants me to do something. Jesus wants me to go home now."

Gypsy sighed and lay back on the bed. He looked up at the ceiling, but he couldn't see who was talking to her. "Jesus also, huh? That's two out of three. What does the Holy Ghost say?"

"I knew you wouldn't understand," she answered sadly.

I understand that you're crazy, he thought. He tried again. "Why don't you smoke a little more dope?" he suggested hopefully. And added silently, Maybe you'll hear things better.

"I don't want any more dope, Gypsy. I just have to go home now, that's all."

Gypsy folded his arms over his face. He couldn't believe how tired he was. It was too good to last, he figured. Karen was a marvelous fuck, but apparently a crazy fuck as well. It was a lousy time to find out about it, though. He crawled off the bed, stumbled to his feet, and stood there, naked and nodding out. "God. What time is it?"

Karen must have thought he was asking her to use her connection. "It's about a quarter to four," she said helpfully. "Go back to sleep, Gypsy, it's okay."

Gypsy rubbed his eyes. He was trying hard to function.

"No," he replied unhappily, "I'll take you down to your car. Unless God wants you to get mugged, too. Let me find my clothes." He walked back and forth in front of the bed, looking for something to wear and trying to wake up. He kept walking into things. A couple of times he smacked his leg on the metal frame of the bed, and that woke him up some.

Karen watched him groping around naked. "You know," she observed incongruously, "you do have a nice body."

"That's great," Gypsy muttered. "It was worth getting up just to hear you say that."

He found his jeans where he had dropped them, on the floor. Putting them on was challenging; he was so tired he kept missing the orifice with his leg. Karen came over and helped him.

"Thank you, Sister." He glared at her.

She looked hurt. Gypsy started hunting around the room again. "Socks," he said to himself, "where are the goddam socks?"

"Gypsy," she responded, in a small, unbid voice, "they're on your feet."

He looked down. "Oh. They're on my feet."

"You wanted to ball me so much you wouldn't stop to take them off. Remember?"

"No." He got disgusted with hunting for a shirt, so he just put on his yellow coat, and his ragged black top hat. And sneakers. He hadn't worn the top hat since Samoa.

"All right," he said wearily, "let's go."

She made a point of holding on to his hand and they left the apartment together. He almost fell asleep in the elevator. Downstairs, the street looked wet and shiny, even from the lobby. They walked out of the front door, and into a cold, black, drizzling rain. She squeezed his hand. "Doesn't the street look pretty?"

"Oh, absolutely," he said. "Egdon Heath." The rain started to drip off the brim of his top hat. She held his arm meekly, and they walked toward her car. She was parked all the way down at the corner. It was really cold and dark out.

They reached her car and she unlocked the door. "Gypsy, I'm sorry, you know. I don't mean to be difficult or anything. It's just that God wanted me to go home."

Gypsy sighed audibly. "Oh, that's all right, Karen. I come down here at four, five o'clock every morning—to warm up my motorcycle."

She looked hurt again, and kissed him lightly on the forehead. She got into the car and started the engine. Then she rolled down her window. "Good night, Gypsy. Thank you."

"Good night, good night," he answered. "You're welcome. Good-bye." He was getting wetter and wetter. She pulled out of her parking spot and drove off down the glistening, deserted street toward Madison Avenue. Gypsy waved his soggy black hat at the taillights of her car. "Good-bye," he called after her. "Get fucked."

He walked back in the direction of his house and passed his parked and chained motorcycle. He also passed a street sign with the message NO PARKING—8 TO 11 A.M.—TUESDAY AND FRIDAY.

He stopped. "Oh, shit," he groaned. This was now Friday morning, and he knew that he was never going to make it out of bed again by eight o'clock to move his bike. Which meant that the New York Police Department was going to move it for him, at about ten after eight.

"Shit, shit," he swore. It was turning into a disastrous fuck. Gypsy decided the bike had to be left someplace legal before he could go back to bed. He hunted through his pockets until he found the right key, and unlocked the big chain. He pulled the chain out from between the spokes of the rear wheel. Then he wrapped it around his waist and snapped the lock back on, since he couldn't carry the six feet of heavy chain in his hand and drive the bike at the same time.

He received another surprise. The rubber sleeve covering the chain had been collecting rainwater, and all of it poured out while Gypsy was wrapping the chain around himself. The water ran down the front of his coat and soaked into the crotch of his jeans. It was nice and cold. Gypsy looked down at himself, wondering if he had suddenly turned incontinent or something. He saw what had happened, took off the top hat, and raised his eyes to the black sky. "Thank you, Karen!" he shouted. "You really put in a good word for me, didn't you?" He replaced the hat on his head, and stepped off the curb into a pile of dogshit.

He stared at his foot. "Very nice," he said slowly, "very nice. This should be in a movie." Muttering to himself, he scraped his sneaker off against the curb. Then he got onto the bike and stuck the key in the ignition. He stood up on the foot pegs, and kicked it over.

Gypsy had the oldest motorcycle in the world. It was big, too, and whatever he tried doing to it, it needed new spark plugs every five days. Wherever he went, he carried his spark-plug wrench with him. All the pockets on his yellow coat were filled with spark plugs. His black doctor bag was laden with spark plugs. He was the Good Humor man of spark plugs. The number was never sufficient. No matter how many he bought, the bike always wanted more. The last time he had gone to the motorcycle-supply house to replenish his stock, the mechanics had asked him whether he was just driving cross-country or all the way to South America. "No," he had told them, stuffing his pockets with the new load of spark plugs, "back to the East Side."

The plugs in the motorcycle now were only a couple of days old, and it started right up. The thing was, it wasn't a very quiet bike, either, and it wasn't very clean. Even with all the traffic in New York, you could hear it coming three blocks away, and it always laid down a heavy trail of dense, oily, black smoke behind it. During the day it was like any cement mixer going by. In the middle of the night, it sounded like a large airplane taking off.

The engine caught on the first kick. It began to sputter a little, and Gypsy gave it some throttle to keep it going. It backfired twice, with two sharp cracks, and then the exhaust turned into a loud howl. Gypsy loved the sound of it, but nobody else in the neighborhood did. Whenever he started the bike, he was obliged to get it off his own block quickly, before his neighbors sent for the police again. He hated discussing the issue with the police, because he usually forgot to wear his helmet, which was illegal, and because he had no motorcycle license, which was also illegal.

The engine was turning over nice and smooth. Gypsy reached down and patted the rusty old bike as if it was a thoroughbred horse, and gassed it again, hard. The howling of the engine became a shattering, deafening roar, and the bike rocked and shuddered underneath him. The sound, now actually painful, bounced off the nearby buildings and echoed along the block. Gypsy stood up again and wrestled the bike down off the stand. He backed it into the street and straightened it out. Then he pulled in the clutch, and gassed it one more time.

"Beautiful, beautiful!" he shouted, carried away by the physical presence of the thundering noise all around him. He couldn't hear himself.

Lights started to come on in some of the apartment windows. Gypsy reached up and jammed the top hat down around his ears. And then he kicked the bike into gear, did a spectacular and unintended wheelie on the wet street, and raced for the corner. The ancient bike still had terrific acceleration. Twenty yards down the block Gypsy was able to clutch once more and put it into second. As soon as it

[148]

caught he gassed it again, and twisted the throttle almost wide open. The sensation was astounding—pure speed and neck-snapping acceleration, with Gypsy just hanging on to the bars and winding it higher, and the bike trying to rocket out from under him. He was no longer even conscious of the noise, and he was pushing almost 11,000 R.P.M. It was glorious.

Just before kicking it into third he opened his eyes. There was a car stopped dead, halfway into the intersection at the corner. Working absolutely out of reflex he clutched, down-shifted, and hit both brakes. The street was too wet, and he felt his rear wheel start to slide out. He figured he was going to drop the bike and decided to stay with it. He stood up on the pegs to try to ride it down. He would scrape off more flesh that way, but perhaps break fewer bones.

The bike didn't go down. The front wheel slid, too, and Gypsy ended up traveling sideways, but he came to a stop upright. He was only a couple of feet from the car. He sat there on the stalled motorcycle, shaking. After half a minute it passed, and he got off.

He realized for the first time there was a girl standing next to the car.

"Oh, wonderful," he said disgustedly. "It's the Wrath of God again. Karen, what the hell's wrong with you?"

"Gypsy," she said with a thoroughly insane look, "Gypsy, I just killed two people." She started to cry noisily.

"No shit. You almost killed me, too. And you made me lose my hat! God damn, I think I ran over it."

"Gypsy," she blubbered, "I'm not kidding. I hit two people. Oh, Jesus, I just didn't see them."

"Yeah, well, kill for Christ. You want to know something, Karen? You're turning into a bad dream. I had that hat for three years before I met you!" He walked around to the front of the car. Sure enough, there were two people lying in the street, getting rained on. They didn't seem that bad off.

"Hallelujah," Gypsy said sourly, kneeling down to check them over. It was hard for him to tell very much in the dark, but they were both breathing and conscious, and nothing important appeared to be broken. They looked more frightened than injured.

"Don't worry," Gypsy said reassuringly. "Everything's going to be okay. I think you might have to go to the hospital, though, just to make sure you're all right." They gave him weak little smiles.

A police car drove past. It made a U-turn, came back to the intersection, and stopped. Two policemen got out. They walked around a little, shining their flashlights on the ground, and they talked to everybody two or three times. They talked to Karen more than anybody else, but, of course, she was the prettiest girl there. An ambulance showed up, and Gypsy and the policemen helped load the two minor casualties on board. Then everyone except Karen drove away.

"Good night," Gypsy said to her. He straightened the mirrors on his motorcycle.

"I'm not driving that car," she announced.

"Karen, don't talk to me. I'm going to park my bike and go to bed. Good night."

"Gypsy, I just can't drive that car any more. Not after I hurt those people." She started to cry again, too.

"Holy shit!" Gypsy exclaimed. "I should have gone to a whorehouse tonight." He pushed the bike over to the curb and chained it up. Then he came back and got into her car, from the driver's side.

"Well?" he said, through the window. "Get in the goddam car!" She climbed in, sniffling. "Thank you," she said quietly. He started the engine, went around the corner, and drove right into the twenty-four-hour garage.

"Wait a minute, Gypsy, you don't understand. You have to take me home. God wants me to go home."

Gypsy turned the engine off and got out of the car. "Sure." He handed the keys to the garage man. "Where do you want to go? Rome? Jerusalem? Mecca?"

"New Brunswick. It's only about two hours from here."

"Karen," he said, "kiss my ass. I'm going to bed. You are absolutely welcome to stay at my apartment, or you can sleep here in the goddam garage. I don't give a shit. Do you understand, Joan of Arc? God wants me to go to sleep."

She decided not to spend the rest of the night in the garage and followed Gypsy up to his apartment. As soon as he walked in the door, Gypsy dropped his clothes onto the floor and crawled gratefully into bed. Karen joined him in the bed, with all her clothes on, and backed herself against the wall. In a little while she started to mumble in a singsong, unintelligible voice. Damp and worn out, Gypsy waited for her to stop. She didn't.

"Karen, now what?" he asked without even turning over.

"I'm praying."

"What language are you praying in? Aramaic?"

"We don't pray in any language," she said. "I'm just talking to God."

It was a long conversation. Gypsy listened to her mumble, sing, chant, and thump on the wall for almost an hour, and then he gave up and drove her out to New Brunswick. He had to hitchhike to Jersey City to get a bus back to New York.

"She was definitely crazy," Vittorio said the following day in the cafeteria. "Where do you find people like that?"

"I found her on the fourth floor," Gypsy answered. "How did I know she was crazy?" Gypsy was having lunch, and killing a little time with his friends, over at the city hospital.

"Did you fuck her in the ass?" Kid Otto wanted to know,

his eyes gleaming. He had missed the whole story, except for the very end. Gypsy grinned at him. "Go ask her, man."

Vittorio gave them both a distasteful look. "What's the matter with you two?" Vic had apparently just acquired a girl friend, a smart ophthalmology resident who liked to sky-dive, and he was feeling very superior.

"I have to amuse myself somehow," Gypsy pointed out. "Do you want me to walk around horny and depressed?"

"You are horny," Kid Otto told him, "and depressed."

"I know," Gypsy agreed, "I know. Aren't you tired of your wife yet?"

"Anyway," Vittorio interjected, "you're not going to have time for all that fooling around much longer. We're going to the M.I.C.U. next month."

Gypsy turned serious. "Vic, you know what that whole fucking private service is? A waste of time."

Vittorio shook his head. "You're never satisfied, wherever they send you. You didn't like the Emergency Room, either."

"I'm just trying to be a good doctor." Gypsy looked discouraged. "Why is that so fucking hard to accomplish?"

"You have to learn to compromise," Vittorio said. "You've got to bend a little, Gypsy. Otherwise you're going to go crazy yourself."

Gypsy stood up, with a sad expression on his face. "Aren't we all."

Gypsy returned to the affiliation hospital after lunch. There was, of course, nothing doing there, and he wound up roaming idly around the floors making social calls on his patients. He at least enjoyed spending time with his people, but then he had always liked being with patients. There were more than a few interns in his year who could not stand patients, and they perplexed Gypsy. It was true, though, that the misanthropes were almost all going into pathology, where they could take care of dead people, or into radiology, where they could take care of machines. There were also a couple of interns who were simply, and obviously, .crazy. And they were going into psychiatry. So maybe things did balance out.

Gypsy walked into one of the spacious, elegant rooms up on the tenth floor to visit Mr. Kennedy. Kennedy was even better at making Gypsy laugh than the other way around. Gypsy seated himself comfortably in the chair next to the bed. The patient was resting in bed reading the *New York Times*, and pretended not to see him.

"Mr. Kennedy?"

No answer.

"Mr. Kennedy, are you drunk again?"

Kennedy looked over the top of his newspaper. "I'm not talking to you."

"You're not?"

Kennedy shook his head.

"Well, why the fuck not?"

"Because," Kennedy informed him, "I don't want to."

"Nah, that's bullshit," Gypsy said. "Conversation is like whiskey for you Irish guys—you can't turn it down."

"That may be," Kennedy agreed, "but if somebody left a seventy-nine-cent bottle of wine in the room, I wouldn't drink that either." He rustled his newspaper at Gypsy.

"Are you telling me my conversation is as bad as rotgut wine? I'm insulted."

"I'm telling you I don't want to talk to you. Me and you are finished."

Gypsy chuckled. "Come on, man, what did I do? Should I change my mouthwash?"

Kennedy put down his paper. "You sent me for that goddam barium enema thing! That's what you did."

"Ah," Gypsy said, "the barium enema. You didn't like the barium enema, huh?"

[153]

Kennedy made a terrible face. "What an invention. They pump you up with that stuff until it comes out your ears, then they roll you around the table to make more room inside you, and then they pump some more of that lousy stuff in! And after that, they have the nerve to hook you up to this balloon and blow air into you! It's disgusting."

"Oh, is that what they did? I meant to send you for the test where they take a little blood sample from your finger and send you back to your room. My mistake."

Kennedy tried to look injured. "I had to get stuck with a brain-damaged intern. Did somebody happen to drop you on your head when you were a baby?"

"My Irish grandmother. She was so drunk one day she thought she was playing Gaelic football. She put the boot to me head, is what she done. I was in a coma for twenty years, and when I woke up again, here I was—an intern."

"I don't believe you. Anyway, what's the point of all these damn tests, Gypsy? Is something wrong with me or not?"

"I'm not sure yet, boss. That's what they're trying to find out."

"Gypsy, I don't want you people lying to me. Do you know what I mean?"

Gypsy nodded. "Okay, man. As soon as we know anything, you got it. I won't bullshit you."

Kennedy sighed. "Now, if only you could learn to read. Then you could figure out what's going on with me, and we'd be getting someplace."

"Listen, patient," Gypsy told him, "just keep in mind who writes the diet orders around here. You hurt my feelings once more, and you'll be eating pureed baby food."

Kennedy made another face, and threw up his hands. "Baby food? Saints preserve us. I better stay on your good side." He reached into the little drawer in his bedside table and produced a red yo-yo in a transparent plastic package. "A present, doctor."

"For me?" Gypsy said eagerly. "Thanks, man."

"It was for my grandson, actually. But my daughter-in-law says you're only supposed to let them play with educational toys today. What the hell's that supposed to be?"

"I don't know," Gypsy admitted, tugging at the impregnable plastic that was molded tightly around his new yo-yo. "How do you open this goddam thing?"

One of the second-year medical students walked into the room, all puffed up with his own importance. He was learning Physical Diagnosis. He stopped at the foot of the bed, going over his list of patients who had interesting physical findings. "Excuse me, please," he asked without looking up, "are you the Mrs. Kennedy with prolapsed hemorrhoids?"

Kennedy laughed. "Do I look like Mrs. Kennedy to you?"

The student raised his head in surprise. "Oh, gee, I'm sorry, sir," he stammered, "I thought . . . I think I've got the wrong Kennedy."

"Yeah," Gypsy said, "it's an easy mistake to make. All those Irish people look the same anyway, laying there drunk."

"Listen to me, son," Kennedy warned the medical student. "If you want to grow up to be a doctor, don't pay any attention to anything this guy ever tells you. The only reason they haven't thrown him out yet is that his father's a trustee here. He doesn't even know how to read!"

"All right, Kennedy," Gypsy announced, "that's it for you. You're through. I'm taking your pacemaker away!"

The second-year student looked back and forth from Kennedy to Gypsy in bewilderment. "Excuse me," he said again, and turned and headed for the door.

"Come over here," Gypsy said, laughing. "We were fooling with you, man. How do you like Physical Diagnosis? Do you enjoy working with patients?"

The medical student hesitantly recrossed the room, still looking doubtfully at both of them. He didn't understand

[155]

what the joke was. "Yes, sure, I like Physical Diagnosis. Only, well, this is my first week in the hospital; I guess it takes a while to get used to certain things."

"Which things are bothering you?" Gypsy asked.

"Well, like I was just down in the Emergency Room doing a rectal on a patient. You know, for occult blood?"

Gypsy nodded. "And?"

"Well," the student went on reluctantly, "the trouble is . . . you know—it takes such a long time to get your fingernails clean after one of those rectal exams. It's really a nuisance."

Gypsy glanced over at Kennedy, who picked up his *Times*. "Didn't you use a rubber glove?" he asked the medical student.

The student stared at Gypsy. "Glove? What glove?"

The *Times* started to shake uncontrollably. Kennedy was trying manfully to keep himself from dissolving totally into hysterical laughter, and the effort was nearly choking him.

Gypsy was very tempted to let the comedy reach its climax, but he decided instead to save his patient by changing the subject. Besides, he had heard something that intrigued him. "I'll explain it to you later," he told the student. "What was that you were saying about an emergency room?"

"What?" The medical student looked even more confused.

"You said you were down in an emergency room."

"Well, I was."

"Where?"

"What do you mean, where? In the basement."

"*Here?*" Gypsy asked.

"Sure, here. Where else?"

"Are you talking about the Outpatient Department?" Gypsy asked him.

"No, of course not. I know what the O.P.D. is. I'm talking about the Emergency Room in the basement."

Gypsy's eyes widened. "You mean I've been on the private service almost three months, and I never knew they had an emergency room? Son of a bitch! This must be some emergency room you got here."

"I'm not following you, exactly," the medical student complained. "You keep losing me."

"Forget about it," Gypsy said. "And remember to get yourself some rubber gloves." Gypsy waved to Kennedy and left to investigate the new wonder. The medical student caught up to him just as he reached the stairs. "Doctor, wait a second."

Gypsy stopped.

"Uh, are you sure about the business with the glove?"

Gypsy smiled. "That's the way I always do it."

"Well," the medical student insisted stubbornly, "I think you're wrong. I don't see how you can palpate anything if you've got a glove on."

"It's not a boxing glove, man; it's just made out of rubber. You can feel everything right through it."

The student was not satisfied. "Then how come they never told us about it when we started Physical Diagnosis?"

Gypsy gave up on him. "Look, dummy, do what you want. You're going to be sticking your finger up people's assholes for the next thirty years. You want to be scraping shit out from under your fingernails all that time, fine, don't wear a glove. Okay?" Gypsy smiled again and departed. He walked all the way down to the first floor, and then found a separate staircase that led to the basement.

When he finally emerged into the basement itself, as he'd expected there was no evidence of anything like an E.R. He wandered around for a while anyway, and discovered only the kitchen, the linen supply room, and a lot of aides and porters sitting and smoking cigarettes. Then he passed through another hallway, and astonishingly, walked right into an honest-to-God emergency room. And the place was in absolute chaos. It was just filled with doctors, and nurses, and cops, and hordes of patients. It was incredible—it was as bad as the city hospital. Worse. Everything was there except Allen Gallberg screaming at some O.D.'d junkie. So, Gypsy thought, this was where all the action had been going on for the last three months. No wonder it was always quiet upstairs; there was enough to do down here for half a dozen hospitals.

Gypsy closed his mouth and stopped gawking, and went to help. There must have been a train crash somewhere, he decided. There were too many maimed, twisted, bleeding patients filling the corridors for the disaster to have been anything else. He walked a little further into the maelstrom of carnage, and almost tripped over a patient with a gruesome head wound who was lying unattended on a stretcher on the floor. The terrible wound was only partially exposed; the staff were so busy that nobody had even finished removing the bloody shirt that was serving as the patient's makeshift bandage.

Gypsy quickly kneeled down alongside the man. "What happened to you, sir?"

"Huh? Nothing happened to me."

Gypsy nodded to himself. Delirium was not uncommon in severe head trauma. He started to unwind the rest of the blood-soaked shirt from the patient's head.

"Hey, what the hell are you doing?" the patient yelled angrily. "That took two hours to put on!" He sat up suddenly on the stretcher and batted Gypsy's hands away from the shirt, which was now fluttering down free over his ears. "Somebody get this jackass out of here!" he shouted.

"It's all right, sir," Gypsy reassured him soothingly, "we're

[158]

going to take care of you, don't worry." Gypsy looked around urgently for an aide to help him control the patient, and then he realized that everyone in the Emergency Room was staring at him. Not just the staff, but all of the other patients as well. Some of the stretcher cases had stood up to get a better view of Gypsy fighting with his patient, and one lady in a crowded corner was standing on her wheelchair. Everybody was grinning broadly, and a few of the patients were even starting to laugh out loud.

Gypsy thought that the world had gone crazy, and then someone came along and grabbed him by the sleeve of his white coat. "What do you think you're doing?" the man demanded, trying to drag Gypsy away from the casualty with the head injury. "You know you ruined this scene?"

Gypsy got to his feet, intensely annoyed, and jerked his arm out of the guy's grasp. "What the fuck are you bothering me about, man? I'm working on a patient!"

The guy glared at him disapprovingly. "Hy, come over here, for Christ's sake. What's this supposed to be?"

A second man, short and fat and sweating, joined them. "Anything wrong, Lenny? What is it?" he asked nervously.

"Who made this one a doctor, Hy?" The first man pointed at Gypsy. "He just fucked up the whole God-damn scene!"

"Jesus, Lenny, I don't know. I didn't do it."

"Yeah? Who did? My old lady?" Lenny sighed. "Christ. All right, make him one of the drug addicts." Then he got fired up with indignation again. "Will you look at him, for Christ's sake. Where's your brains, Hy? The kid looks exactly like a drug addict. Christ, he probably *is* a drug addict. And you make him a doctor!"

"I am a doctor," Gypsy said to him. "Who the hell are you?"

"You don't know who I am?" Lenny answered condescendingly. "You've got a great future, kid. I'm the assistant director on this movie."

"Movie? You mean you're only making a *movie?*"

"What do you think?"

"None of these people are hurt?"

The assistant director threw his hands in the air. "What am I wasting my time with this bullshit for? We're losing money here."

"Some schmuck, huh, Lenny?" Hy sniggered.

Gypsy turned around slowly, looking mean, and stepped up very close to Lenny's friend. "Fat boy, how would you like to spend a few weeks in a real hospital?" Hy backed away from him quickly and decided he had something to do somewhere else.

"Excuse me," the assistant director said, suddenly made courteous by the possibility of some genuine violence. "If you don't care to work, could you leave the set, please?"

Gypsy walked toward the hallway he had come through before—like Alice in Wonderland—to discover the train-crash-turned-movie. He was talking to himself. "Yeah," he said, "I'll leave the set. You know what else I'll leave? I'll leave this goddam useless fucking private service!" He stopped and gave some sort of big microphone stand a good kick, and walked out of the usurped Emergency Room.

A few days later, goaded by curiosity, Gypsy stopped down at the basement E.R. again. The movie crew was gone. The population of the ludicrous place now consisted of two bored nurses, one female medical student, and a lone patient. The patient didn't look very sick.

# The M.I.C.U.

TRUE TO HER WORD, Karen quit her job on the private service —and then joined the Jesus freaks. Gypsy never saw her again. And several weeks after his brush with the movies, Gypsy returned to Manhattan County Hospital for good. The winter brought him to the halfway point of his internship, and to the Medical Intensive Care Unit; Kid Otto and Vittorio were assigned to the Unit with him. That had taken some fancy maneuvering.

Gypsy had bribed a crucial secretary in the Department of Medicine with an outrageous amount of Moroccan hash, and she had juggled the appropriate schedules. But then some intern had gotten himself shot by an irate patient in the E.R., and Allen Gallberg was suddenly left short of house staff. He had press-ganged Kid Otto for another tour of duty in the Emergency Room.

"Oh, no," Kid Otto yelled when he heard about it, "not me! I'm not going back to that hole again. I'm going to the M.I.C.U. with you guys."

Gypsy went to see what had happened to his investment. The secretary said that she was very sorry, but it was out of her hands. She had gotten the three of them onto the same M.I.C.U. rotation, as promised, but Allen Gallberg himself had come up to the Department office and just picked out a name on the board, and it was Kid Otto's. She offered to give some of the hash back. Gypsy told her to forget about it.

Kid Otto was not so cavalier. "I'll quit," he threatened.

[161]

"I'll punch that bastard Gallberg in the mouth—I'll break his fucking ass!"

"Otto, be calm," Gypsy said. "We'll take care of it."

"Yeah?" Vittorio asked, when Kid Otto had walked off muttering and cursing. "How?"

"I don't know yet," Gypsy admitted. "I'll think of something."

"Why don't you get some more hash," Vittorio suggested sarcastically, "and bribe the Chief? It worked great with his secretary." Vic was losing his hair, and was therefore something of a cynic.

"I thought of that already—I don't have any more money. Look, meet me over at my place tonight. Around midnight."

"Midnight?" Vittorio said suspiciously. "What for?"

"I want to look around. Something'll hit me."

"Look around where?" Vittorio persisted. "What are you talking about?"

"I'll tell you tonight. See you later."


At a quarter after twelve, Vic rang his buzzer. Gypsy came downstairs carrying a couple of large screwdrivers, a big hammer, and a putty knife. He got into Vic's car.

"Now what?" Vittorio said, eyeing the tools.

"Let's take a drive over to the hospital."

"What's that junk for?" Vittorio asked, putting the car into gear.

"I think," Gypsy said cheerfully, "we're going to do a little breaking and entering."

"I knew it. You lost your mind altogether. We're going to end up on the prison ward."

Gypsy chuckled. "Drive, Vic."

Vic insisted on parking a block away from the hospital so nobody would notice his car. "Ah, who's going to notice your car at this hour?" Gypsy said as they walked to the hospital. "You're too nervous."

[162]

"You're crazy," Vittorio told him. "The problem isn't that I'm too nervous, it's that you're crazy."

They got to the hospital and took the elevator up to the Medicine office. Vic tried the door that said "Chief, Department of Medicine." "Too bad." Vittorio sounded relieved. "It's locked."

"Yeah, I figured it would be locked." Gypsy went to work with the putty knife and one of the screwdrivers.

"Jesus," Vitorrio said under his breath. He started peering anxiously up and down the corridor.

There was a loud, spronging sound, and Gypsy pushed the door open. "Okay," he instructed Vic as he walked into the office, "you're the lookout. You stand guard and let me know if anybody's coming."

Vittorio leaned against the wall, trying to appear casual for the benefit of the empty hallway. He heard some scraping and crashing around from inside the office while Gypsy bumped into things until he found the light switch. Then a light came on, and the illegal activities grew quieter. After a few minutes of silence Vic got so jittery alone he tiptoed cautiously into the office.

Gypsy was putting the big, magnetic master rotation board back up on the wall.

"What are you doing?" Vic whispered.

"Some lookout you are," Gypsy whispered back, grinning. "Suppose the cops come?"

"What are you doing with the board?"

Gypsy seemed pleased with himself. He pointed at the board, which was a schedule of all the interns' rotations for the year. He had moved the little magnet with Kid Otto's name on it from the Emergency Room, back to the M.I.C.U. "I just transferred Kid Otto."

Vittorio stared at the board. "You idiot," he whispered, turning back to Gypsy. "What's the matter with you?"

"You think they'll notice it?"

"Of course they'll notice it," Vic hissed, *sotto voce.* "They'll just move it back again."

"You're right," Gypsy agreed after a little reflection. "I've got a better idea." He walked over to the secretary's desk and began prying at the locked drawer with a screwdriver.

"What are you doing now?" Vic whispered excitedly. "You can't break into the desk!"

"Sure I can," Gypsy grunted, "if I can get a little more leverage on it."

An Indian resident walked into the room, and stopped in his tracks when he saw them. "Oh, Christ," Vittorio groaned.

"Hello," Gypsy said pleasantly. "We're breaking into the Medicine office." He picked up the hammer and started to hit the end of the screwdriver with it.

"I see," the Indian resident replied in polite, formal, colonial English. "You are breaking into the Medicine office. Yes."

"You want to help?" Gypsy offered.

"No, thank you very much." The Indian resident left.

"I like those guys," Gypsy said. "They've got nice manners."

"Let's get out of here." Vittorio was becoming more agitated. "What if he calls the guards?"

"You can hold them off," Gypsy answered, "while I escape." There was another spronging noise. The desk drawer slid open. Gypsy fished around in the drawer for a minute, and came up with a little piece of paper. "Got one!" he said happily. "Let's split."

"You got one what?" Vittorio asked, mystified, but following him with relief out into the hall.

"A parking sticker," Gypsy explained. "An attending's parking sticker. Now we got a bargaining point."

"Bargaining point?" Vittorio repeated. "You crook, are you going to screw somebody?"

"Arthur Nerd," Gypsy said, looking crafty. They walked over to the elevators, Gypsy said good night to the Indian resident, and Vic drove him home.

The next day they had a hurried conference with Kid Otto right before lunch, and then went to look for Arthur Nerd in the cafeteria. They found him sitting at a table by himself, and descended on him.

"Hello, Nerd," Gypsy said. "How you been?"

"Terrible," Arthur complained. "Terrible. Why do I always get more admissions than any other ward? Every time I'm admitting I get bombed. I think the guys in the Emergency Room all hate me."

"Nah," Gypsy said. "Who would hate you?"

"Did you hear what happened last night?" Kid Otto asked. "This aide got mugged right across the street. The junkies kicked the shit out of him."

Arthur put down his fork, and his face became pale. "They did? Why'd they do that?"

"How the fuck should I know? They just wanted to kick the shit out of somebody, I guess."

"Jesus Christ," Arthur said indignantly, "it's getting dangerous here. One of those guys tried to kill me last month! Over in the parking lot. Di Bello beat him up."

"No kidding?" Vittorio said solicitously.

"Sure." Arthur grinned. "Di Bello really pounded him."

Vittorio looked worried. "I think you're in trouble, Arthur," he said ominously.

"Why?" Arthur asked quickly. "What's wrong?"

Kid Otto tried to look concerned. "Boy, have you had it, Nerd."

Arthur's eye started to twitch. "What are you talking about? What did I do?"

"Those junkies really stick together, Arthur," Vittorio told him. "You better not let them catch you."

Kid Otto confirmed the warning vigorously. "Yeah, they'll kill you for sure. No question."

"Oh, Jesus," Arthur said, turning dead white. "I never thought of that! What am I going to do?"

"I guess I'm pretty lucky, then," Gypsy announced, rejoining the conversation. "Look what I've got." He took out his wallet and carefully unfolded the parking sticker. "I can park right next to the hospital as soon as I put this on my windshield. I won't even have to go across Third Avenue to the parking lot."

"Holy shit," Arthur exclaimed enviously, "an attending's sticker! Where'd you get it from?"

"I got friends," Gypsy said smugly. "You know how hard it is to get one of these?"

"It's impossible," Arthur said, staring at the sticker. "They never give them to interns."

"True," Vittorio agreed. "That's why they call them attendings' stickers."

"I wish I had one, too," Arthur whined. "Look," he blurted out suddenly, "I'll buy it from you! I'll give you ten dollars for it."

"Ten dollars?" Gypsy echoed in a shocked voice. "You mean your life is only worth ten dollars to you? You must be a brave man, Nerd." Kid Otto and Vittorio nodded solemnly at Arthur's courage.

"A hundred dollars," Arthur yelled, getting hysterical. "Anything! Just give it to me!"

"Well, Nerd," Gypsy protested, "I couldn't actually take any money from you. I mean, money for a guy's life—that really wouldn't be right."

"Please," Arthur pleaded, "I gotta have that sticker! They're gonna kill me!"

"You know," Gypsy said offhandedly, "I guess there is a favor you could do for me, Arthur. You could work the

Emergency Room for Kid Otto, so we can hang out together in the Unit. If you want to, that is."

"Anything, anything," Arthur cried, his voice cracking, "just give me the sticker!"

"Wait a minute," Kid Otto said thoughtfully. "I like the Emergency Room. I don't think *I* want to trade."

"You got to," Arthur begged. "You got to! Big guys like you don't have anything to worry about. I don't stand a chance out there. They'll kill me if I don't get that sticker!"

"Oh, do him a favor," Vittorio urged. "He's a nice guy."

Kid Otto looked at the ceiling, prolonging the agony. "All right," he said finally, "I'll trade rotations with you. But listen, Nerd—I'm in enough trouble with Gallberg already. If I mess up his schedule once more, he's really going to have it in for me. So don't come around complaining that you want to trade back again. This is final, okay?"

"Yes, yes," Arthur said quickly. "I promise. Gimme the sticker!" Gypsy gave him the parking sticker, and Arthur jumped up and ran toward the cafeteria exit with it.

"Nerd," Gypsy called after him, "you didn't finish your lunch."

"I got no time," Arthur yelled back. "I want to go over and put it on my car while it's still light out." He disappeared through the door.

"What a schmuck—it's twelve-thirty in the afternoon," Kid Otto pointed out. "He's got six hours before it gets dark!"

"You know," Vittorio commented, "I wouldn't have minded having that sticker myself."

"Well, I don't think it would have done you too much good," Gypsy said. "It's a blue sticker. That's last year's color."

\*      \*      \*

[167]

The medical resident in the Unit was a smart, abrasive doctor named Hugo. He was a very structured person who believed in people playing their traditional roles. Hugo was only a couple of years older than his interns, but as soon as he met Gypsy and his friends, he was convinced the revolution had come.

Their first day in the Unit, Hugo sat down with them in the nursing station. "You're a gypsy?" he said to Vic. "You don't look like a gypsy to me; you look Italian."

"I am Italian," Vittorio Mazzoli told him. "That's the gypsy over there." Gypsy was playing with his red yo-yo and looking around for nurses.

"Hey," Hugo said, this time to Gypsy, "we'll get along better if you put that away and listen to me."

"Sure," Gypsy said agreeably. He put the yo-yo in his pocket and smiled at Hugo.

"What about those things? Are you going to wear those in my Unit?"

"Wear what in your Unit?" Gypsy's voice was less friendly.

"Those earrings."

"Earring," Gypsy corrected him. "Earring. I only wear one. It doesn't bother anybody, man. Are you going to wear that thing in the Unit?"

Hugo looked down at himself nervously. "What? What thing?"

"That skinny little brown tie. It's kind of cheap-looking, don't you think?"

"This is a necktie!" Hugo said, his voice turning shrill. He was scared that he was losing control of his interns already.

"I know what it is," Gypsy agreed. "What I'm trying to figure out is what you are."

"He's probably an insecure anal-compulsive," Vittorio volunteered. "You better leave him alone."

[168]

"Shut up, all of you." Hugo was getting a little red in the face. "And I don't need any help from you, Mazzolo."

"That's Mazzoli."

"Everybody listen to me—you all have to take a copy of these rules. They tell you what you've got to do and what you can't do in the Unit." Hugo was trying to reassert his authority. He was feeling threatened.

Everyone smiled except the medical resident. "You know, Hugo," Kid Otto said, "Gypsy doesn't like guys telling him what to do."

Vic glanced at a few of the rules. "Who wrote this nonsense down?"

"Clancy did." Hugo got up to leave. "She's the head nurse. You better keep those; I'm not going to give you any more copies."

Vittorio looked tolerant and amused. Gypsy folded his copy of the rules into a paper airplane and sailed it out the window. Hugo went to look for Clancy to tell her about the new crew.

Kid Otto read his copy. The rules were ordinary head-nurse horseshit. Where you could hang your coat. Where you couldn't hang your coat. Where you could write your orders. When you could write your orders. Which telephone you were allowed to use if you wanted to call your girl friend. Everything except when you could crap.

Kid Otto stopped reading and started to make a speech. "Did you see this? Did you see this bullshit? What is this? Am I supposed to be the doctor or the grocery boy? I'll take this fucking resident and this fucking nurse and I'll break their goddam asses."

"Well, I think Clancy's nice," Vittorio observed. "I heard she gives good blow jobs."

"I think they're both fucking assholes!"

"Relax, Otto," Gypsy said. "You haven't even met Clancy

yet, and Hugo's very smart. He'll probably teach you a lot of medicine. Anyway, you can just ignore him. Let's go have lunch."

They ate lunch together, with Kid Otto grumbling and cursing through his french fries. After lunch, they spent the rest of the day reading over the charts of the patients they were picking up. "Scum," Kid Otto complained suddenly, in the middle of a chart. "Scum and more scum. Alcoholics with staph pneumonias, overdosed drug addicts, and criminals with holes shot in them! It's a scum farm here."

Gypsy laughed. "Why don't you guys beat it and go home? It's getting late anyway." He took Kid Otto into the corner and gave him half an ounce of grass. "Otto," he said, "look, this is my emergency stash. I got to work here tonight, so I certainly can't use it. You take it home and smoke it with your wife. You'll feel much better, and I have to stay straight anyhow."

Kid Otto smiled. "Okay, Gypsy, you talked me into it. Thanks. What do you say, Vic?"

Vittorio pulled his coat on and looked around at the respirators and tubes and EKG monitors. He put his hand on Gypsy's shoulder. "Good night, man; good luck."

It was a good night. No one died.

The next morning Vic came in at twenty to eight. He commiserated with Gypsy about his night in the Unit, and then they sat down in the nursing station to drink coffee and wait for Kid Otto.

"Gypsy, I think you gave him too much pot. He probably has himself on Thorazine by now."

"Nah," Gypsy said. "He's an Episcopalian. Episcopalians don't get paranoid when they smoke dope."

"Are you kidding? Episcopalians are terrific paranoids."

Hugo walked into the nursing station and took his coat off.

[170]

"Hugo," Gypsy asked, "are Episcopalians paranoid much?"

"What?"

"Never mind," Vittorio said, "here comes Kid Otto."

Indeed it was. They could see Kid Otto's grin all the way down the corridor. He walked up to the nursing station. "Boy," he announced from the doorway, "did I get fucked last night." Hugo ran into the closet with his coat.

"Good stuff, huh, my man," Gypsy said.

"Wow, that pot is great," Kid Otto said in a booming voice. "Joanie loved it. Man, we got stoned and then she wouldn't stop fucking." Hugo disappeared deeper into the closet.

Gypsy laughed. "We can talk about it later. I think you're embarrassing Hugo."

"I told you it was too much for him," Vic said. "He's out of control."

Kid Otto was prancing around the nursing station. "Oh, boy, Joanie went crazy. She kept sucking me off, and screwing, and sucking me off again!"

One of the little Catholic nurses from the Philippines was standing there getting the morning meds ready, and she dropped half of her pills on the floor. The pills were all different colors, and they went bouncing and rolling around Kid Otto's feet. The nursing station was emptying out, except for Hugo, who stayed hidden in the closet.

Kid Otto was very excited, and kept right on with the play-by-play. "Man," he said happily, "she wanted me to fuck her in the ass and everything. I couldn't come any more after a while." The little Filipino nurse dropped the rest of her pills on the floor, said something in Tagalog, and ran out the door.

"He's your friend, Gypsy," Vic said. "Do something with him."

"Shit on you, Vittorio—he's your friend, too. You do something with him."

"You gave him the pot."

Hugo appeared out of the closet, trying to look like he hadn't heard anything. "All right, let's make rounds, shall we?"

"Hugo, what are you embarrassed about?" Vic asked.

"Get the chart rack," Hugo ordered. "We're going to make rounds now."

Gypsy obediently trundled the chart rack into the hall. "Hey, Hugo," he said, "did you hear what happened to Kid Otto last night?"

"We're making rounds now, doctor."

Vittorio sighed and shook his head. "Poor old anal-compulsive."

Kid Otto was still ebullient, but a little more restrained. They left the nursing station to make bedside rounds, and the nurses started to drift back, looking strangely at Kid Otto. Kid Otto smiled at all of them. The M.I.C.U. house staff were occupied until twelve making rounds, and then they went to lunch. In the afternoon they had to change trach tubes.

A tracheostomy is basically a hole in the throat. An incision is made in the skin of the neck, a little below the Adam's apple. This incision is carried down through the subcutaneous tissues until the trachea is dissected free. Bleeding vessels are, of course, clamped off on the way. When the windpipe, or trachea, is reached, it is immobilized and a hole is stabbed through the front of it, in between the rings of cartilage. The hole in the trachea is reamed out to make it a little bigger, a tracheostomy tube is slipped in, and you're done. A quick check is made again for bleeders, and the wound is closed with a few sutures.

Half the patients in the Unit had tracheostomies. Either

[172]

they weren't breathing well enough on their own or else they were breathing spontaneously but couldn't clear their own secretions, so they were in effect drowning themselves. The trach tube was a curved, plastic little tube about four inches long. It had a kind of flange or guard close to one end that divided it into a long and short part. The long part was inserted through the hole, down into the patient's trachea. The tube was pushed in until the guard was up against the skin of the patient's neck, and the whole business was tied in place with a string, like a bib.

The patient was left with the stumpy end of the trach tube sticking out through the front of his neck. The tube could then be hooked up to a respirator, which would help him breathe more easily, or, if necessary, do all of his breathing for him. Also, long rubber catheters could be passed through the tracheostomy and quickly snaked down into the patient's lungs. Hooked up to suction machines, these catheters were used to suck out secretions that very sick patients could not bring up. Without good suctioning in such patients, pneumonia, respiratory failure, and death were what usually resulted.

Tracheobronchial secretion is normally fairly copious, and the presence in the windpipe of a foreign body, like a trach tube, stimulates even more secretion. Unlike the real trachea, a tracheostomy tube has no cilia, and these secretions just stick to it. This glop built up quickly on the inside of the trach tubes and so they all had to be changed every two or three days.

Changing his first patient's trach tube was not a big deal: Gypsy just cut the string, deflated the pressure cuff, and pulled the thing out. Then he threw the old tube away, suctioned the patient for a minute, and slid the new tube in. Unfortunately, the rest of the patients were not as deeply comatose as the first one was, and all this fooling with the

[173]

inside of their windpipes set off their cough and gag reflexes. They started to choke and cough and turn blue as soon as Gypsy removed their trach tubes, and each time one of these patients gasped Gypsy got sprayed with spit from the hole in the patient's throat. It was unsettling as hell.

Then Gypsy came to an apneic patient. This was a man who was so sick he had no spontaneous respiration at all; the respirator that he was on had to trigger itself, automatically.

When Gypsy disconnected the respirator from this patient's trach tube, his breathing simply stopped. He just lay there. And, beyond that, the patient hadn't had his tracheostomy very long, and once Gypsy pulled the trach tube out, the soft tissues of the patient's neck immediately closed over the hole in his windpipe. What Gypsy had to do then was quickly fish around in the man's neck with a long metal probe that had a hook on the end, something like what the dentist uses in your mouth. Gypsy finally hooked the hole with his probe, pulled the trachea up to the surface, and hurriedly pushed another trach tube in. During the time Gypsy was trying to get the old trach tube out, and the new one in, and the respirator connected again, the patient wasn't breathing. And while all this was going on, no oxygen was getting to his brain, or his heart, or anywhere else. There is no worse sight in medicine. No spectacle of gore and blood is as final, as irrevocable, as a patient quietly lying there, not breathing.

Gypsy was sweating when he finished. He got a cup of coffee in the nursing station and sat down, holding the coffee in his lap with both hands. Vittorio came in and looked at him.

"What's wrong, Gypsy?"

"Nothing, Vic. I'm okay. I think I'm a little ragged from last night, is all." He took a deep breath. "I don't know, man, this is some fucking place . . ."

Vittorio glanced at his watch. "Come on," he said.

"Crazy Hugo's working tonight, anyway. Let's just get out of here."

Gypsy nodded. He threw the coffee away and put on his coat. "Where's Otto?"

"He's probably in the cafeteria again. We'll pick him up on the way out."

They walked through the corridor toward the elevators, which were around a corner. Halfway there, they heard Kid Otto start yelling and cursing. Gypsy smiled. "Kid Otto, I think." They turned the corner. Kid Otto was standing in front of one of the elevators, banging on the metal doors with both fists and yelling.

"Fucking lazy scumbag elevator operators—they should take them all out and break their fucking asses!" He beat on the doors once more.

"Otto," Gypsy said, "relax, would you? Those doors are only made out of steel. You're going to fall down the fucking elevator shaft."

Kid Otto stopped banging and turned around. "Oh, hi. I was looking for you guys, but this elevator operator got me aggravated." He smiled broadly.

"I noticed," Vittorio said.

"Well, anyway, what I wanted to tell you was, Joanie liked her present so much she wants both of you to come out to Bay Shore for dinner tonight. Okay?"

"Joanie made dinner for us last time," Gypsy said, moved by some kind of vague vision of ingratiating himself with Kid Otto's piece-of-ass wife. "Call her up and tell her that we're coming, but me and Vic are going to bring dinner over. She won't have to cook anything."

"Oh, great," Kid Otto said. "I'll see you about seven o'clock." He went off in the direction of the Unit.

Vittorio looked at Gypsy. "Are you crazy? What can you cook?"

Gypsy laughed. "Get fucked, Vic. Just make a giant pot

[175]

of spaghetti. I'll buy some caviar; I think Joanie likes that."

"You get fucked; I have to take The Angel to the vet today. You've got to make the dinner."

"Me? I can't cook anything!"

"Learn," Vittorio said, "learn. I'll be at your place around six."

"My God," Gypsy said to himself, "what have I done?" He thought about the problem all the way home. No ideas. As soon as he entered his apartment, he took off his whites and threw them on the couch, and then he started to walk back and forth in his underpants.

"Shit," he said out loud. "Shit, shit." He put some Grateful Dead on the stereo and turned it up. No inspiration. Four o'clock. Four-thirty.

"Jesus. Eight years of college and I can't handle dinner for four people and one dog." He looked in the refrigerator, not very hopefully. There was no help there. Some moldy green bread, two-month-old chocolate pudding, stuff like that. He called Vic up, to chicken out. Vic wasn't home.

"Crap," Gypsy said. He didn't know what to do, so he pulled out his water pipe and got stoned. Once he was high, he couldn't even focus on the problem, but it didn't seem so important any more. Five o'clock. Five-thirty.

"Five-thirty?" Gypsy said to his clock. "Five-thirty? Oh, boy, half an hour! This is stupid. I have to get dinner." He managed to navigate himself through the door and pushed the button for the elevator. He realized he was waiting for the elevator in his underpants.

"Hah," he said, "they're going to throw me out of the A.M.A.—I don't have any pants on." He wandered back into the apartment to try to get dressed.

Finally, he made it down to the street. There was not a lot of time left. He selected the first store he passed with a neon sign in the window: the Hoo Hop Take Out Restaurant. A Chinese man at the counter gave him a very complex menu. Gypsy looked at it carefully, but he couldn't figure it out. He was much too stoned.

The elderly Chinese smiled at him. "What you like?" Gypsy smiled back, and looked at the menu some more. It was hopeless. Everything had a pretty name. "What you like?" the man asked him again.

"Uh," Gypsy said, "uh, egg rolls. Egg rolls."

"Egg roll. What else you like?"

"What else? Ribs. Spareribs."

"Sparerib," the Chinese man repeated. "What else?"

It was a little too fast for Gypsy. "Egg rolls," he said.

The Chinese man grinned. "Egg roll? Egg roll. What else you like?"

Gypsy bought nine orders of spareribs and twenty-seven egg rolls, and went home to wait for Vic.

When he returned to his apartment, the egg-roll bag was dripping grease, so he put it in the sink. A few minutes later Vittorio came up and rang the doorbell. "Jesus," he said when he walked in, "it smells like an opium den here. Did you get something for dinner, druggie?"

"I got a lot of spareribs," Gypsy said proudly. "I hope The Angel likes spareribs."

"I fed The Angel already, before I took him to the vet. It puts him in a better mood that way. Let's go, Gypsy, we're late again." Vic picked up the spareribs, and they left.

They climbed into Vic's car and Gypsy immediately nodded out, with his arms around the bag of spareribs. He began to snore quietly. Halfway across the Brooklyn Bridge, Gypsy woke up. "Vittorio, I think I forgot something."

"That figures." Vic kept his eyes on the traffic in front of him. "All that pot finally rotted your brain. You forgot the caviar, didn't you?"

"Caviar?" Gypsy said. "I didn't get any caviar. I think I

[177]

got a whole lot of egg rolls." He looked inside the bag of spareribs. "Vic, I don't see any egg rolls in there. I think maybe I left them all home."

"Gypsy, what's egg rolls between friends? Go back to sleep."

"I'm not stoned," Gypsy insisted. "I just forgot the egg rolls, is all." He put his head down on the bag and passed out again. Vittorio drove east for an hour on the Belt and the Southern State Parkway, and they arrived at Kid Otto's home. Vic parked the car and then walked around to Gypsy's side.

"Gypsy," he said, pulling the door open, "we're here."

"Right." Gypsy stumbled out of the car and looked around. "Where are we?"

"Kid Otto's. Come on."

Gypsy made it across the lawn okay, but he had some more trouble with his balance on the stairs. He started to tip backward. Vittorio, who had foreseen this, was two steps behind him. Vic reached up and tilted Gypsy forward again. "Almost there, Gypsy. Don't nod out yet."

Gypsy got to the top of the narrow stairway. "Vic," he said, "I can't ring the bell."

"What now? Why can't you ring the bell?"

"I'm holding the spareribs," Gypsy explained. "There's no place to put them down here."

"My God," Vittorio said. "What's wrong with you?"

Somebody inside the apartment heard the discussion and opened the door. It was Joanie. "Gypsy and Vittorio! Welcome. How are you?"

Vic grinned at her. "Hi, Joanie; I'm fine. He's stoned."

Gypsy wandered around the living room a little bit, and then he came back to Joanie and presented the big paper bag to her. This bag was now pretty greasy also. "We brought you dinner," he announced, with as much ceremony as he could assemble.

[178]

She took the bag from him. "That's very sweet. Thank you, Gypsy."

"Gypsy's dinner is dripping all over your white rug," Vittorio pointed out accurately. "You better put it in the kitchen or something, Joanie."

"Oh, yeah, you're right. Excuse me a minute." She went into the kitchen, holding the bag out in front of her.

"Hey, you guys!" Kid Otto's voice rang through the apartment. "I'll be right out. I'm taking a crap!"

"My other elegant friend," Vittorio observed crabbily. "Joanie, what do you see in these two?"

Joanie walked back into the living room. "What are you bitching about, Vittorio?"

"My friends," he said, "my friends. What's a nice Italian boy like me doing with these crazies?"

Kid Otto came out of the bathroom pulling his pants up and smiling happily. "Hey, what's happening? Good to see you guys; it was a great idea for you to come over." He turned philosophical. "You know, taking a shit is the only uncomplicated gratification left to man. It's true. I learned that from Gypsy."

"Who else?" Vittorio said.

"Joanie, bring the grass in here for Gypsy," Kid Otto requested. "Let's get high."

"More pot?" Vittorio frowned. "Fine. You can just intubate Gypsy and put him on a respirator for a few days—until he's conscious again." Kid Otto's wife had gone into the bedroom. She returned with a plateful of joints. "I hope there's enough grass left," she said. "I think Gypsy likes to get really stoned."

"He is really stoned," Vittorio corrected her. "Aren't you, Gypsy?"

Gypsy was lying flat on his face, inspecting the carpet up close. He said something unintelligible to the floor.

"That's pretty good," Vittorio said. "He can still talk."

[179]

Joanie lit some of the joints and passed them around. She and Kid Otto both became involved enthusiastically in getting wasted. Vic took his customary two or three quick hits to be polite and went into the kitchen to find some liquor to drink. He brought the bottle back with him.

"Joanie, what do you have cooking in the oven out there?"

"Wow, the lamb chops," she remembered suddenly. "You know, I didn't expect Gypsy to be able to produce a dinner. I'll go turn the lamb chops off."

"You better go look at Gypsy's dinner before you do that," Vittorio suggested.

"At Gypsy's dinner? Why?"

Vic shrugged. "Go look."

Joanie was weaving a bit, owing to the grass, but she made it into the kitchen. She came back giggling. Kid Otto started to laugh, too. "What did he do now?" he asked.

Joanie was laughing harder. She went over and shook Gypsy. "Gypsy, what did you do?" Gypsy rolled onto his back and tried to sit up. He was too stoned.

Joanie sat down on her husband's lap. "Do you know what? Your friend is crazy." She was still laughing. "The whole bag is filled with spareribs. The whole bag. Nothing but spareribs. Hundreds of them, I think."

"Then I guess we're going to have lamb chops and spareribs for dinner," Kid Otto said. He kissed Joanie. "So what?" He thought about that menu a little while. "Vittorio, how come Gypsy bought all those spareribs?"

Vic was getting drunk. "Well, I'll tell you. Gypsy is my friend and I love him, but I don't know why he does anything. Now, if you wanted me to speculate, I would say it was probably a toxic psychosis from all the drugs he has on board."

Gypsy was finishing off a roach. He propped himself up

[180]

on his side. "Vic, get fucked," he mumbled, with his voice hoarse from too much dope-smoking.

"Ah, he's out of coma," Vittorio said. "Gypsy, concentrate. Everybody wants to know why you bought so many spareribs."

Gypsy was drifting off once more. "Joanie," he said slowly, trying with difficulty to construct an explanation, "I bought egg rolls for you. Egg rolls. I bought all these egg rolls, I think. Only, I forgot them. I forgot the egg rolls. Am I making any sense? I think I bought a lot of spareribs, too."

"Correct," Vittorio said.

"I'm sorry, Joanie. I forgot the egg rolls."

"Poor Gypsy." She came over and patted him on the head. "Poor baby. Don't worry, it's okay. We'll give you a nice lamb chop to have with your spareribs."

Gypsy lay down on the floor again. "I feel so guilty . . . I wish I wasn't stoned. I could show you what happened."

"Gypsy, everybody forgives you," Kid Otto told him.

"I feel terrible," Gypsy said.

"What is this, group therapy?" Vittorio muttered. "I liked it better when he was unconscious." Vic got up and went over to Kid Otto's stereo. He hunted through the records until he came to one that put a pained look on his face. "Good, you have some here." He started the record, switched the speakers off, and plugged the set of earphones in. Then he brought the earphones back to Gypsy, who was still trying unsuccessfully to explain about the egg rolls. He dangled the headset in front of Gypsy's face.

"Gypsy," he said, "Rolling Stones!"

Gypsy stopped talking and grinned slyly. "No shit? Not some of that Italian crap?"

"No, no opera; the Rolling Stones."

Gypsy pulled the earphones on, closed his eyes, and turned oblivious.

Vittorio laughed. "So much for how terrible he feels."

"Let's eat," Kid Otto decided. Everyone was stoned except Vic, who was drunk. Joanie, Kid Otto, and Vittorio moved to the dinner table, bumping into each other as well as the furniture. The three of them ate a large number of spareribs and lamb chops.

"Wow," Joanie said when they had finished stuffing themselves, "Gypsy didn't eat anything yet." She stood up to go check on him.

"Forget about it," Vittorio said, "I plugged him into the Rolling Stones." He certainly had. Gypsy was just where Vic had left him, prostrate on the floor, and connected to the world outside his head solely through the earphones.

Joanie nudged him tentatively. "Gypsy? Don't you want your lamb chop?" Gypsy was far away. Vic took a snort from his bottle. "Leave him alone, Joanie, he can't even hear you."

Kid Otto belched and walked over to his wife. Vittorio joined them, and they all stared down at Gypsy as if they were standing around a bier.

"He's crazy about the Rolling Stones, isn't he?" Joanie said finally.

"He's crazy altogether."

"Yeah, I guess he is," Kid Otto said. "You remember what happened when Janis Joplin died?"

"Sure. He was in love with Janis Joplin. Just like this Brian Jones thing."

Joanie studied Gypsy's face. "Why does he like Brian Jones so much? Why doesn't he like anyone who's alive, Vic?"

Vittorio took another swallow. "How should I know? He's probably trying to drown out the voices in his head." Vic looked at his stuporous friend. "You know something?" he added after a moment. "Maybe it's the damn hospital

[182]

that's driving him up the wall. He's trying to be Albert Schweitzer or somebody. I don't think Gypsy's a very happy person." Vic put his bottle down. "Well, what the hell," he said. "Wake him up in the morning, would you? Good night, everybody."

Right after they finished making rounds on Wednesday, Kid Otto stopped Gypsy outside the staff bathroom.

"Gypsy, how do you feel?" he asked.

"I feel fine. How do you feel?"

"You looked terrible this morning. Are you sure you're all right?"

Gypsy sighed. "Otto, I'm starting to get a little deaf in one ear from listening to rock and roll all the time. Except for that there's nothing wrong with me, man. I'm fine. Okay? Can I go to the bathroom now?"

Kid Otto looked at him suspiciously. "You going in there to crap?"

"What is this, a new fetish? I was going in to urinate, actually, if that's all right with you."

"Are you sure you're not shooting up in the bathroom?" Kid Otto said. "You look very pale."

"I'll tell you a secret—I'm going in there to drown myself in the toilet."

"Gypsy, I'm serious. All those drugs are bad for you. You're going to hurt yourself."

"Jesus Christ!" Gypsy said. "Vic, would you take this schmuck for a walk someplace so I can piss in peace?" He slammed the bathroom door. Vittorio came over to the bathroom. "Watch your needles, Gypsy," he cautioned in front of the door, "he's on to you. He knows what you're doing."

"Get fucked, the both of you," replied Gypsy's voice from the bathroom, punctuated by the flushing of the toilet.

[183]

Gypsy reappeared, looking surly. "God damn it, Vic, don't encourage him."

"You know, I think you hurt his feelings," Vittorio said, smiling. "He was concerned about your health."

"Oh, Christ," Gypsy complained. "Why does everybody say I'm the one that's crazy? You and him are the schizophrenics. Otto, hey, I'm still alive. I didn't drown myself."

Kid Otto was trying to appear preoccupied with a chart. Gypsy approached him. "Otto, I'm sorry I called you a schmuck."

"I was just worried about you." Kid Otto looked hurt.

Gypsy sighed again. "I know, I know. You got me at a bad moment, is all. Otto, when you've been drinking coffee and walking back and forth on rounds all morning, and somebody stops you right before you get to the bathroom, it's a bad thing, man. Okay? I'm not mad at you, Otto; it was only my bladder you offended."

Kid Otto was still pouting. Gypsy laughed. "This is ridiculous. All this conflict between two mature physicians over one piss? Here, look what I brought in." Gypsy reached under Kid Otto's chair and produced a large brown bag, identical to the one he'd been carrying around the night before. By now, however, it had gotten really greasy, from sitting in Gypsy's sink overnight. He stood the bag on the table, on top of the chart Kid Otto was pretending to be reading.

"Go ahead," Gypsy told him. "They're for you."

Kid Otto kept trying to look injured, but the bag had started to drip into his lap, anyway, and after half a minute he broke down and opened it. He stuck his head inside. "Egg rolls!" he said excitedly, pulling his head out of the paper bag. "A whole bag of egg rolls." His appetite immediately got the better of his pride. "This is wonderful," he proclaimed. "We can eat them for lunch."

[184]

"Well, I don't know. I brought them in for you."

"That's ridiculous. I can't eat all these egg rolls by myself."

"Well, yeah, there are a lot of them, I guess," Gypsy conceded elaborately. "Look, you're right, why don't we take them down to the kitchen later and heat them up for lunch?"

"Great," Kid Otto said. Then, smitten with an idea, he jumped out of the chair and clapped his hands together once. "Wait a minute. Fuck lunch! I can heat them up right now in the back, on Clancy's hot plate."

Vittorio and Gypsy looked at each other. "Otto," Vittorio reminded him, "you know Clancy gets pissed off about the interns hanging around back there."

"Fuck Clancy" was Kid Otto's response. He lugged the bagful of egg rolls through a door with a sign on it that said:

NURSES ONLY
ALL OTHERS KEEP OUT!
THIS MEANS YOU!

"You did it," Vittorio said to Gypsy.

"Me? I didn't do anything. I just figured he'd stop sulking if he saw some food."

Vittorio made a sour face. "Clancy's going to cut his balls off when she finds two hundred egg rolls cooking in there."

Gypsy laughed, but somewhat halfheartedly. "Vic, there's only about thirty egg rolls in the bag."

"Oh, excuse me, that changes everything."

"Maybe she won't notice anything anyway," Gypsy said hopefully.

"She's going to cut his balls off. You'll see."

Kid Otto returned from the Nurses Only room. "Holy shit, what a mess. There was an awful lot of egg rolls in that bag, Gypsy. I had to kind of pile them up, one on top of the other, you know? I had a hard time getting them all on the hot plate."

"Otto, you can't cook all those egg rolls at the same time —on one lousy hot plate!"

"I think I can," Kid Otto said, with an intrigued look. "It's an experiment."

"Don't say anything else," Vittorio warned him. "I don't want to know anything about this one. I'm innocent." He walked out from behind the chart racks and almost got run over by the portable X-ray machine. "Goddam faggot X-ray technician," Vittorio muttered, and retreated back behind the chart racks.

"Cut it out, Vic," Gypsy said, coming to the technician's defense.

"He's a goddam faggot," Vittorio grumbled.

"Yeah, I suppose he's a queer, all right," Gypsy agreed, "but that's got nothing to do with anything. That's just his thing, man. Besides, he's bigger than you; you better be careful."

"He's not bigger than me," Kid Otto pointed out belligerently. "I'll break his ass."

"What's the matter with you guys? You're really getting hostile. Maybe it's your own masculinity you're a little worried about, huh?"

"Come off it, Gypsy," Kid Otto protested. "When did you go into the fruitcake business?"

"I'm not in that business, man. I just think that as long as this dude doesn't hit anybody with a blackjack, he can fuck whoever he wants to."

"Crap," Vittorio said. "Look at him, will you? Watch how much the goddam faggot cares about the patients!" Gypsy had never heard such intense animosity in Vic's voice.

Every day most of the patients in the Unit had a chest

[186]

X-ray taken on a portable machine. This was because it was either impractical or impossible to disconnect them from all their tubes, monitors, and life-support systems and send them down to the X-Ray Department. Accordingly, every morning an X-ray technician was dispatched to the Unit along with a large, impressive-looking portable X-ray machine. Sometimes the machine was more impressive than the technician.

This was what the X-ray technician, Mr. Green, was supposed to be doing—obtaining chest X-rays on the very sick M.I.C.U. patients. He got the first patient propped up in bed, with the film cassette behind the man's back. Then he set the collimators on his portable machine, slouched off to the very end of the cable, ordered "Hold your breath" indifferently, and fired. Unhappily, the patient was comatose, intubated, and being breathed for by a mechanical respirator. When the technician gave the instructions "Hold your breath," the machine, of course, did not know it was being addressed, and kept right on ventilating the patient. The X-ray, therefore, was undoubtedly going to turn out blurred and useless.

"Did you see that?" Vittorio asked angrily. "That's really intelligent, isn't it?" He and Gypsy walked over to talk to the technician, whose hair style consisted of a narrow, bristling hedge arising above the center of his forehead. The hedge bisected his otherwise shaved scalp. "Vic, behave yourself," Gypsy said, trying to play peacemaker.

Vittorio confronted the technician. "What's the matter with you?"

Mr. Green was already moving to his next patient. "You got a problem, man?"

"No," Vittorio replied, "you got a problem. That film has to be taken over again."

The technician went on propping up the second patient.

[187]

"One X-ray a patient. You want more, send another request downstairs."

"Look, Mr. Green," Gypsy said reasonably, "the respirator cycled just when you made your exposure, and the film's going to be blurred. This patient's been on a respirator for a long time, and he's a setup for an aspiration pneumonia. It's really important that we get a good film; otherwise we wouldn't ask you to shoot it over again."

"Uh-huh," the technician answered. "One X-ray a patient."

"Mr. Green, the X-ray was no good. The patient might have pneumonia, and he needs the film. Can't you understand that?"

"One X-ray a patient. That's it."

"You lousy faggot," Vittorio fumed, "are you the doctor now, or what?"

"You watch your mouth, boy!" The technician glowered at Vic. "I'm in the union. You talk to me like that and we gonna strike this whole motherfucking hospital, and you and the patients can drop dead together. You hear?"

Kid Otto came over and poked the technician in the chest with his finger, hard. "I think you should shut up now," he told him. Gypsy pulled Kid Otto away. "Come on, we'll go down and talk to Debbins."

Vittorio, Gypsy, and Kid Otto all went downstairs and marched into Dr. Debbins's office. Debbins cringed. He was a very bright, academic radiologist who wanted to be left alone to do his research, which he liked. Being Chief of Radiology, he also had to run the Radiology Department, which he did not like. "Hello," Dr. Debbins said, trying to look confident.

"We have a problem with one of your technicians," Gypsy informed him.

"Oh," Dr. Debbins answered, looking less confident. "Well, perhaps you should talk to the Chief Technician."

[188]

"No, we don't seem to be communicating with the technicians. This is for a physician."

"I see. I'll get the Chief Resident for you, then."

"Dr. Debbins, we don't want to talk to your Chief Resident. We want to talk to you."

"Me?" Dr. Debbins said. "Why didn't you say so? What's the trouble?"

"I think you got him cornered, Gypsy," Kid Otto said scornfully. "You want me to block the door if he tries to get away?" Gypsy gave Kid Otto a stern look and turned back to the Chief of the Radiology Service. "Dr. Debbins," he said succinctly, "this guy Green has to go."

"Oh, yes, Mr. Green. He's a funny one, all right."

"He's a faggot," Vittorio stated.

Debbins cringed again. "You gentlemen are from where?"

"The Medical Intensive Care Unit," Vittorio answered, "and we don't want your faggot technician up there any more."

Debbins cleared his throat. "Doctor, uh . . ."

"Mazzoli. Vic Mazzoli."

"Dr. Mazzoli, the man's sexual preferences are neither here nor there as far as we are concerned."

"Didn't you hear Vittorio?" Kid Otto interrupted. "We don't want your goddam faggot in our Unit."

"This guy really is an awful X-ray technician," Gypsy insisted to Debbins. "He doesn't care about the films, he doesn't care about the patients, and he won't listen to anybody. I don't think he should be working in a hospital, with sick human beings. I think you should fire him."

Dr. Debbins quailed. "Fire him? Oh, no, he couldn't possibly be fired."

"Why not?" Vittorio asked. "Is he your brother-in-law?"

Debbins looked uncomfortable. "Well, Mr. Green is a union delegate."

Gypsy and Vic exchanged glances. "So?" Gypsy said.

"Every moron who cleans out the toilets is a vice-president in the goddam union. So what?"

"I'm sorry," Dr. Debbins said. "I know the man's an incompetent. I know he doesn't give a damn about the patients. But I just can't fire him; I can't. I'll transfer him away from the Intensive Care Unit for you; he won't have anything to do with M.I.C.U. patients any more."

"Oh, that's fine," Gypsy shot back. "Send him up to some ward that doesn't happen to have three doctors with big mouths around to complain about him. Who cares about those patients? Dr. Debbins, the man doesn't belong in a hospital—he needs to be fired!"

Debbins raised his voice for the first time. "Doctor, don't you understand what I'm telling you? This technician is in the union. Not only is he in the union, but he's even a delegate. There's no way to deal with these people in the union. I have no control over them any more. Fire him? My God, they can't be fired! Why, they can't be disciplined, they can't even be reprimanded." He stopped and wiped his brow with a handkerchief. "I'll transfer Green away from the M.I.C.U., if I can talk him into it. If I'm lucky."

"That's marvelous!" Gypsy yelled. "That's how to run a hospital, all right. Tell me something, would you—what do I need to get a decent X-ray on one of these poor bastards in the I.C.U.? Arbitration? A ninety-day cooling-off period? A fucking injunction?"

Vittorio stood up and grasped Gypsy's arm. "Gypsy, let's go. You're not accomplishing anything. He said he'd transfer the son of a bitch."

"Jesus!" Gypsy uttered. He walked as far as the door, and turned around again. "What should I tell my patient, Dr. Debbins? I'm sorry, patient, you can't have a chest X-ray; the fucking technician is a union delegate, and he doesn't think you need an X-ray today."

[190]

Kid Otto took hold of him by his white jacket and steered him out of Dr. Debbins's office. They walked over to the elevators together. "Ahh, fuck this place," Gypsy said. An elevator stopped, and they all went back upstairs.

As soon as they stepped off the elevator, it was apparent something else was wrong. The hall was full of smoke. "Now what?" Vittorio said.

They headed for the Unit. As they got closer, the smoke got thicker. Twenty feet from the Unit the three interns passed the female-staff bathroom, out of which the head nurse emerged looking the way people look when they have to cut short a visit to the bathroom.

"What the hell is going on?" Clancy demanded.

"Don't ask me," Vittorio told her, stealing a line from Gypsy, "I just work here."

All four of them hurried into the Unit. A steady stream of peculiar-smelling smoke was flowing out from under the "Nurses Only   All Others Keep Out!   This Means You!" door.

"Shit," Clancy swore, running for the door. She pushed it open and disappeared into the smoke. "Fire!" she shouted from inside the room. "Fire, fire!"

"Oh, Jesus," Kid Otto yelled, flooded with sudden understanding, "the egg rolls!" He ran into the room after her.

"You better go help them," Vittorio said to Gypsy, straight-faced.

Gypsy shook his head. "Shit on you, man."

There was a lot of yelling from inside the room, followed by the sound of a window smashing. More yelling and screaming. The smoke diminished slightly.

Then there was a short pause, and Kid Otto and Clancy both came bursting out of the room, raving. "Do you know what she did?" Kid Otto shouted, jumping up and down in front of Gypsy. "Do you know what she did? She threw all the egg rolls out the window!"

"You schmuck," Clancy said, "the egg rolls were on fire, for Christ's sake."

"They were not on fire—they were only smoldering. And don't you call me a schmuck."

"You schmuck," Clancy replied.

"I told you not to call me that. And keep your rotten hands off my food, you understand?"

"Schmuck!" Clancy repeated. "If I catch you in that room again I'll throw you out the fucking window, too."

Clancy was a big strong girl, and she looked serious. Kid Otto was beginning to look genuinely angry, which was an unheard-of thing for Kid Otto. "Listen," he warned, "you just keep your goddam hands off things that don't belong to you. I'll break your ass otherwise."

"Fuck you! The trouble with you fucking doctors is you can't read English. It's against the rules to cook anything in this Unit. It's against the rules for you to be in that room at all!" She was yelling right into his face now. "Do you hear me, schmuck? There's rules here. You bring any more goddam egg rolls into my Unit and I'll stick them up your ass! You schmuck," she added.

It was one schmuck too many. Kid Otto's vast good nature had been exhausted. The veins were standing out in his neck. "You stupid, ignorant nurse," he said in a thick voice, and held one of his great fists up in front of her face. "I'm going to break your head."

She was crazy as well. "Schmuck," she told him, "go fuck yourself."

Kid Otto grabbed her by the throat with his left hand and lifted her off the floor. He cocked his right fist, shaking with rage. "I'm going to kill you," he grunted.

It looked like he might. Gypsy ran over and clutched Kid

Otto's arm with both hands. "Otto," he yelled, "Jesus Christ! Put her down, will you? Somebody's going to get hurt here." Kid Otto freed himself with one jerk of his shoulder and a guttural "Let go of me, God damn it!"

Clancy tried to claw at Kid Otto's eyes.

"Vic, my God, he's going to murder her."

"Five dollars on Kid Otto," Vittorio said thoughtfully. "But you got to give me odds."

Gypsy didn't know what to do. Clancy was hanging from the end of Kid Otto's arm, kicking and turning a dusky purple, and he hadn't even smacked her yet. Her eyes started to bulge.

Gypsy picked up the telephone and dialed 9-9. He got a response on the first ring. "Good morning," a voice said briskly. "Cardiac-arrest operator."

"Good morning yourself," Gypsy said. "Call a Code Ninety-nine in the M.I.C.U."

"Medical Intensive Care Unit," the operator repeated, "right away, sir." A few seconds later the Code was paged.

A circus quickly gathered in the M.I.C.U. The Code Cart, which is a six-foot-high cardiac-resuscitation unit on wheels, rolled in first. The Code Cart was accompanied by the three nurses assigned to responding to Codes, who also supplied the horsepower to push the Cart down the hall. A surgical resident and a chief resident in internal medicine ran in, panting, followed by the senior cardiology Fellow. An anesthesiologist arrived with his set of tubes. A group of nursing students wandered in to watch. Not too many medical students had come, but it was the middle of the day and most of the medical students were already busy eating lunch and advocating community control of medicine to each other. A few stray porters joined the show, apparently finding it more entertaining than washing the floors.

The Unit had become packed with people looking for

[193]

someone to save. What they found was Kid Otto strangling the head nurse. There were so many people pushing and hollering and shoving, though, that Kid Otto and Clancy just got jostled aside. Some of the clamor penetrated Kid Otto's head. He shook himself and put Clancy down.

"Where is it? Where's the Code?" everyone was asking everyone else.

"There's no Code here," Gypsy announced. Nobody could hear him. He climbed up on the nurses' desk. "No Code!" he yelled. "There's no Code here; it's a mistake. Nobody called a Code," he lied.

There was a general murmur—of relief from some people, and of disappointment from others. The mob began to thin out. The porters picked up their mops and left. Like firemen after a false alarm, the nurses who had brought the Code Cart started to reel in the tangle of tubes and wires that had sprouted from the Cart.

Gypsy put his hand on Kid Otto's shoulder and led him over to a chair. "Why don't you sit down?" he suggested.

Kid Otto sat down slowly. His breath was still rasping through his teeth. There were mottled patches of red across his face, but his eyes didn't look wild any more.

"Are you okay, lunatic?" Gypsy asked him.

Kid Otto took a few deep breaths and rubbed his face with his hands. "Yeah, I guess so." He looked across the Unit at Clancy. "Damn, I never got so mad at anybody in my life."

Gypsy shrugged. "Well, she was asking for it. You know, I never saw you try to hurt someone before, Otto. Remind me not to fight with you."

"Jesus, I really wanted to kill her," Kid Otto said, sounding amazed.

"Man, I don't think you're the first person who ever wanted to kill Clancy. You're probably just the first guy who actually tried to do it, is all."

Clancy was also sitting down now, on the other side of the Unit. She was talking to one of her nurses. Her face was no longer purple—it was quite white. After telling so many interns to fuck off for so long, this sudden display of independence and initiative on Kid Otto's part had evidently astounded her.

Hugo arrived. He was upset, because the Code had made him leave his parasitology conference early.

"Who Coded?" Hugo asked.

"No one," Gypsy told him. "It was a mistake."

Hugo looked around at the mess. "I smell smoke. What happened here?"

Vic was standing in the center of the Unit, midway between Clancy and Kid Otto. "Nothing happened," Vittorio said unconvincingly. Hugo took in the scene. His head nurse and one of his interns—a Doctor of Medicine—were glaring at each other from their seats, looking like a pair of prizefighters resting in their corners after a tough fight and waiting to hear who had won.

"Oh, fine." Hugo started to edge his way out of the Unit. "As long as nothing's wrong. I'm going back down to the parasitology conference, then. Just page me if you need me for anything." He left to return to conference, which was where he felt physicians belonged anyway.

Vittorio was still standing center-ring, between the two combatants. He watched Hugo retreat down the corridor. "There goes the fearless leader, all right. It's a good thing he showed up to help us out."

"Who was that masked man?" Gypsy said. He left the Unit and took a slow, brooding walk to the solarium at the other end of the corridor. Along the way he passed the vegetables who were gradually decomposing on the neurology ward.

# A Little
# Blood and Guts

THE WEEKS WENT BY. Almost two-thirds of the way through
the year, and four months away from a license to practice
medicine and surgery, Gypsy still did not know how to cook
anything. He could never cope with making dinner, good as
he was at putting it into his mouth. All he ever had for
breakfast was orange juice, instant coffee, and sometimes a
joint, so the first meal of the day was no problem. Lunch he
ate at the hospital, if there was time. Any other meal was
McDonald's.

One night he went over to Vic's house for dinner,
equipped with Vittorio's keys and a boring social-worker
date named Maryann. Maryann was kind of typical for
Gypsy. He was very hard to please. He was always complaining bitterly that some girl he'd seen in D'Agostino's
wouldn't go home with him, or else he was complaining
that the girl who was going home with him was an igno-
ramus. And he would periodically start sending roses he
couldn't afford to girls who wouldn't have anything to do
with him.

Vic was supposed to have a date, too, but he was tied up
at the hospital. The Unit had gotten an admission about
five o'clock, and Vic was still putting tubes into the patient
when Gypsy left. The plan was for Gypsy to take The Angel
out for his walk, make very simple preparations for dinner,
and then wait for Vittorio. After he left the Unit, Gypsy
stopped at Social Services to get Maryann, and drove to
Vic's house.

"Look," he said while they were climbing the stairs, "The Angel is very big, but he won't hurt you. He just gets excited when he meets strangers."

"I don't like dogs," Maryann said. "I'm afraid of them."

Get fucked, Gypsy started to say, and then changed his mind. Gypsy loved dogs in general and The Angel in particular, but Maryann had great legs. He closed his mouth.

They reached Vic's door, Gypsy unlocked it, and as soon as he pushed the door open The Angel came bounding out. The enormous white German shepherd took one look at Maryann, growled, and made a wild rush for her, slipping like mad on the linoleum in his eagerness to chew her arm off. Maryann ran halfway back down the stairs.

Gypsy grabbed The Angel as he tried to get by and wrestled him back into the apartment. "Angel!" he yelled. "Cut that out! This is Maryann; be nice." He leaned over and whispered in the dog's ear. "Be nice or I'm not going to get laid, you hear?" The Angel thumped his tail and licked Gypsy in the face.

"Come in, come in," he said to Maryann, holding The Angel tightly by his chain collar. "It's all a big bluff," he assured her, untruthfully, "the dog wouldn't hurt anybody." Maryann walked cautiously in. Actually, The Angel was sitting there quite calmly by then. He was very pleased with himself. He loved scaring the shit out of strangers.

"This is a very rare albino dog, Maryann," Gypsy began.

"Something stinks in here."

Something did stink. Gypsy hunted around the apartment a little and found what stunk. It was behind Vic's big leather easy chair. "Heh, heh," Gypsy said, coming out from behind the chair and trying to look casual, "I have to clean something up."

The Angel did not like living in an apartment, having essentially grown up in a large backyard in southern California. He did not like being kept waiting to go out for his five o'clock walk, either. Although he was completely house-broken, once Vic moved him into the apartment he had elected to forget that part of his training. If no one came home to take him out at what he considered was a reason-able hour, he would just shit on the floor. And he was a big dog.

"You're a bad dog," Gypsy said to The Angel. "Bad!" The Angel let his big pink tongue hang out and thumped his tail again. He looked like he was laughing. Gypsy collected a pile of newspapers and a roll of paper towels and busied himself picking up dogshit.

"That's disgusting," Maryann said from the other side of the room.

"Yes, it certainly is. Why don't you read a magazine or something?"

"I don't like to read."

"Are you able to?" Gypsy muttered to himself. He came out from behind the chair once again, this time with a healthy amount of dogshit wrapped precariously in paper towels and newspapers. Gypsy hopped across the room try-ing to get to the door with his bundle intact. The Angel had apparently had a touch of diarrhea. "Quick," he said, "open the door."

Maryann came reluctantly over to where Gypsy was stand-ing, with her nose in the air, and opened the door for him. Gypsy ran for the incinerator and met Vittorio and Barbara coming the other way. It was a narrow hall.

Barbara was the ophthalmology resident who liked to sky-dive. "Gypsy," she said, "hello there."

"Look out, look out, dogshit!" Gypsy made it to the in-cinerator, but barely. He slid the disintegrating package into the chute and returned down the hall.

"Gypsy, what are you doing?" Barbara tried to kiss him hello.

[198]

"Don't touch me." Gypsy moved out of her reach. "Let me wash my hands first. There was an accident inside." Barbara stared at him blankly.

"Uh-oh," Vittorio said. "You got here late, didn't you?"

"Jesus, Vic, I got here as soon as I could. I didn't know the damn dog could tell time."

Vittorio shook his head. "I warned you. The Angel won't wait much past five o'clock to crap."

Barbara laughed. "I don't believe that the two of you went to college."

"Well, you're half right," Vittorio told her. "Gypsy went to correspondence school."

"Get fucked," Gypsy said cheerfully. "Come on in and meet the cretin."

"Oh, thanks for inviting me in. Is it okay if I pet my dog, too?"

"What cretin?" Barbara asked, and they all walked into the apartment.

"Maryann," Gypsy started out, "this is my friend Dr. Vittorio Mazzoli..."

"Hey," Maryann immediately interrupted him, "you're Italian, huh? I'm Italian, too. Are you from the Bronx?"

"Barbara," Gypsy said under his breath, "that's the cretin. Go be friendly, would you? I have to wash the dogshit off my hands." Barbara gave him an unkind look. "Gypsy, don't talk like that," she whispered back. "She seems like a nice girl."

"Uh-huh. Nice cretin." Gypsy went into the bathroom. Maryann began telling Vic about her Italian relatives all over the Bronx. After a few moments of regarding her haughtily, Vittorio drew himself up and said, "Miss, I am Yugoslav."

"Vic, stop that," Barbara admonished him. "He's just screwing around," she said to Maryann. "Of course he's Italian."

Vittorio smiled. "But I'm not from the Bronx—I'm from Staten Island."

Gypsy walked out of the bathroom, wiping his hands. Conversation had ceased. "Gypsy, where are you from?" Barbara asked him. She seemed a little desperate for anything at all to say.

"Me? Yugoslavia. What are we going to do about dinner?"

"I don't know," Vittorio complained, "I'm sick of Yugoslavian food."

"Yeah, so am I," Gypsy agreed, nodding. "Day after day, Yugoslavian food. It's not natural."

Barbara laughed. "Yugoslavian food? You're both crazy. All you ever eat is pizza and beer."

"Excellent idea," Vittorio decided immediately. "Much better than Yugoslavian food. We'll send out for two pizzas and four six-packs."

"Vic, I think we should cook a real dinner," Gypsy said. "You have guests."

"Three pizzas?"

"I'm going to make a spaghetti dinner for everybody," Gypsy announced. "And we can drink wine with it." Barbara and Vittorio snickered in unison. "Have you gone crazy again?" Vittorio said.

"No, man. I just think it would be nice if we made dinner for the broads, for a change."

"Gypsy," Barbara said, "the broads wouldn't mind eating pizza at all."

"Oh, come on, Barbara, me and Vic can do it."

"Wait a minute." Maryann joined the discussion. "You're going to make dinner for us? After you picked up all that dog do?"

Vittorio grinned. "Dog do?"

"Dog do?" Gypsy repeated, grinning also. "Dog do? You

mean dogshit, Maryann? I washed my hands about six times. Here, smell them." He held his hands up in front of her nose. Maryann backed away from him, looking abused.

Barbara gave in. "Okay, Gypsy, we'll have spaghetti for dinner. I think you better let Vic supervise, though."

"Hah," Vittorio said. "You better let Vic make the dinner."

"We'll make it together," Gypsy compromised, very excited about his idea. Vic filled a huge pot with water and dumped two big boxes of spaghetti into it, grumbling the whole time.

"What should I do?" Gypsy asked.

"You should go downstairs and buy some tomato paste. Can you handle that?"

"Of course I can handle it." Gypsy went downstairs and bought tomato sauce. By the time he came back, Vic had decided the spaghetti was ready.

"Now, look," Vittorio told him, "this pot is really heavy. You go hold the colander over the sink. I'll carry the pot."

"The what? What do I hold?"

"That thing," Vittorio said patiently, "the strainer."

Gypsy got the strainer ready. Vic wrapped a towel around the pot, tried with no success to pick it up, and dragged it, instead, across the stove to the sink. He managed to tilt the pot up on its side and started to pour the spaghetti into the colander.

"Hold it up, Gypsy—hold the strainer up. I can't see anything." He couldn't see anything because of all the steam billowing out of the pot.

"Watch out for my hand," Gypsy warned, "that stuff is hot."

"Hold it higher," Vittorio said, "I can't see."

"Watch out for my hand," Gypsy said again.

The more Vic tilted the pot, the less he could see. The

sink, the strainer, and the spaghetti were all hidden in a cloud of steam. Vic tilted the pot a little too much, and sent a cascade of scalding water and spaghetti sliding down Gypsy's arm.

Gypsy shrieked and jumped in the air, dropping the strainer and all the spaghetti on the floor.

"God damn it," Vittorio shouted, "I told you to hold it higher!"

Gypsy was running cold water over his arm. "Ahh, blow it out your ass. I told you to watch out for my hand."

The Angel had been pretending to be asleep in the corner, figuring to lay low for a while after crapping in the apartment. As soon as he saw the spaghetti hit the floor, he abandoned his act and raced into the kitchenette.

"Angel, get away from that!" Vittorio yelled.

"Oh, what the hell, Vic," Barbara said, "let him eat it." The Angel didn't know that anybody was on his side. The spaghetti was too slippery for him, and he was trying to hold it still with one of his front paws and gulp down as much as he could.

Gypsy laughed. "Poor old dog. It's hard for you to eat that stuff, isn't it?" He got down on his hands and knees and helped The Angel shovel up their dinner.

"Okay," Vittorio informed everyone, "I'm calling the pizza place."

"Come on, Vic," Gypsy protested. "I promised the girls a spaghetti dinner. What's a little accident? I'll boil some more water, and everything will be ready in fifteen minutes." Gypsy used his good, unburned hand to fill the tremendous pot with water once again.

Vittorio shook his head sadly. "My God," he reflected wistfully, "we could have had two big pizzas by now—with mushrooms, and anchovies, and sausage, and green peppers. And pepperoni."

"Quiet," Gypsy ordered. "This is better for you. Look how big and strong The Angel is."

"Shit," Vittorio said, but it was futile. Gypsy was already opening.up two more of the large boxes of spaghetti. He emptied them into the pot.

"It's a good thing you keep all this spaghetti in the house, Vic."

"Yeah, well, spaghetti is the backbone of Yugoslavian cooking."

Maryann spoke again. "I don't want any Yugoslavian food," she told them. "I want to go out for a cheeseburger."

"Go pet the dog," Gypsy said to her. Maryann chose not to pet the dog. She watched Vittorio, Barbara, and Gypsy watching the spaghetti cook. After a while Gypsy peered into the pot. "I think the spaghetti is done," he noted.

Barbara got up. "Gypsy, let me take care of it now."

"You sit down and relax. Me and Vic are in charge of dinner."

Vittorio gave his girl friend a helpless look, shrugged, and stationed himself in front of the sink next to Gypsy. "All right," he instructed, "now, listen, Gypsy, we're doing it different this time. I'm going to work the strainer. All you have to do is pour the spaghetti out of the pot and into the strainer. You can't possibly get hurt."

Gypsy appeared doubtful. "I don't know. You could get burned that way instead of me. There must be an easier way to do it."

"Gypsy," Vittorio said impatiently, "this is not a heart transplant here. All we've got to do is drain a pot of spaghetti."

Gypsy wrapped the towel around the pot. "I wish it wasn't so goddam hot. Whose idea was this?"

"Pour," Vittorio coached. He held the strainer out.

[203]

Gypsy glanced worriedly at Vittorio and tilted the pot an inch or two.

"Christ," Vittorio said, "tilt the pot."

"I am tilting it." Gypsy turned the steaming pot another inch on its side. "I just want to control the flow, is all."

Vic rolled his eyes up toward heaven. "What flow, Gypsy? What flow? Do you see one lousy piece of spaghetti in the strainer yet? Pour the damn spaghetti!"

Maryann leaned closer to Barbara and said, sister to sister, "What's wrong with them? Are they both insane?" Barbara smiled thinly at her. "Maryann, wouldn't you like to look at some comic books?"

Maryann declined. "I don't like comic books."

Gypsy was moving the pot imperceptibly, with an expression of intense concentration frozen on his face.

"For God's sake," Vittorio shouted, "tilt it more! Tilt it more!"

"Ah, get fucked," Gypsy said. "I am tilting it." He illustrated getting fucked, with his middle finger. Unfortunately he had to let go of the pot to do that. The pot, of course, immediately flopped over and spilled two pounds of spaghetti and a lot of hot water onto the ·floor. Gypsy stood there holding his middle finger up, with the dripping pot dangling from his other hand.

The Angel, who thought it was Christmas in February or something, was instantly on his feet and running. He came skidding across the wet floor near the sink and went to work on his second two pounds of spaghetti in thirty minutes. The dog liked to eat.

Barbara burst out laughing. Maryann didn't say anything.

Vic looked at the empty strainer he was holding, and put it down slowly in the sink. "Gypsy," he said in a careful, controlled voice, "you're my best friend in the world, but sometimes you are just a hopeless asshole."

"I'm sorry, man. I guess I fucked it up again."

"You guess? You *guess* you fucked it up?"

Barbara came over and tried to make him feel better. "Oh, it's not so terrible, Gypsy. This is better than the Marx Brothers."

"Well, what are we going to do for dinner now?" Gypsy asked contritely.

"Nothing!" Vittorio said quickly. "You don't have to do anything at all. Not a thing. Barbara and I are going to handle everything. You take The Angel, and your girl friend, and go for a walk."

"Can't I even watch?"

"Gypsy," Vittorio said vehemently, "take The Angel out for a walk!"

Gypsy looked at Barbara for support. She shook her head. "We're going to starve otherwise, Gypsy. Take The Angel out like Vittorio says, and come back in half an hour."

Gypsy searched everyone's face for sympathy, found none, and sighed forlornly. "Okay, you win." He picked up The Angel's leash. "Come on, dog. Come on, Maryjane, let's go for a walk."

"My name is Maryann," she said.

"Well, come on anyway." Gypsy hooked The Angel to his big leather leash and the three of them marched downstairs: The Angel first, pulling Gypsy behind him, and Maryann dragging along last and looking pissed off.

"Vic," Barbara said when the door closed behind them, "how come Gypsy's going out with an idiot like that? He's really smart, isn't he?"

Vic was heating and stirring yet another potful of water and muttering under his breath about the spaghetti. "Yeah, he's a regular genius."

"Hon, I'm serious. Gypsy's got nothing at all in common

[205]

with that girl. I don't think he even likes her. Would he put up with someone that dumb just for some sex?"

Vic turned away from the stove to face his girl friend. "No," he said. "Not exactly." He gestured with the big spoon he was holding, searching for the right words. "It's more like, well, like he's passing a judgment on himself. It's as if he's saying, 'This girl is the best I can do—this is all I deserve.'"

"Vic, what are you talking about?"

Vittorio played with the spoon. "It's hard to explain, Barbara. Gypsy's whole life is really that damn hospital, and he's very tough on himself about it. He thinks being a doctor is the same thing as being the Pope. He thinks everything he does has to be perfect; he can't make any mistakes. And he can't stand the idea of any of his patients dying. It doesn't matter if they're ninety years old—it's his fault anyway."

"But what's that got to do with who he goes out with?"

Vittorio shrugged. "I'm not sure, exactly."

As soon as they got outside, The Angel ran over to the curb, did a little perfunctory sniffing around, and started to take a gigantic shit.

Gypsy watched him crap. City people who have big dogs like to look everywhere except at their dog when the beast is polluting up the street with excrement. Their behavior for that moment is supposed to imply somehow that the dog is an utter stranger they've never seen before in their life. Gypsy thought that was ridiculous. The animal was, after all, attached to his arm by five feet of thick leather leash. However, even though Gypsy liked dogs at least as much as he liked people, shit was nonetheless shit.

The Angel was a virtual shit factory. Maybe all the spaghetti had stimulated his insides, but it began to look like he was going to have to move over and start a second pile. The first mound was already brushing the underside of his tail, and he was a great big dog. Gypsy watched, very much impressed. Maryann edged away. Something caught Gypsy's eye then, and he leaned over the dog to inspect it. The Angel had just defecated a condom.

"Wow, Maryann, look at this." Gypsy pointed at the condom on top of the pile of rank dogshit. "The dog is nuts. He must be stealing Fourexes from Vic and eating them up. Isn't that strange? I didn't think anyone was still using those things."

"That's disgusting," Maryann said. "You look at it, if you think it's so wonderful."

Gypsy was fascinated by his discovery. It set him off thinking of a whole catalogue of fanciful perversions. After some moments of pornographic introspection, Gypsy turned around casually and asked, "Maryann, have you ever done a dog?"

"What?" she said, blinking.

"You know, did you ever ball a dog?"

Maryann gave him a horrified look. "That's disgusting! That's so disgusting . . . My God!" She ran a few steps away from him, as if Gypsy was contaminated by some dangerous and quite contagious disease. "I'm going home," she announced. She stalked off in the direction of the bus stop.

"Hey, come back," Gypsy called out, "I was just asking." He was thinking, a little too late, of her great legs. He tried to run after her, but The Angel was still unloading and in no position to run after anybody. Gypsy's love life was being sabotaged by a German shepherd taking a shit. "Dog, are you trying to tell me something?" he said to The Angel. Then, with mixed feelings, he watched Maryann go. In a way he was almost relieved. "Maryann," he said grandly, "you got no style. Go get fucked."

[207]

She didn't look back.

The dog finally finished his monstrous crap, and Gypsy returned upstairs with him.

"Gypsy," Barbara said to him when he walked in, "what happened to your date? Where's Marybeth?"

Gypsy grinned. "I must have said something wrong. She got angry and left."

"She just walked away? Oh, poor Gypsy."

"I'll survive, Barbara. Us gypsies are tough."

Vittorio came out of the bathroom. He looked around quizzically. "Where's what's-her-name? Marylou."

"Don't complain, man," Gypsy told him. "I brought your dog back, didn't I? Oh, yeah, Vic, by the way, how come you always get mad when I give The Angel pizza? You been feeding him Fourexes."

"Let's have dinner," Barbara said.

One morning in the Unit, late in March, the telephone rang while Gypsy was changing Mrs. Scharfstein's tracheostomy tube. Clancy was sitting right next to the telephone, playing deaf. Gypsy sighed. "Clancy, answer the phone, will you? I'm a little busy right now."

Clancy smiled innocently. "Oh, of course, doctor. I didn't hear it ringing." She picked up the telephone. "Medical Intensive Care Unit," she said, "Miss Clancy speaking." There was a pause.

"No, you fucking schmuck," she snarled into the telephone suddenly, "there's nobody here at all!" She slammed the receiver down.

Gypsy tied Mrs. Scharfstein's new trach tube in place and walked over to the desk. "Clancy," he asked patiently, "who was that?"

"Some schmuck," Clancy responded without looking up. That meant it was a doctor. The telephone rang again, and

Gypsy answered it himself. "M.I.C.U.," he said, "Gypsy."

It was Arthur Nerd, still stuck down in the Emergency Room. "Jesus," Arthur whined, "what's wrong with Clancy? Do you know what she just called me?"

"Nerd, you are a schmuck," Gypsy explained. "Why do you always say 'Is anybody there?' whenever you talk to a nurse? They don't consider themselves part of the equipment, man."

"Gypsy, she shouldn't talk to *me* like that. I'm a doctor, you know."

"Arthur, what do you want? We're busy up here."

"Okay, okay," Arthur said. "We've got this patient in the Emergency Room, and we think he's a candidate for the Unit. Do you want to come and see him?"

"Who thinks he's a candidate for the Unit, Arthur? You?"

"Are you going to come and see the patient or not?" Arthur demanded, trying hard to sound effectual. His voice, however, was cracking.

Gypsy laughed. "All right, don't fall apart, I'm coming down. I just have to get my resident first. We'll be there in a couple of minutes."

"Hurry up," Arthur whined. "I want to send the lousy drug addict to a ward or something. I'm afraid of him. It's all your fault they're making me work here again, anyway."

Gypsy located Hugo, and they rode down to the Emergency Room together to look for Arthur Nerd and his patient. They discovered them in the second examining room they checked. Arthur was standing at one end of the room, close to the door. A cluster of policemen were standing at the other end. Hugo started going over the patient's chart with Arthur, who insisted on reviewing it out in the safety of the hallway. Gypsy went to talk to the cops.

The policemen were grouped in a close little circle around

a big, nasty-looking boy who had his arms handcuffed behind him. Gypsy tapped a sergeant on the shoulder. "Hello," he said. "What do you have here?"

"Doc, we got a real beauty. A real son of a bitch."

"What did he do?"

"Well, this prick is a junkie," the sergeant said. "He grabbed an old lady on a Hundred and Second Street yesterday, right after she cashed her Social Security check. He beat her up with a piece of pipe and cracked her skull open. He must have scored right after that. We found him O.D.'d in an alley this morning and brought him over here."

"Did you smack him around any?"

"Believe me, doc, if we smacked this scum bag around he'd be in the morgue by now."

Gypsy nodded. "How's the old lady?"

"She died," the sergeant told him. "She was seventy-three."

Gypsy examined the boy briefly. His high had just about worn off, and he was awake but drowsy. He started to complain. "Hey, man, make these bastards turn me loose. Them fucking handcuffs hurt, man."

"Close your mouth," Gypsy said. The boy had the usual abscesses along both arms from shooting up with dirty needles. His left arm and his left leg were both swollen and ugly-looking. Gypsy walked out into the hallway to confer with Hugo and Arthur Nerd. Hugo was studying some Emergency Room lab reports on the boy. He raised his eyes.

"Do you know the story on this patient?" Hugo asked.

"Yeah," Gypsy said, "he's a murderer."

"I mean the medical story."

Gypsy shrugged. "Just that he O.D.'d last night. And his left side looks like a crush injury. It's probably from lying unconscious and not moving for a long time."

"Precisely!" Hugo said quickly. "I think when he O.D.'d

he just collapsed right where he was shooting up. It wasn't a big enough overdose to knock out his breathing, so he didn't die. But he was comatose, and he probably stayed there on that left side without moving at all the whole night. Until the cops found him. I think that's what gave him the crush injury. And you know what else?"

"What?" Gypsy said.

"Arthur catheterized him, and there was no urine in his bladder. And he hasn't put any urine out since he's been here. I think he's in acute renal failure!"

"So?"

"So I'm going to admit him to the Unit."

"Hugo, we have no empty beds in the Unit."

"All right," Hugo came to the obvious conclusion, "we'll have to send someone down to the wards, then."

The basic purpose of an intensive care unit is to provide the constant attendance, in the unit itself, of a good doctor and good nurses. Such a unit, by its nature, is limited in capacity. It does not take that many physicians to provide twenty-four-hour coverage for the unit, if they're bright and willing to work hard. What it does take is a lot of expensive equipment and, much more important, a whole lot of nurses. Often, neither is available. There were over a thousand beds in Gypsy's hospital, and perhaps thirty of them were in the various intensive care units. Certainly every patient in the hospital did not need to be in an intensive care unit at the same time, but it was a good bet that more than thirty of them did. However, you cannot just push a bunch of beds together, assign some interns and residents to it, and call it an I.C.U. You have got to have good nurses and money. Both were in short supply, particularly the nurses. The nursing capacity of the Medical Intensive Care Unit was nine patients. Of course, more patients than that could be brought into the Unit. Hugo could have made it a ten-bed Unit, or even a hundred-bed Unit, merely by admitting a hundred patients who he thought ought to be in the Unit. But doing that, since each M.I.C.U. patient required a tremendous amount of nursing time, would only have hopelessly diluted whatever nursing care was available, and the I.C.U. would then have no longer been an I.C.U. All this left somebody with terrible decisions to make. Who should be admitted to a unit, and who should not? This was what Hugo and Gypsy were talking about.

"Hugo," Gypsy said, "who are you going to send out?"

Hugo thought for a while. "I'm going to send Scharfstein out," he decided finally.

"No, you're not," Gypsy immediately objected. "Mrs. Scharfstein has bad emphysema and bad bronchitis. She needs to have her trach changed every day, and she needs to be suctioned all the time. The nurses on a ward aren't going to have the time to suction her. You know that, Hugo."

"She's not going to get any better," Hugo said coldly, with harsh objectivity. "She's an old woman with a chronic disease, and this patient is a young boy with an acute, curable disease who needs to be in the Unit."

"Hugo, Mrs. Scharfstein never hur: anybody in her life. If you send her down to a ward, she's going to die there."

"What you're trying to do is pass a moral judgment on this boy," Hugo said impersonally. "I'm making a medical judgment."

"That's bullshit! You can't separate those two things. You're doing something that's wrong, Hugo. I'm not telling you to throw the patient out on the street—acute renal failure can be managed on a ward. This kid just got finished murdering somebody, and when we're done curing him he's probably going to go out and murder somebody else!" Gypsy was hollering. "I don't see why you have to kill that poor old lady so this filth can go on murdering people!"

[212]

"That's why you're the intern and I'm the resident," Hugo responded. "And I'm not killing anyone."

"The hell you're not!" Gypsy shouted. "The hell you're not!"

Hugo admitted the boy murderer to the Unit, and three separate shifts of policemen sat by his bedside the entire time he was there. His acute renal failure was managed very nicely.

Mrs. Scharfstein had to be sent down to a ward. One afternoon about a week later, Vittorio came back from collecting lab reports looking depressed. He walked over to Gypsy.

"You remember Mrs. Scharfstein?" Vic asked quietly.

Gypsy nodded.

"I was just down getting the lab reports," Vittorio told him slowly, "and I went into the morgue to see if they had any autopsy results for us. Mrs. Scharfstein was there, Gypsy."

"Damn," Gypsy breathed—much more in frustration than in surprise. "I knew that was going to happen. I knew it. The son of a bitch killed her."

"It's a pity," Vittorio said. "I know. I really liked Mrs. Scharfstein; she was such a nice old lady."

Gypsy felt impotent with useless anger. He shook his head helplessly. "Jesus, Vic. It's just not right. It's not fair."

"Fair?" Vittorio said. "What's fair, Gypsy?"

Gypsy and Vic and Kid Otto went on working the Unit. It remained their feeling that no one who made it into the M.I.C.U. alive should ever die after he got there. They did not think they should lose anyone. This was not arrogance; it was inexperience. And this iron conviction that the interns held reflected the confidence that they had in the doctors who were there to help them, rather than in any extraordinary skills of their own. The great strength of the city hospitals has always been their doctors. The occasional half-wit like Arthur Nerd, who would never even have been there a few years ago, was invariably rescued by his betters. The plaster might be falling off the ceiling, but most of the guys walking around with plaster in their hair were excellent physicans. All the intern had to do was yell, and he was swamped by whatever types of specialists he yelled for. Giving up was very hard for these people. And it was as if the gods wanted them to remember who, finally, held the powers over living and dying. Because the last patient the three of them had before they left the M.I.C.U.—a boy of twenty-one—got sick, came into the Unit, and died, all in the space of five hours.

The boy had gotten up that morning and told his nineteen-year-old wife that his head hurt. She made him breakfast, and by the time she was done he was talking funny and walking into things. She became frightened then and called an ambulance, and when the ambulance arrived her young husband was almost incoherent. They brought him to the E.R. with his wife riding next to him in the ambulance. The Emergency Room people immediately called the Unit. "We've got a bad one here" was the message. "You guys have a bed?" They had a bed, and Hugo told the Emergency Room to bypass the ward completely and send the patient straight to the Unit.

They met the boy coming off the elevator. He was tied to a stretcher, delirious, and wrestling wildly against the straps. Someone had gotten an intravenous line into his arm, and an intern from downstairs was holding the I.V. bottle in the air and helping to push the stretcher. The boy's wife was following them, carrying some of his clothes. She looked terrified.

Gypsy, Hugo, and Vic ran the stretcher into their treatment room. They unstrapped the boy to try to do a neuro-logical exam on him, but he was thrashing around like a wild animal. Hugo ran out into the hall again and grabbed the huge resident, Di Bello, to hold the boy down. Between all of them, they managed to test his pupils with a light. "No good," Hugo said, "we have to do a spinal tap on this kid."

"Jesus, how are we going to hold him?" Gypsy asked. "He's going to roll all over the table."

"I'll help Di Bello hold him," Vittorio said. "You two try to tap him."

Di Bello relaxed his grip on the patient and waved Vic away. "Just tell me when you're ready to do the tap. He won't move."

Hugo paged neurology, neurosurgery, anesthesia, and the infectious disease consult, all stat. While Vic was opening a spinal tray and putting on gloves, the treatment room was filling up with consultants.

The neurologist and the neurosurgeon both agreed that the boy should be tapped, in order to establish a diagnosis. It looked like he was dying, and at least a probable diagnosis had to be made. Treatment could then be directed rationally at whatever was killing him, and not blindly at the hundred different things that might be killing him. Neither physician felt that transtentorial herniation was present yet, and they thought that a very cautious spinal tap with a small-bore needle, although dangerous, was imperative if they were going to save the boy's life. It was decided that the man with the most experience, the neurosurgeon, would perform the spinal tap—a procedure that normally could be more than adequately handled by a medical student. Vic, who already had his gloves on, would help him.

Di Bello, who had been rather loosely containing the boy's writhing arms and legs, now hooked one ape arm be-hind the boy's neck, and the other one around his knees,

[215]

and bent him double into a fetal position. He held him like that on his side, with the boy's back in almost perfect alignment for a spinal tap. The patient, who was heavy-muscled and very powerful, aside from being completely wild, didn't move.

"Thank God," Gypsy said, "at least we can tap him now. I thought for sure he was going to be too strong for you."

"Nobody's stronger than me," Di Bello said in a flat voice.

Vic swiftly prepped the boy's back, and the neurosurgeon got a long spinal needle ready. The boy's wife, who must have been going crazy with fear watching all these people running into the treatment room, chose this moment to walk into the room and find out what was happening to her husband. She found him—naked and doubled over on his side, surrounded by close to a dozen doctors, with a six-inch needle about to be thrust into his back.

She turned white and made a choked, gagging noise deep in her throat, and threw up. Gypsy went over to her and hastily led her out of the treatment room. He asked someone to clean her clothes off and sit with her a little while, and then he dashed back to help inside.

The neurosurgeon had already made his puncture and passed through the thick layers of muscle in the boy's back. He was advancing his needle only a millimeter at a time now, stopping after each tiny bit of progress to remove the stylet from the hollow needle and check for spinal fluid. Normal cerebrospinal fluid is absolutely crystal clear. It contains a lot of complex substances, but all of these particles are much too small to be visible. It is so completely free of cellular elements that you worry if you see just a few white blood cells in somebody's spinal fluid—under a microscope.

"Okay," the neurosurgeon said suddenly, "I think I'm in." He straightened up to rest for a minute. Vic opened the package of sterile test tubes and prepared to collect the specimens of spinal fluid. The neurosurgeon bent over the patient again, and pulled the stylet out of his needle. Vic quickly handed him the first test tube, and lined the rest of the tubes up with their tops off to be filled in turn.

Spinal fluid dripped into the tube for a few seconds. Then the neurosurgeon whispered, "Oh, Jesus," very softly. Gypsy couldn't tell what the trouble was. The surgeon turned to Vic. "Forget about the other ones. The pressure's too high. Give me the stylet back." In one motion he reinserted the stylet, stopping the flow of spinal fluid, and pulled his needle. He held up the small transparent tube for everyone else to see.

It looked like a tube of gray-colored pea soup. The boy's spinal fluid was almost pure pus. The roomful of doctors stared at it.

"Well, he's a dead man," Di Bello finally said, putting into words what everybody else was thinking.

"No, maybe we can do something," the neurosurgeon said desperately. "Look, start him on mannitol and urea. Somebody call the O.R. in case we have to put a ventricular shunt in to decompress him." He poured off about half of the muddy spinal fluid into another one of the specimen tubes. "I'm going to Gram-stain some of this stuff right now —then we can decide what to put him on. Page a messenger to take the other tube to the lab for protein and glucose right away. And culture it for everything."

"We won't get a messenger for forty minutes," Gypsy told him. "I'll take it up to the lab myself." He ran out of the treatment room clutching the tube and found the girl waiting there in front of the door, looking like a ghost. She was trying very hard to stay in control of herself, but there was terror behind her eyes. "Doctor," she said with her mouth trembling, "I'm scared. Please, what's happening? What's wrong with my husband?"

[217]

Gypsy couldn't look at her. She was practically a child. "He's very sick," Gypsy said gently. "He has meningitis."

"Oh, God." Her voice broke. "Oh, my God."

"Please, go and sit down. We're trying to help him." Gypsy didn't know what else to say to her, and escaped toward the labs.

He ran up the three flights of stairs to the laboratories, and was about to run into the chemistry lab through the front door when he realized the shifts were changing. The laboratory technicians like to bullshit for at least an hour or so when the shifts change. If they see you coming with any work for them to do during these self-appointed rest periods, they simply shut down the autoanalyzer. Meningitis or no meningitis, they just finger their union buttons pointedly and say, "Sorry, doc, we're cleaning the machine now. Come back later."

As soon as he noticed that the shifts were changing, Gypsy backed out of the front door and hurried around to the side entrance to the lab. Then he slipped inside and walked quickly over to the autoanalyzer before the technicians had a chance to turn the machine off. He set his little tube down right in front of it.

"I have an absolutely stat spinal fluid for you guys to run," he announced.

Two shifts' worth of technicians sat on their asses and glared at Gypsy like he had suggested they go scrub the urinals in the bathrooms. Finally one of them said, "Okay, doc. You can leave it there. We'll take care of it in a few minutes." Gypsy knew that trick, too. He stayed where he was, with a cynical expression on his face.

When the technicians are really irritated, they will use a less subtle, but more effective technique to get out of work. They pour the specimen into the sink. Then they write "Quantity Not Sufficient" on the request slip and laugh.

Once it became evident that Gypsy wasn't going to let them fox him, one of the technicians got up with a surly look and started to run the spinal fluid. After it was diluted and actually inside the machine, and when part of the sample had also been sent for culture, Gypsy left. He did not leave any friends behind among the technicians, but he didn't give a shit. He walked back toward the stairs, reflecting on the wonderful devotion to patient care evidenced by the "paraprofessionals," as they called themselves, of the technical staff.

Suddenly, as he reached the stairwell, the hollow, metallic voice of the loudspeaker on the wall began calling a Code in the M.I.C.U. Gypsy ran. He knew instantly who it was. "Damn it!" he swore helplessly as he rushed down the stairs. "God damn it!"

He covered the three flights very fast and came racing into the treatment room. There was bedlam inside. It was one thing to know that a patient was probably going to die, and another thing entirely to have to watch, powerless, as he died there in front of you. The room was filled with bright, young, talented physicians, and this kid was dying despite anything they could do for him. It was making them crazy with frustration.

The boy had finally stopped his twisting and writhing. An anesthesiologist had barely finished intubating him, and somebody from inhalation therapy was trying to push a respirator around to the head of the treatment table. Vic climbed up on top of a chair to pump the boy's chest. Gypsy dragged the EKG machine across the room and someone connected the leads for him. He turned the machine on, and got no tracing at all. Just a long straight line. The boy's heart was without electrical activity.

"Flat line!" Gypsy yelled. "Flat line!"

Hugo had been about to shock the boy. He threw down

the defibrillator paddles and shouted for epinephrine in a cardiac needle. One of the nurses quickly drew up half a c.c. of epinephrine and handed it to him with an eight-inch intracardiac needle. Hugo hesitated for a moment, feeling for landmarks on the boy's chest, and then plunged the needle through the chest wall and into the boy's heart. He got arterial blood back, and injected the epinephrine.

There was a spasm of idioventricular complexes on the EKG, and then nothing again.

"Jesus," Gypsy said, hunched over the EKG machine, "it's still a flat line!"

"Shit!" Hugo kept trying. He called for more epinephrine, and then, one after another, he injected a string of other drugs. He gave the boy epinephrine, lidocaine, calcium chloride, and isoproterenol, all directly into his heart.

"I'm not getting a rhythm, I'm not getting a rhythm!" Gypsy cried, almost pleading.

Vittorio was pumping the boy's chest so furiously he was cracking ribs. Somebody offered to take over the cardiac massage, but Vic didn't even hear him. There was a terrible, wild look in his eyes, and sweat was flying off him. It was like he was in a physical struggle with someone for the boy's life.

The surgeons had gotten two cutdowns going, and they were pouring sodium bicarbonate into the veins they had exposed. The anesthesiologist was bagging the boy continuously. Without interrupting this artificial breathing, he checked the boy's pupils with a small light. He shook his head. "Come on, come on! His pupils are up!"

"Damn," Hugo said. "Let's try to pace him. Give me a wire." He was handed a transthoracic cardiac pacemaker lead. Hugo shoved the big needle through the boy's chest and hooked the pacing wires to the hub. Everyone's attention turned to the dials on the Unit crash cart's pacemaker while one of the medical residents tried to get capture.

"It's not holding," Gypsy told them, ripping the tracing off the EKG machine. "There's only pacemaker signal!"

The medical resident worked with the pacemaker settings feverishly. "I don't know what's wrong. We should be getting capture."

"All right," a surgical resident interrupted, "let's stop fucking around. I'm going to open his chest." He grabbed a scalpel from a discarded cutdown set. "Get me a thoracotomy tray," he ordered, stepping up to the treatment table. He made a long, ragged intercostal incision and, working very quickly, he slashed the chest wall open and hacked his way into the mediastinum. They got some rib retractors into the chest to hold the ribs apart, and then the surgical resident was able to reach the dying heart. He held the boy's heart in his hand, deep in the bloody chest, and started squeezing it rhythmically.

"Okay, I'm doing open massage now. Maybe we'll get some better perfusion this way. Let me have the epicardial leads."

He placed the epicardial pacemaker leads, and somebody attached the other end of them to the pacemaker on the crash cart. The frenzied activity around the boy momentarily ceased.

Gypsy moved aside to let a cardiology Fellow read the EKG. The cardiologist shook his head. "It's no good," he said. "You better keep pumping."

No one wanted to give up. They kept the Code going for almost two hours, but it was useless. They were working on a dead person. The boy's whole central nervous system was bathed in pus. They finally stopped.

Gypsy stared at this human being who had just turned into a lifeless slab of meat, right before their eyes. He wanted to cry.

"We have to try to get a post," Hugo pointed out. For

[221]

him it was no different from trying to save the patient. You were the doctor and you did it. Preferably well.

"Hugo, I can't," Gypsy said. "I can't talk to that girl about autopsies. Hugo, my God, she's only nineteen years old."

"It's very important that we get a post," Hugo insisted. "You know that."

Gypsy couldn't bear to be in the room any longer. He walked out into the corridor with his head down, and the nineteen-year-old widow came up to him hesitantly, looking very afraid. She was ashen. "Doctor, what happened?"

Gypsy took her by the arm. "Come and sit down with me for a minute," he said softly.

She looked at Gypsy's face, and she knew. She gave a little cry and pulled her arm away from him, and tried to run into the treatment room. Vic met her halfway through the door and pushed her out. He and Gypsy both grabbed her, and they guided her over to a chair in the nursing station. It was like holding a rag doll.

"Let me see him," she kept pleading, "let me see him. I'll make him better. Please let me see him."

Gypsy appealed mutely to Vittorio for help, but Vic wasn't able to say anything at all.

"I'm very, very sorry," Gypsy said in a small, wretched voice, "but your husband passed away. We tried to save him, we really tried. We just couldn't."

The girl recoiled from his words, gripping the edge of the chair. Then she made a dreadful wailing sound and started to sob. Once she broke down, she got completely hysterical, and her sobs became long, wracking, awful cries of agony. She flung herself out of the chair and beat her fists against the wall.

"He's not dead," she began to whimper piteously, shaking her head and crying. "He's not dead!"

[222]

Gypsy and Vittorio stood there silently. There was nothing on God's earth they could say to her. After about ten minutes her crying stopped, and then she just stared out the window, chewing on the tissue she was holding.

She finally turned away from the window, and gazed numbly at Gypsy for a long time with her tearstained, child's face. Gypsy was ready to come apart himself. She touched his arm with her hand. "Thank you. . . . Thank you very much for everything you did. I know you all tried very hard. Please thank everyone for me."

She went as far as the hallway, and seemed utterly alone. "I think I have to go home now." She started to weep again.

Gypsy didn't know what to do to help her. He followed her out to the bleak corridor. "Look, isn't there somebody you can call or something?" he tried to suggest.

"No," she said. "No. There's nobody." She couldn't stop crying. "I'm sorry. . . . I have to go home."

She walked away, painfully, as if she'd suddenly been left crippled. She was sobbing uncontrollably into her frayed tissue. When she reached the elevators she sagged against the wall and remained there like that, holding her face in her hands. Gypsy could see her body shaking.

He couldn't stand it any more and fled back into the nursing station. Hugo was sitting at the desk starting to make out a death certificate for the boy. He stopped writing when Gypsy walked in.

"Well," Hugo said, "did you get permission for a post?"

Gypsy just looked at him.

# The Wards

GYPSY WENT THROUGH the final initiation rites of internship in the spring. The first Monday in April found him driving up Third Avenue, at seven-thirty in the morning, with a dejected look on his face. This was it. The last three months of the year. The wards. This was what he'd been hearing about since his first day in the Emergency Room.

He wasn't happy. Not with the hospital, or with the internship, or with himself. He was dissatisfied with the caliber of his work, and he was disappointed by how little he'd been able to learn; he felt he had accomplished nothing. Actually, he had performed fairly well, and he'd learned a lot more than he realized, but it was his nature to count his failures and not his successes.

And, in truth, medicine did not exist the way Gypsy wanted it to. People got sick, they got old, and they died. Sooner or later it happened to everyone. Once in a while you were able to cure someone, but much more often all you could do was run them through a lot of fancy tests and then just hold their hand. It ripped the guts out of Gypsy. And the wards—the wards were supposed to be the times that tried men's souls. He didn't know if he was going to be able to handle it.

It took Gypsy almost forty-five minutes to park his car, because the streets around the hospital were filled with TV trailers and newspaper cars, and he couldn't get near the parking lot. He finally found a nice, semilegal spot on Lexington Avenue and walked over to the hospital. Then he headed for one of the side entrances near the ambulance dock, and almost walked into somebody backing around a corner of the building. It was a kid waving a long butcher knife. "Stay away from me, man," the kid said threateningly to someone. "You just stay away from me." Gypsy stopped.

Jim MacKinley came into view, slowly approaching the kid with the knife. MacKinley made eye contact with Gypsy for an instant, and Gypsy reached forward and tapped the boy politely on the back. He whirled around, slashing wildly with his knife, and Gypsy scrambled out of the way.

MacKinley was on top of the kid in one bound, and the knife went flying into the gutter a second later. MacKinley picked him up in both hands and raised him over his head.

"Hey, brother, put me down!" the kid yelled. "Put me down, man!"

"You jive-ass, I'll put you down," MacKinley rumbled. "I'll put your ass down in the fucking river!"

MacKinley marched toward the corner of the block, carrying his yelling and flailing assailant above his head, with Gypsy following curiously several yards behind them. At the corner, MacKinley folded the erstwhile knife-fighter forward at the waist, bending him in two, and stuffed him ass-first into a garbage can. "You little motherfucker, I catch you near my car again, and you had it, man!" He turned and started to walk away. Gypsy followed him once more.

There was a tangle of arms and legs sticking up out of the garbage can, with a head in the middle. "What you doing to me?" the head said. "Get me out of here, brother."

"Brother my ass," MacKinley growled, without looking back.

"Hey, blood, I didn't know it was your short. We doing this for you!"

MacKinley stopped dead. He walked back to the garbage can. "Boy, you ain't doing shit for me. I work two fucking jobs, man, and anything I want I go out and buy. I don't ask nobody for nothing. You want something in this world, you gotta work for it."

"Shit!" the kid snorted contemptuously, trying to pry himself out of the can. "You dumb as a white man."

MacKinley didn't deign to answer this. He reared back and gave the garbage can a tremendous kick that sent it rolling and clanging down the street. Along the way, the kid shook loose and tumbled out into the gutter. "Where you belong, man," MacKinley said with some satisfaction, "where you belong."

He returned toward the hospital with Gypsy. "Well?" Gypsy asked. "What's going on? That guy almost stabbed me."

"You?" MacKinley said. "They can patch you up again. Look what the bastard done to my car." They walked over to the small parking area next to the ambulances. All four tires on MacKinley's car were flat. They had been slashed.

Gypsy laughed. "No wonder; they must have thought you were one of the doctors or something. That'll teach you to drive a Cadillac."

"What the hell am I gonna do now? I'm already late for my day job."

Gypsy held out his car keys. "You want to take my car?"

"Yeah, okay," MacKinley said after a moment. "I guess I got to." They walked back down the street, and then went west to Lexington Avenue.

"Jesus Christ," MacKinley exclaimed when he saw the Fiat. "Look at this car! How old is it?"

"Ten years," Gypsy answered proudly. "It's a pisser, isn't it?"

MacKinley didn't say anything. He glanced at Gypsy with the same expression he'd worn at the beginning of the year—when Gypsy had asked him why he carried a gun. Then he shoehorned himself into the little car and smacked his head against the large hunk of metal that was jutting out from the rear seat. "Gypsy," he demanded, rubbing his head, "why the fuck is your goddam bumper in the back seat?"

"It fell off." Gypsy smiled. "I didn't know what else to do with it."

"Christ," MacKinley said, starting the engine. "You crazy, for sure. All I hope is nobody don't see me driving around in this shit wagon."

"Say, Mac, you want to tell me what's going on here?"

MacKinley frowned. "It's just a bunch of guys who don't want to get a job, man. Thanks for the car." He waved and drove off, looking like he was sitting in a toy car. Gypsy walked up Lexington Avenue to the hospital once again. Then he couldn't even get through the lobby, because a large, noisy mob had completely displaced the usual three or four dozing, overnight bums. There were a lot of bright lights.

"Excuse me," Gypsy said to a girl with a clipboard and wire-frame glasses. "What is this? Are you making another movie?"

"Oh, no," the girl told him. "Don't you watch the six o'clock news? It's the Young Pagans."

"The young which?"

"The Young Pagans. They want community control of the hospital and more methadone."

"I see," Gypsy said. "Now I understand; must be a good market for methadone these days."

He edged his way into the crowd. It took him a long time to get to the elevators. The great horde of reporters and cameramen, it turned out, were all fighting to interview about a dozen members of the Young Pagans, who had thoughtfully set up their community-control table right in front of the main hospital elevators. The interviewing was going pretty slowly, Gypsy noted once he had worked his way through the crush. This was because the Young Pagans of course knew nothing about anything, and had nothing at all to say beyond tiresome, anti-Semitic, and unimaginative tirades against the doctors.

They had a big box in the center of the table, that said, "Workers and Patients Complaints."

"Can I put a complaint in the box?" Gypsy asked one of the Pagans who was not busy being interviewed. "I'm a worker."

"Sure, man. You put it in the box, and we fix it, guaranteed. We going to change things around here."

"Uh-huh," Gypsy said, "far out." He picked up a sheet of their notebook paper and wrote:

> Please do something about the gangs of hypocritical, misinformed, and illiterate nonworkers who are cluttering up the lobby of the hospital. Us workers cannot get to work.
>
> Sincerely,
> Gypsy

He folded his complaint in half and dropped it into the box. "Are you really going to take care of it?" he said to the Pagan.

"You know it, man. Power to the people."

"Right on," Gypsy seconded, and walked into an elevator. The elevator starter herded as many people as he could on board the elevator, and then the Pagan reappeared in front of the doors. "Hey," he inquired suspiciously, peering into the stuffed car, "you a doctor, man?"

"Who, me?" Gypsy said. "I'm going upstairs to get my orange juice—I'm in the Detoxification Program." He rode up to the twelfth floor to start Male Medicine on the wards.

He was, of course, late. He went looking for the people

he was going to be working with and found Hugo, also newly arrived on the ward service, leading a small group of interns and medical students through the hallway. They were making work rounds. Gypsy fell into step with the last student in line and followed everyone else into a small, cheerless, four-bed room. They halted at the foot of a bed that held a very emaciated old man, with sunken eyes and the look of death about him.

"What's wrong with him?" Gypsy whispered to the medical student he was standing next to.

"He's a real mess," the student whispered back. "He has an inoperable carcinoma of the lung with bone metastases all over. Last week a couple of his vertebral bodies collapsed, and it crushed his cord. Now he's paraplegic."

"My God," Gypsy murmured.

"Doctor," the old man said with a heavy accent, and paused. He swallowed, wincing in pain. "Doctor, excuse me."

Hugo snapped the man's chart shut and looked up impatiently. "What is it?"

"I'm sorry to bother you." The old man paused again, and then asked haltingly, "Please, am I going to be able to walk again soon?"

"What?" Hugo said incredulously.

"I have to be able to walk, doctor. I want to go home to Germany with my brother."

Hugo's personality had curdled somewhat. "Walk?" he repeated. "Walk? You can't walk. You're paralyzed." He turned around and left. Gypsy stalked into the corridor after him.

"Hugo," he said angrily, "do you know you're a prick?"

Hugo blanched. "Gypsy, just don't bother me. You're not one of my interns this time. You belong to the other resident on the ward, okay?"

[229]

"Oh, yeah? Did you arrange that?"

Hugo looked uncomfortable. "Yes," he admitted finally.

Gypsy smiled. "Thank you," he said, and departed to search for his own resident. His resident turned out to be Irene, who was also making work rounds, and smoking and coughing.

"Hello," Gypsy greeted her. "I think you've inherited me, Irene."

"I know," Irene acknowledged, trying to find her matches. "Hugo told me already. This is my other intern." She introduced Gypsy to a stocky, middle-aged man whose name he couldn't make any sense out of.

"How are you do, sir," the middle-aged man said. He had several gold teeth. "It is being from Bulgaria that I am."

"Oh," Gypsy said.

"Yes, Pathology man in Bulgaria I am. Having Boards."

"Oh. I don't understand. If you've got your Boards in Pathology, what are you doing this for?"

"I am not having Boards in this country."

"Aha," Gypsy sympathized.

"Yes," the Bulgarian intern agreed. "Aha."

"Irene, where's the rest of our team?"

"This is it," Irene said, lighting another cigarette.

Gypsy looked around. "Don't we have any medical students?"

"Well, we're supposed to, but, you know, it's spring, and they're all seniors."

"Hugo has medical students," Gypsy mentioned.

"Hugo is a hard-ass."

"Hugo," Gypsy corrected her, "is an asshole."

Irene grinned. "I guess he is, that's true, but he's a good doctor." Then she had a coughing fit and had to go into the bathroom to get her breath back.

"Sir Gypsy, excuse me, please," the Bulgarian intern said, "but I am having here a problem."

"Just Gypsy is fine. What's the trouble?"

"I am having here a patient with fever." He smiled and held the patient's chart up for Gypsy to see, acting like the fever was some kind of personal accomplishment of his. The chart confirmed that the patient had indeed had a fever for the last two weeks.

"Yeah, he's been febrile for a long time, too," Gypsy noted. "Do you have a source for the fever?"

The Bulgarian intern gave him an odd look. "No, I am not having a source for the fever." He cleared his throat. "I am not wanting to bother Irene with this, but I am asking please, is better I should give him ampicillin or penicillin?"

"Oh," Gypsy said again. "Uh, you see, you can't just sort of pick out an antibiotic and start him on it. You have to find out why he's got a fever first."

The intern with Bulgarian Boards in Pathology looked at him even more strangely.

"Sure," Gypsy attempted to encourage him. "You know, you listen to his lungs, you check his throat, you do a urinalysis. And it probably wouldn't hurt to get a sputum culture and send a urine for culture and sensitivity. And get about three sets of blood cultures. You do a regular fever work-up, is all. That way you'll have an idea what you're treating."

The Bulgarian intern was staring at him with his mouth open. Then he said something hostile-sounding in Bulgarian, wrote a brief order for ampicillin, and closed the order book. "So. Now is the next patient." He moved off down the corridor.

Irene came out of the bathroom looking a little blue and lit another cigarette.

"You know, you're going to make yourself a chronic lunger with all those cigarettes," Gypsy said.

"I know." She shook her head sadly. "I'm going to quit tomorrow. Anyway, I've got friends in the pulmonary

I.C.U." She gestured in the direction of the middle-aged intern. "What do you think of your colleague over there?"

"I think he's an idiot."

"Well, he's not so bright," she conceded charitably.

"Does he really have his Boards in Pathology?"

"Positively," Irene nodded. "He's an attending in Bulgaria."

"Okay, maybe he is, but I don't think he went to medical school."

Irene laughed. "Actually, he's got a pretty good sense of humor. You just have to watch him whenever he does anything. Otherwise he gets a little dangerous sometimes."

"Thanks for telling me," Gypsy said.

The Bulgarian intern, Irene, and Gypsy continued making work rounds. It was slow business, because all the patients were new to Gypsy, and Irene had to give him a summary of all the problems of each of the patients he was going to pick up. As far as the rest of their patients were concerned, the Bulgarian intern by and large at least knew which ones belonged to him. Once in a while, though, Irene would come upon a patient of his she would have to introduce him to. Each time this happened, he would look annoyed and say, "Is very strange. I am not seeing this patient ever before." Which was probably true.

The work rounds dragged on into the afternoon, and the Bulgarian intern became very restless. They were in one of the foulest multibed rooms, filled to far past capacity with malodorous alcoholic derelicts, when it proved too much for him. He drew a deep breath and made a theatrical face of long-suffering disgust.

"I am not liking this," he announced. "Terrible it is in this place!"

"Nah," Gypsy objected, "this is wonderful."

The Bulgarian intern took the charts he was carrying and

began stuffing them haphazardly into the chart rack. "Sir Irene, smelling it is here, of vomit, feces, urine, pseudomonas, and feet! I cannot standing it more today, and home I am going now." And he walked off the ward.

Irene lit a cigarette. "Damn. We're admitting today, too."

"You mean you're just going to let him pull that on you?"

Irene took a long drag on her cigarette. "Well, they have a different concept of medicine in Bulgaria. And he usually behaves himself the days we're admitting."

Gypsy held his hands out. "You're admitting today. What are you going to do for an intern?"

Irene shrugged.

"Christ," Gypsy said, shaking his head. "Look, I'll work for this schmuck tonight, and he can take one of my nights."

"Would you? I'd really appreciate it. I better warn you, though—he doesn't like paying people back nights that they worked for him."

Gypsy smiled a tight, assured little smile. "Oh, I think he'll pay me back. Me and Vittorio'll talk to him about it."

"Hey," Irene said, "I think Vittorio's admitting downstairs tonight. You'll be able to bullshit with your friend, anyway."

"Really? Vittorio's on call also?"

"Uh-huh. I think so."

Gypsy grinned. "See, everything's turning out fine."

"Who's admitting? Who's admitting?" It was the cowlike bellow of the very fat ward secretary. Gypsy left Irene and walked over to the secretary. He was no longer grinning. "I guess that's me," he said unhappily.

She handed him the telephone. "Emergency Room," she informed him.

"Good afternoon," Gypsy said politely into the telephone. "This is the admitting intern."

It was Allen Gallberg, all right. "I have an interesting case I'm sending up," he said without preamble. "His hematocrit is six."

"A G.I. bleeder?"

"Yeah," Gallberg answered. "Good-bye." He hung up. He was still a real charmer, Allen was.

Gypsy hung up, too, and rejoined Irene. "We're getting an admission; a G.I. bleeder."

"Hmm." Irene knew there had to be more than just that involved. "What else?"

Gypsy looked at her quizzically. "What do you mean, what else? Gallberg didn't mention anything else."

Irene chuckled. "I forgot, you haven't been on the wards before. Well, you'll see."

Five minutes later their admission was trundled off the elevator on a stretcher. The ward secretary added his papers from the Admitting Office to the chart she had made up for him and handed the whole thing to Gypsy.

Gypsy examined the information gleaned by the Admitting Office clerk: "Name—Abraham Lincoln. Address—not known. Nearest relative—not known. Provisional diagnosis—alcoholic drunk."

"Abraham Lincoln?" Gypsy said. "Really?"

"Lincoln?" the charge nurse, Miss Cuyler, repeated. "Is Lincoln back already?" She walked out of the nursing station to take a look. "Yep, Lincoln's back again." She turned to Gypsy. "Doc, it's his own fault. Lincoln was just discharged last Thursday. Weren't you, Lincoln?"

"Fuck you," Lincoln said to her.

"Doc," Miss Cuyler went on, "I've seen this bum every single morning, from the day he was discharged, sitting over there in the park and drinking that cheap wine. Seven o'clock in the morning and him drinking that wine! No wonder he's sick again!"

[234]

Besides being a chronic alcoholic, a heroin addict, and a barbiturate addict, when he was up to it Lincoln was also a car thief, an armed robber, and a rapist. Since his discharge the previous Thursday, he had been living in the small, dirty park across Lexington Avenue from the hospital, drinking wine and shooting up. These activities were being financed by money from a little gas-station holdup, which Lincoln had carried out to celebrate his discharge from the hospital. The steady diet of cheap wine and no food had given him an erosive gastritis, secondary to which he had bled down to his present hematocrit of six—normal being about fifty. He had probably been vomiting blood for at least a couple of days but, judging from the stench, that experience had not appreciably interfered with his wine intake.

Gallberg had passed a naso-gastric tube, in the Emergency Room, to see if there was fresh blood in Lincoln's stomach. The proximal end of this tube was now sticking out of Lincoln's nose, and was folded over on itself in several loops and safety-pinned to the sheet. Lincoln was very unhappy about the tube.

"Mr. Lincoln," Gypsy asked, "how long have you been throwing up blood?"

"Get this fucking tube out of my nose, you cocksucker," Abraham Lincoln said. "And give me some methadone!" He began to shout. "Goddam it, I'm gonna pull the fucking tube out myself!"

"Mr. Lincoln, if you touch that tube you'll die," Gypsy lied to him.

Irene had just returned from a fruitless search for an I.V. setup. "Come on, don't talk like that; you're going to scare him. Let's move him into the treatment room."

Lincoln raised his head from the stretcher and glared at her. "Who the fuck are you? I want methadone!"

"Shut your mouth, you bum," Gypsy said. "This is my

resident, Irene, who would like to keep you from bleeding to death." Lincoln's hollering and complaining had started him bleeding again. A column of bright-red blood appeared in the naso-gastric tube where it exited from his nose. The blood traveled quickly through the loops of tubing safety-pinned to the sheet and started to drip onto the floor. Lincoln watched the growing puddle his blood was making and shut up.

"Damn, he's still having active bleeding," Irene said. "We better transfuse him up to something reasonable before he has an M.I."

"Absolutely," Gypsy agreed. "Six isn't so good for a hematocrit."

"My God, six? His hematocrit is only six? Maybe that's his hemoglobin."

Gypsy shook his head. "Gallberg said it was his hematocrit."

Irene ran over to one of the cabinets lining the walls and started collecting tubes and needles. "Let's get an I.V. into him, quick," she instructed. "And type and cross him for some whole blood." She came back to the stretcher with a long, vicious-looking C.V.P. needle and cannula. "Mr. Lincoln, hold out your arm, please."

Lincoln bolted up on the stretcher. "Get the fuck away from me! I want my methadone!"

"Mr. Lincoln," Irene said solicitously, "you've lost a great deal of blood, and the rest of your blood has gotten very thin. That's very dangerous for you. You could have a heart attack, or a stroke, just from your blood being so thin. We have to give you some blood back, and we can't do that without an I.V. All right?"

"Fuck you," Lincoln answered. "Stay the fuck away from my veins!"

Mr. Lincoln had of course completely sclerosed most of

[236]

his veins from his years of shooting dirty drugs with dirty needles. A usable vein is a dear possession to a junkie, and Lincoln was not about to part with one of the few he had left for the sake of a mere blood transfusion.

"Mr. Lincoln," Irene began explaining once more, "you're very sick. We have to give you a transfusion to help you, and we aren't able to do that unless we start an I.V. Do you understand?"

"I don't want no fucking I.V.'s in me, you piece of shit!" Lincoln yelled. "I want my methadone!"

"Lincoln," Gypsy interrupted this dialogue, "let me tell you something: if there is a piece of shit in this room, it isn't one of us. Now, listen, you have a choice. You can let us start this lousy I.V., and we'll give you your damn methadone, or you can get the hell out of here and go cop some more smack and bleed to death. It's up to you, man. I don't really care what you do."

Abraham Lincoln looked at Gypsy for a moment, sizing him up. "Shit!" he said finally, and held out his arm for the I.V.

Gypsy and Irene quickly got a large-bore central venous pressure line into the one good vein they could find. They used it to draw their routine bloods and, most important, an extra tube for type and cross-match. Irene hung a bottle of plasma expander.

"Gypsy, can you bring that to the blood bank?" she asked. "It's going to take forever to get a messenger."

"No problem. I'll go down right now and wait there for the blood."

"Fantastic. I'll do everything else up here meanwhile."

Gypsy ran down to the blood bank with his hard-won sample of Lincoln's blood. He hounded the technicians into leaving their pizza long enough to type and cross-match the

[237]

sample, and in fifteen minutes the first two units were ready. He carried the blood upstairs.

"Okay," he said when he got back to the treatment room, "here it is."

"Great." Irene was standing next to the stretcher, irrigating Lincoln's naso-gastric tube with ice water and saline. "He's still got a tachycardia, but I think the bleeding's slowed down."

"Good," Gypsy said with relief, hanging the first unit of blood. "Did you finish working him up?"

"Just about." She stirred the ice around in the stainless steel basin. "The lab reports are back," she added; "they're over there on top of his chart."

"Hey, doc," Abraham Lincoln announced, "I gotta piss!"

"Gypsy, give him a urinal, would you? And why don't you get some urine for a urinalysis; I didn't have time to do one yet."

"Sure." Gypsy fished through a supply cabinet and produced the standard metal urinal with a handle on the side, and a small plastic bottle.

"Hurry up, man," Lincoln demanded. "I told you I gotta piss!"

"I'm coming, I'm coming. I don't carry urinals around in my pocket." Gypsy returned to the stretcher and held up the two receptacles for Lincoln to see. "Abe," he said, "now pay attention to me. I want you to let me have a urine specimen in this little bottle here"—he waved the small plastic bottle—"and then you can urinate all you like in this big one." He shook the big metal urinal.

"Gimme that fucking pot to piss in!" Lincoln yelled.

Gypsy handed him a pot to piss in. "Lincoln, remember, I need some urine in the little bottle, too." Gypsy picked up Lincoln's chart and started to go through the lab results. Irene remained occupied irrigating the tube hanging out of

Lincoln's nose with iced saline; that was supposed to be of some help in controlling upper G.I. bleeding.

Oblivious to all of this activity, Lincoln took hold of his penis and aimed it more or less in the direction of the urinal he was holding between his legs. A long yellow stream arched out from the end of his penis, missed the urinal completely, and continued toward the floor. Lincoln was unconcerned; he went right on placidly pissing. The stream landed squarely on Irene's foot. Her shoe began to fill up with urine, and a pained expression spread over her face. She looked down at her feet.

"Good Christ!" she said unbelievingly, and hopped away from the stretcher and beyond Lincoln's range. She took her shoe off and slowly poured the urine out of it, looking infinitely disgusted. "Uh, Gypsy . . ."

Gypsy put the chart down and came over to the stretcher. "Okay, is he through? I'll do the urinalysis, then." He retrieved the little plastic bottle. It was empty.

"Lincoln," he said, holding up the empty bottle, "what's wrong with you. Couldn't you go, or what? Was it too complicated for you to piss in the bottle?"

"Gypsy, he went."

"He didn't do anything," Gypsy insisted. "Look—there's nothing in the urinal, there's nothing in my bottle, there's . . ." It struck Gypsy that Irene was standing on one foot, and the foot she wasn't standing on was dripping. The shoe from that foot was in her hand, and that was dripping, too.

"Uh-oh." Gypsy looked suspiciously at Lincoln. "You lousy bum, did you piss on my resident?"

"That's what he did, all right," Irene said caustically, trying to wring out the end of her stocking. "That's what he did."

"Lincoln, you piece of shit, are you so stupid you don't even know which way your prick is pointing?"

[239]

"Ahh, fuck you," Lincoln replied. "Take this fucking tube out of my nose!"

"I'll put my foot up your ass in a minute, is what I'll do!" Gypsy yelled.

The doctor-patient relationship was deteriorating.

"Gypsy, leave him alone," Irene said resignedly, beckoning Gypsy aside. "You're wasting your time anyhow; you're not going to teach him manners."

"Manners? Jesus, all I asked him to do was piss in the goddam bottle. My God, Vittorio's dog could piss in the bottle if you told him to!"

"Well, Vittorio's dog is a smart dog, I guess, and this is a dumb bum. Besides," Irene reminded Gypsy, "he needs a lot of things done. I don't think he's bleeding any more, but I'm going to lavage his stomach for a while longer. Give him three more units of blood when this one's finished, but slowly, all right? And watch his C.V.P. You don't want to put him into pulmonary edema."

Gypsy nodded.

"Oh, yes, see if you can find a Blakemore tube somewhere," she added, "in case we need it. And schedule him for an emergency upper G.I. series, and after that get hold of the gastroenterology Fellow to endoscope him if he bleeds again. Can you manage all that?"

"Sure," Gypsy said.

At a quarter to seven, he was still busy managing things for his bum. Lincoln had eaten dinner, after a fashion. Gypsy had not. He was on the telephone trying to locate the gastroenterology Fellow. Irene came into the nursing station and waited for him to put the telephone down.

"Gypsy," she told him when he did, "I think you should give the seven o'clock pushes now."

"In a couple of minutes, okay? Just let me finish up this stuff for Lincoln first. It's not seven o'clock yet anyway, Irene."

Irene shrugged. "All right. But I don't think you should wait until seven to give the pushes."

Gypsy got back on the telephone and ran down the gastroenterology Fellow at about ten after seven. He told him all about Lincoln. Then he went to give the pushes. A "push" is a large syringe filled with any drug that has to be given directly into a patient's vein, regularly, around the clock. Pushes are traditionally a job for the medical student, once the drug regimen has been determined. Irene, however, had set her medical students free. That left Gypsy.

There were on the ward a whole slew of patients—most of them drug addicts with bacterial endocarditis, thanks to filthy needles—who were receiving, as pushes, tremendous doses of antibiotics every six hours. Gypsy prepared about a dozen of these antibiotic pushes and set off down the corridor to look for patients.

He was back in less than five minutes, still carrying his armful of loaded syringes. He placed the syringes next to the telephone and walked over to his resident.

"Irene, what's going on?"

"Trouble?" she asked. "Who died?"

"Nobody died. Everybody disappeared. I was trying to give the seven o'clock pushes, and except for Santos everybody was gone."

Irene twisted around in her chair and looked at the clock on the wall. "You know what, it isn't seven o'clock. It's after seven. See?"

"Yeah, I see it's twenty after seven," Gypsy agreed. "I still don't see where all the bums went."

Irene took out a cigarette. "Gypsy, you have to understand that most of these patients are junkies."

"No kidding."

"Well," she went on, "seven o'clock is when visiting hours start. So, actually, you have to give the seven o'clock pushes before seven."

"Why?"

"Because at seven o'clock sharp their friends come around with their heroin," she explained, "and they all beat it into the bathroom to shoot up."

"You mean," Gypsy said, stunned, "I'm standing here waiting to give them their penicillin, and they're in the bathroom shooting up all over again—with the same goddam dirty needles?"

"That's it, I'm afraid. Right into their I.V.'s"

"My God," Gypsy said slowly. "Well, fuck it then!" He gathered up the syringes and threw them into the trash can.

"Gypsy, sometimes it's a real fight to try to take care of these people. You have to compromise. You can't break their thumbs to stop them from using drugs."

"Somebody should break their heads," Gypsy said.

The resident from the ward one flight beneath them, big and fat and named George, materialized out of the stairwell. He looked harassed. "Irene," he said, sitting down heavily, "I'm too old for this. It's unreal down there."

"Yeah, we were just talking about that. Oh, have you met my new intern? George, this is Gypsy."

George smiled weakly. "Hello. I think I've got your buddy downstairs with me."

"Vittorio?" Gypsy inquired. "Vittorio's working on your ward? How are you guys doing?"

Fat George sighed audibly. "Son," he said, "I'm a very patient man, but this bullshit is starting to get to me. They just sent us up another admission and this one is addicted to absolutely everything. Plus which he's in D.T.'s." George rose to his feet and laughed bitterly. "Why don't you pay us a visit for a little while—take a look at this mental-defective psychopath."

"No, thank you. We've got a nice selection of them up here."

[242]

"Not like this one, you don't," George told him, shaking his head despondently. "Come on down and say hello to your friend Vittorio, anyway."

Gypsy shrugged. "Well, I guess it's worth one more bum to say hello to Vittorio." He looked over at his own resident. "Irene," he said, "I'll be back in a few minutes." Then he followed George downstairs.

They discovered Vittorio in hot pursuit of a wildly incoherent drunk.

Vittorio was wielding a big syringe filled with paraldehyde and trying to corner the drunk. The drunk, for his part, was in florid D.T.'s and hallucinating like mad. He apparently thought he was hallucinating Vittorio, too, because he kept backing away from him and muttering something about cockroaches.

George rejoined the chase. "Listen, bum," he said to the patient, "take it easy, will you? We're trying to help you."

The bum scurried back and forth between Vittorio and George. "Help!" he yelled. "Help, help! The giant roaches are after me!"

Gypsy laughed. "George, you better lose some weight. Your patient is mixing you up with his fantasies."

George was feinting charges at the bum and starting to perspire. "Fuck you, Gypsy. Why don't you help?"

"Vic, you want some help?" Gypsy asked, grinning.

Vittorio was looking grim. "I don't believe it. Four years of medical school, for this!" He made a determined run at the patient. The bum, in his haste to escape from medical therapy, moved back too fast and stepped into a pool of urine he had left on the floor a short while earlier. Hoist with his own petard, he slipped and went down. Vittorio dived for him, and the bum scrambled underneath one of the beds. Vic looked up at Gypsy from the floor. "It's kind of

[243]

like treating a mad dog, you know?" Vittorio disappeared under the bed, too.

There were the noises of a brief struggle underneath the bed and then a small shriek.

"Vittorio?" Gypsy said. "You okay?"

"I think so," Vic's muffled voice answered. "He's sedated now, anyway."

Vittorio crawled out from under the bed. "The only thing is," he added, "I think he decided to shit. Help me pull him out of there."

"No chance," Gypsy replied quickly, and chuckled. "This big strong resident will help you. Go get your patient, George."

George tried gamely, but he was much too fat to fit underneath the bed. Gypsy relented, and together he and Vic dragged the bum out of his warren. The bum had indeed shit.

"Well, I did my part," Gypsy said, and went into the treatment room to wash his hands. Vittorio and his fat resident somehow carried their patient into the room and lifted him up onto the treatment table for the mandatory spinal tap. It was a little too much for George, and he suddenly had to sit down, holding his crotch and looking sick. He was a few shades whiter than he'd been before.

"Wow," he complained, "that was some heavy bum. I think I ruptured myself."

Vittorio shook his head hopelessly. He gestured back at the patient, who was now giving off a strong smell of paraldehyde and feces. "Here I am, risking my ass trying to practice veterinary medicine, and who have I got to help me? An overweight resident with a hernia, and a tone-deaf rock-and-roll musician." Vic went out into the corridor and returned with a very surly-looking aide.

"Gypsy, do me a favor," Vittorio then requested. "I want to tap this guy while he's still snowed, and one of the damn asthmatics is wheezing and gasping out there. Would you take care of him?"

"Sure. Have fun with this beauty." Gypsy walked into the corridor and followed the wheezes to an end room. He found a man who looked to be about thirty sitting comfortably in the middle bed, smoking a cigarette and hacking away.

"What's wrong, sir?" Gypsy asked.

"I got asthma," the man informed him. "I can't breathe." He coughed on cue and made some more wheezing sounds.

"Why don't you put out your cigarette? You'll probably breathe a lot better."

"Cigarette ain't the problem," the man assured him. "I get bad asthma every night unless I get enough methadone."

"Oh," Gypsy said.

The man smiled. "Yeah, terrible asthma. Sometimes it keeps the doctor up the whole night." He gave Gypsy a knowing look and blew a smoke ring.

"Let me see what we can do," Gypsy said pleasantly. He walked down to the nursing station and selected the biggest Foley catheter he could find. It was almost as thick as his thumb. Then he went back to the asthmatic's room.

"Where's the methadone?" the man demanded irritably, eyeing the Foley.

"Well," Gypsy answered, lubricating the business end of the catheter, "I'm just the medical student, but I talked to Dr. Mazzoli, and he said that this works better than methadone for asthma. Pull down your pants, please. I'm going to put this little tube up into your bladder."

"Fuck you, you are. Get the fuck away from me with that pipe!"

Gypsy smiled innocently, holding the gargantuan catheter out in front of him. "What about your asthma? Dr. Mazzoli said this would make your breathing much better."

"Fuck you and Mazzoli!" the man yelled. "My breathing's

fine. You stay away from me with that fucking thing, you understand?"

Gypsy shrugged agreeably. "As long as you can breathe okay," he said. "That's what counts. Now, you be sure and call us if you have any more trouble, all right?"

"Drop dead," the grateful patient said.

Gypsy walked out of the room and decided it was time to go back upstairs and see how Irene was making out. He headed for the stairs, carefully skirting the treatment room, but as he tiptoed by a shouting match erupted inside. Vittorio's voice, aghast and outraged, came through the door: "What the hell do you think you're doing? Get your ass back here!"

The aide's voice answered him, just as angry: "I'm ten minutes late already! I'm going on my coffee break now, period!"

"Are you crazy?" Vittorio shouted. "There's a needle in this man's back. Get the fuck over here!"

The door to the treatment room was shoved open and the aide marched out, looking indignant. "Imagine!" she exclaimed self-righteously when she saw Gypsy. "It's time for my coffee break and he wants me to stand there holding that nasty patient! All shit everywhere, and everything. It says right in the union rules, two fifteen-minute coffee breaks. Some of you doctors just got no consideration for nobody!"

Gypsy was trying to think of something mollifying to say to her when more hollering broke out in the treatment room, followed immediately by a tremendous crash.

"Grab him!" Gypsy heard Vic shout. "Grab him, grab him!"

The treatment room door opened again and the naked bum, his hospital gown discarded, rushed out. He ran past Gypsy, stopped, and spun around with a crazed look in his

[246]

eyes. "Run for your life!" he warned Gypsy desperately. "Giant bugs! Giant bugs! Run!"

Gypsy tried to edge closer to him. "Sir," he said reassuringly, "nobody's going to hurt you."

The bum looked at him warily. "Who are you?"

"I'm a doctor. I want to help you."

A small cloud of uncertainty drifted across the man's face. "Doctor?" he repeated. "Where?"

"Right here," Gypsy said. "Let's go back inside."

Then the bum's thinking equipment broke down again. "You're the devil, you bastard," he announced. "You work for the giant roaches."

"Well, sort of," Gypsy admitted. "I work for the city."

"Lord have mercy," said the aide, who had been watching the exchange wonderingly. "The man got no clothes on!" She hurried away toward the elevators, adding as her parting comment, "Man, I'm sure glad I'm on my coffee break."

The bum was now holding a ramshackle conversation with some phantoms that had been invented by what was left of his mind. Suddenly he looked up at the ceiling and threw his arms over his head to protect himself. "Cockroaches!" he screamed. "Here they come again. Giant cockroaches from the sky!" He dashed by Gypsy, who made a lunge for him but missed, and raced off down the corridor.

Gypsy regained his balance and watched him run. Right above the bum's naked ass the entire lower part of his back was painted orange-brown with antiseptic, and protruding from the middle of this was the big spinal needle. He dripped spinal fluid as he ran.

Vittorio and George had been sneaking around through the utility room where the bedpans are emptied out, figuring to come up behind the poor old bum and at least get their needle out of his back. They arrived in time to watch the

[247]

bum disappear, bare-assed, through the fire door at the end of the hallway. George resumed the chase, favoring what seemed to be his ruptured side as he lurched along. "Do you realize," he said to Gypsy as he passed him, "I could have gone into my father's wholesale dress business?"

Vic was fuming. The faintly cynical look he usually wore was gone and his face was showing blotches of deep crimson. "Gypsy, where is she?" he asked with his voice shaking. "Where is that fucking aide?"

"Vic, forget about her." Gypsy was making a stab at being reasonable. "The damage is done already." He saw his friend's face and decided Vittorio was past reasoning with. There was going to be some more damage done. "I think she went to the cafeteria, Vittorio. Vittorio?"

Vic peeled off his sterile gloves without another word, dropped them on the floor, and left looking murderous. Gypsy watched him go, and shrugged. "Well, what the fuck," he said to himself, "she deserves it." Gypsy walked back upstairs.

His own ward appeared calm. Irene was sitting in the nursing station writing up another admission. "Hello, Gypsy. Where have you been all this time?"

"I was downstairs with Vittorio and that fat resident," Gypsy said. "He thinks he's got a hernia."

Irene laughed. "What's going on down there?"

"Nothing. We busy here?"

"Not really," she answered, gesturing at the chart she was working on. "They sent up this fifteen-year-old junkie as a rule-out bacterial endocarditis."

"Does he have it?"

"I don't think so," Irene said. "He most likely has a febrile drug reaction, from that crap he was using. But he won't let me examine him anyway."

"Of course not. We might be able to help him or something if he did that."

Irene shrugged. Everyone had started to shrug quite a bit, entering this final quarter of the year. The calm did not last. It was broken by a very short man who came scurrying into the nursing station in an actual nightshirt. The garment was much too small for him, and his miniature, skinny legs stuck out from underneath it, but it was his own. It didn't even have "Department of Correction" stamped across the back. The little patient wearing it looked terrorized.

"Why, Mr. Murphy," Irene said, "what's the matter?"

Mr. Murphy was sweating. "There's a crazy man in my room! He took all his clothes off and I'm afraid of him. He says he's going to throw me out the window!"

"It must be Preston again," Irene said disgustedly. "Go back to your room, Mr. Murphy. We'll take care of it."

"He seems like a nice little guy," Gypsy commented after Murphy left. "What's he doing here?"

"Oh, he's not a bum," Irene explained. "He has a job and everything. He was just visiting in New York, and he got thrombophlebitis. His leg blew up like a balloon and he didn't know any doctors, so he asked a cabdriver to take him to a hospital. The cabbie brought him here."

"All right. What about the crazy guy, then?"

"That, no doubt, is Preston Hicks. He lives here. He's a chronic alcoholic with Wernicke-Korsakoff syndrome."

"Is he really going to throw Murphy out the window?"

"Oh, no, of course not," Irene said. "Poor Preston is harmless. It's just that he's got no brain left, and he gets confused sometimes at night. I guess they didn't bother to restrain him in bed again. I'll go see." She stood up to attend to Preston Hicks, but she promptly had a coughing spell instead. Choking and coughing explosively, she went rummaging through her pocketbook for a cigarette. Her lungs had apparently become more or less dependent upon nicotine for their normal functioning.

Gypsy sighed. "I'll do it," he said, getting up also, "if I'm able to tell everybody apart."

There was no trouble telling who Preston Hicks was. Gypsy met him halfway down the corridor, shuffling slowly along in the direction of the nursing station. He had cloth restraints tied to his wrists and his ankles, and the long strips of cloth were all trailing out behind him on the floor. Except for the restraints, he was naked. In the dark corridor, he could have been the spirit of some crucified martyr bum, torn loose from his moorings and come to haunt the hospital.

"Jesus," Gypsy said to himself, "why doesn't anybody wear any clothes here?"

The naked patient was on the point of drifting right past him, so Gypsy grabbed one of the wrist restraints and pulled. "Excuse me. Are you Hicks?"

The man turned around apathetically and looked at Gypsy blankly.

"Are you Preston Hicks?" Gypsy repeated.

The patient without clothes went on looking at him, with as much comprehension as a turnip.

"I shouldn't have asked," Gypsy muttered. Still clutching the restraint, he turned the man's other wrist over and examined his identification band. "P. Hicks," it read.

"Okay, Preston," Gypsy said wearily. "Back to bed." Leading him by his wrist restraint, Gypsy returned Preston to the room he shared with Murphy. "Let's go, boss," Gypsy instructed, pointing him at his bed, "it's getting late." Preston climbed dutifully into the bed and Gypsy tied his restraints to the bed rails. Then he covered Preston with a blanket. "Are you all right?"

"Somebody took my cigarettes," Preston said in a sad monotone.

[250]

"Sure," Gypsy agreed. "You behave yourself now."

Murphy was sitting up in the other bed with his blanket gathered around him, looking nervous. "Doc," he whispered, "can I have a bed that's not next to the window, please?"

"Mr. Murphy, this patient is well restrained, and he won't bother you any more. Go to sleep, it's late." Gypsy walked out of their room and headed back toward the nursing station. When he passed the treatment room, he paused and then went in. He ran his eyes over the empty treatment room. It was a real mess. All the paraphernalia he and Irene had used in stabilizing Lincoln was still sitting there. The metal basin, with its ice now mostly melted, was on the floor in the center of the room, between separate pools of blood and urine. Gypsy crossed the treatment room and stood in front of the window. Twelve stories beneath him and off near the river, he could see the two streams of lights flowing in opposite directions along the F.D.R. Drive. It was an odd thing, but whenever he looked down at the Drive, there was always traffic on it. Even in the middle of the night.

In med school, he had usually used the F.D.R. Drive when he came into the city to escape from the double boredom of medical school and the Bronx. He remembered looking out of his car, in the spring of his senior year, and gazing up at the building he was now standing in. Maybe even at this particular window. He used to think, Man, once I get in there, once I'm an intern, things are going to be different. I'm finally going to be a doctor, not a glorified schoolboy four years after I finished college. I'm going to love it—I'm going to be the best fucking intern they ever had. Gypsy laughed quietly. This was it? This was the great learning experience? This was how he was going to help people? Somebody had played a bad joke on him.

[251]

Irene walked into the treatment room. "Gypsy? What are you standing in here for?"

Gypsy turned away from the window. "Hello, Irene. Anything happening?"

"No; everybody's okay. Did you take care of Preston?"

"Uh-huh. I tied him up in bed."

"Well, I guess that's it then. I think we're through for the night, unless we get another admission."

Gypsy nodded, and returned to staring out the window. Irene came over and joined him. "If it's any of my business, what are you thinking about, Gypsy?"

"You know," he answered slowly, "I really looked forward to this year, Irene. After all that time in school, I figured this was going to make it worth it. Jesus, I expected so much out of interning. And then, every rotation I went on here, I kept saying to myself, 'Well, shit, this is an exception—the next rotation is when I'm going to start liking it; the next rotation is going to be better.' Only it never was."

Irene looked sympathetic. "I understand what you're talking about Gypsy, exactly. But you've got to remember that being a doctor isn't ever what any of us thought it was going to be. It's not an ordinary job—it's something special. It's like a calling, almost, and some of the time it just gets kind of depressing. That's not your fault."

Gypsy sounded very melancholy. "I wonder if I'm cut out for this, Irene."

"Gypsy, do you know what it means when you start asking yourself questions like that? All it means is that you care about what you're doing. You care about your patients. If you didn't feel that way once in a while, you probably wouldn't be much of a doctor."

Gypsy looked away from her and stared out the window again. "I don't feel like a doctor at all. I just feel useless. And this is the beginning of my last rotation, too." Irene could see his glum face reflected in the window. "You know what else I feel like, Irene? I feel like the methadone king." He sighed. "Ah, what the hell. Say, do you want to send out for a pizza or something, maybe?"

Irene shook her head and lit her first cigarette in five minutes. "Has anybody told you what time it is? We have to present these guys in a couple of hours." She patted him on the arm. "Get some sleep, Gypsy. I'll see you at rounds."

# Beggars and Peddlers

By FIVE AFTER EIGHT the next morning, they were going through the ceremony of presenting the new patients to their boss, the ward's attending. Each morning in the hospital, every patient admitted to a ward during the past twenty-four hours was presented to at least one, and sometimes two, attending physicians. Gypsy's opinion of the interminable academic nit-picking that invariably comprised attending rounds anywhere was that it was all a stupendous, pointless bore. Accordingly, he let himself doze off as often as he could manage to during the droning monologues.

A porter came banging through the room, completely oblivious to the presence of the entire complement of the ward's physicians holding formal rounds with their attending. He dumped the garbage cans upside down in the middle of the room, and then made a casual effort to sweep up part of the pile of garbage thus created. One of his less well directed swipes with the broom gave Gypsy a sharp crack in the ankle and woke him up. Gypsy blinked a few times and looked around.

The middle-aged Bulgarian intern hadn't even been there the night before; Gypsy didn't really know any of the patients yet, and with none of their medical students in evidence either, Irene was presenting all the new patients herself. She was talking rapidly, trying to divide her time between presenting the patients, coughing, and chain-smoking. "The next patient," she said, lighting a fresh cigarette, "is Abraham Lincoln."

Hugo reacted loudly from across the room. "Lincoln! Lincoln's here again? Di Bello just discharged that bum last Thursday. What's he doing now, drinking lighter fluid?" Hugo shook his head with superiority and considerable loathing; he was evidently not such a big fan of the bums any more. "What a piece of shit that man is."

Gypsy looked over at Hugo and smiled. "Now, isn't that a coincidence? That's the very same thing Lincoln said about you. He remembers you, Hugo."

"Young man!" said the attending, who had the longest, sourest, unhappiest face of any attending Gypsy had ever seen. He was wearing two hearing aids and a Phi Beta Kappa key. "What kind of thing is that for you to say to a resident?"

Gypsy looked hurt. "Oh, sir, I didn't call Hugo a piece of shit. I would never call Hugo a piece of shit. It was Mr. Lincoln who called Hugo a piece of shit."

Irene gave him an annoyed glance. "Gypsy, stop it." She turned back toward Hugo and the miserable-looking attending. "Actually," she told them, "the patient called *me* a piece of shit. And then Gypsy called the patient a piece of shit. All right? Do you mind if we go on, please?" Everyone was properly chastised, Irene resumed the presentation, and Gypsy tried to go back to sleep.

He hardly ever slept well during rounds. The room they were held in was inevitably hot, someone was always talking, there was a new argument every ten minutes, and people persisted in asking him questions he couldn't answer. So Gypsy was still awake when Irene finally finished presenting Lincoln. He realized that he hadn't listened to more than ten words of what she'd said, and that his ass was starting to hurt. The ward had a bunch of shoddy, molded-plastic chairs that were collected in the treatment room every morning for rounds. The seats of these chairs were designed to fit some sort of mythical, average, universal ass; Gypsy had no such ass. He shifted around uncomfortably in the plastic chair and looked across the treatment room at their attending, who was doing the talking now. The attending seemed too unhappy even for a sore ass. Gypsy nudged Irene's chair with his foot. "Hey—I think I know what's wrong with that sunshine attending over there."

"What did you say?" she whispered. "I can't hear you."

"He can't piss," Gypsy announced.

"What are you talking about?"

Gypsy leaned towards her. "Sunshine can't piss," he repeated. "I think he's one of those seventy-year-old guys with a big prostate. He probably hasn't been able to piss for a month. That's why he's got that terrible expression on his face."

Irene briefly managed to remain solemn-appearing, but as soon as she looked at the attending again she began to giggle. Then she broke out laughing: She tried too hard not to laugh and choked herself, and that started her coughing. Once she'd begun to cough, she couldn't stop without a cigarette. She went digging in her pocketbook for her cigarettes, but she was laughing and coughing too much to see what she was doing.

The stolid, dull attending had continued with his pompous discourse through the beginning of this exchange, but when Irene really got going she couldn't help drowning him out. Sunshine finally stopped talking and glowered at Gypsy. "You there," he said, "are you attached to this ward in some capacity?"

Irene had found her cigarettes and gotten her breath back. "That's the new intern," she explained, her voice still a little wheezy.

"Well, doctor, have you any idea what I've been discussing?" Sunshine asked.

"Nope," Gypsy admitted.

The attending looked pleased with himself. "Would you like to tell us what you've been doing, then?"

Irene made a silent appeal to Gypsy for peace.

"I was thinking that my ass hurt," Gypsy said distinctly, "and that you probably don't piss enough."

Sunshine's expression became even more unhappy, and he almost started to say something to Gypsy. He stopped himself, deciding not to play Gypsy's game. "All right," he said instead, "let me examine this patient Lincoln." Everyone got up, with much scraping of chairs, and the assemblage trooped off to Lincoln's room for the ritual laying on of hands. There was no sign of Lincoln. All the other recuperating felons were snoring peacefully, but Lincoln's bed was empty.

"Where is this patient?" Sunshine demanded, turning petulant. "The patients are supposed to be right here when I make attending rounds."

"Well, I don't have him," Irene said.

"Maybe he just packed up and went home," Gypsy suggested.

"He's a bum," Hugo said disdainfully. "He doesn't have any home."

One of Hugo's medical students came up to Gypsy and tugged on his sleeve. "You better take a look at this," he whispered. "I think I found your patient." He led Gypsy into the patients' bathroom and pointed at the bathtub. Gypsy walked over to the tub. His eyes grew big and he quickly walked out of the bathroom.

Everybody was standing around in the corridor, griping at the delay. "Irene, we've got trouble," Gypsy said. "I think Lincoln drowned."

"Drowned?" Irene stared at him. "Drowned? Gypsy, what are you talking about now? This isn't Coney Island. No one *drowns* on a male medical ward."

"Lincoln drowned," Gypsy said once again in a toneless

voice, and walked back into the bathroom. The whole group crowded in after him and lined up along the tub, gaping. Abraham Lincoln was lying at the bottom of the bathtub, covered with dirty water and dead as a doornail. It was hard to tell whether he had overdosed and then drowned, or simply overdosed. The needle was still in his arm.

"I think I'd better call the administrators," Sunshine said, and hurried out of the bathroom.

Hugo peered into the bathtub for a moment and then straightened up, looking snotty. "This has to stop, Irene. Those needles are expensive."

"Hugo, why don't you fuck yourself," Irene said with rare and uncharacteristic venom. She turned to Gypsy, shaking her head slowly. "The poor bastard. I guess it had to happen sooner or later."

Gypsy knelt alongside the bathtub. He looked at the bloated, motionless face, and then reached in and pulled Lincoln's hand out of the water. It felt like the flesh of a cold dead fish. He dropped the arm back into the water.

Nothing else happened that day. The following morning was pretty quiet, too, except that Irene got attacked during rounds. The fifteen-year-old junkie grew impatient with being worked up for bacterial endocarditis and told Irene he was going home. Irene told him that she was sorry, but he was still sick, he was a minor, and he couldn't go home unless his parents were willing to sign him out of the hospital against medical advice.

"Oh, yeah?" the fifteen-year-old junkie said to her. "Fuck you!" He picked up the telephone and tried to fight his way out.

He was a small fifteen-year-old and Irene fought a pretty good holding action for a while. Eventually, though, he got in a hard shot to her head with the corner of the telephone, and it staggered her. At that point, reinforcements reached the two big hospital guards who had been watching the fight from the safety of the far end of the corridor. With their numbers boosted to five, the guards charged the adolescent junkie and disarmed him of the telephone. They handcuffed him to his bed for further medical attention and then marched off in a bloc, slapping each other's hands and whooping—"Way to go, man, way to go."

"Are you okay?" Gypsy asked Irene, who was rubbing the side of her head gingerly.

"I think so. Where was my intern?"

"Oh, I'm a pacifist," Gypsy said, smiling.

Irene laughed. "You mean coward?"

"That also."

A nurse in Delivery Room greens appeared on the ward, leading Preston Hicks along behind her. "Do you people have a Hicks on this ward?" she inquired.

"Yeah," Gypsy answered defensively, "he's ours. Uh, where did you find him?"

"He was wandering around Obstetrics. You ought to control your patients a little better, doc." The Delivery Room nurse left, and Hicks sat down on the floor and started to take his pajama bottoms off.

"Preston, what are you doing?" Gypsy asked reprovingly.

"What?" Hicks said, with the pajamas tangled around one ankle and his ass hanging out.

"What are you doing, Preston? What are you doing now?"

Hicks lolled on the floor, slack-jawed and uncomprehending. "My cigarettes," he said finally. "They took my cigarettes."

"All right." Gypsy sighed. "Let's go." He helped Hicks put his pants on and got a nurse to escort him back to his room. Then he went looking for Irene again. "Irene," he said to his resident, "what are we going to do with Hicks?"

Irene raised her eyebrows at him and shrugged. "I don't know. I suppose he'll just stay right here with us."

"He can't lay here on the ward and rot forever. We're not accomplishing a damn thing for him."

"No, we're not," Irene said. "But there isn't much of him to work with any more. Nobody's going to accomplish anything for him."

"Does he have a family?" Gypsy asked hopefully.

"He's got a wife. Mrs. Hicks and I already had a couple of discussions about Preston. She says I can keep him."

"I think I'm going to call her up," Gypsy said. "She married him for better or for worser, didn't she?"

"This is pretty worser. I don't think she'll even come in to talk to you."

Mrs. Hicks not only agreed to come to the hospital to talk to Gypsy, but she said she'd be in that same day. She showed up toward the end of the afternoon. Gypsy introduced himself and thanked her for taking the trouble to come to see him. It appeared as if he'd had a fruitful idea. "There's something I want to talk to you about," he began.

"Good," Mrs. Hicks replied. "I got something to talk to you about, too."

"Oh? What's that?"

"Well," she told him, looking smug, "I just found out Preston been in the Army once." She stopped.

"Uh-huh," Gypsy said politely, and waited for her to go on.

"Yeah," she continued after a little throat-clearing. "I figure if you write to the government they ought to give me some money now. I mean, he's a veteran."

"If Preston was in the Army, then he's a veteran all right," Gypsy agreed. "Only, I don't really see why the government should give you money if I write to them, Mrs. Hicks."

She got indignant. "You ever talk to Preston? That man is sick. Damn, he can't even work no more." Gypsy wondered whether Preston Hicks had ever worked, either before or after he was in the Army.

"That's true, he does have a problem," Gypsy conceded. "But I think his problem has more to do with his drinking than being in the Army."

"Problem, shit! He weak in the head!"

"Yes, I suppose he becomes a little confused sometimes," Gypsy said with marvelous understatement. "The thing is, though, he's very devoted to you."

She looked at him narrowly. "What you getting at?"

It was Gypsy's turn to clear his throat. "We thought you might like to take Preston home with you, Mrs. Hicks."

She laughed in his face. "I ain't never taking him home with me."

"Mrs. Hicks, he's your husband. You can't walk off and leave him here until he dies."

"Oh, no? That's exactly what I'm gonna do. And the government owe me money for him! I'm no fool, man."

"Look," Gypsy said, attempting a new tack, "there's no medical reason why Preston has to stay in the hospital. He's not sick, and the poor guy's been sitting here for months and months already. We can't give him his mind back, Mrs. Hicks; he drank it away. What if we just discharge him and send him home?"

"You try that, you wise-ass, and I'll lock him out of the goddam apartment. I don't care if he starve, you hear? I don't want the son of a bitch in my house!" Mrs. Hicks got up and put on her coat, and waved her finger at Gypsy. "Don't you forget," she said, "I want a letter to the government about that bum. You understand?"

"Mrs. Hicks, I don't think I can help you with that. Maybe you should write to the V.A. about it."

[261]

"Bullshit artist!" she called him, and walked away in the direction of the elevators. Gypsy followed her through the corridor.

"Aren't you going to talk to Preston, Mrs. Hicks?"

"What for?"

Gypsy held his hands out to her. "Just to talk to him," he said despairingly. "To say hello. Don't you even want to see him?"

"You like him so much, you talk to him. I think the both of you weak in the head. Hah," she added, nodding to herself, "that's right—bum patient, bum doctor. Man, you as bad as he is." She laughed again and disappeared into an elevator.

Preston had been watching silently from the other end of the corridor. Gypsy walked over to him, and they went into Preston's room together and sat down. Mr. Murphy looked at them suspiciously and hobbled out of the room. They sat and stared at each other for a while.

"Preston, your wife was here," Gypsy said finally.

"My wife," Preston answered with a faint flicker of recognition. "My wife. I seen her."

There was another pause.

"She was real busy," Gypsy said lamely; "she couldn't stay very long today. She's going to come back another time to see you."

Preston shook his head. "She don't want to see me. She used to bring me cigarettes, but not no more. Not no more." He picked one of his tattered slippers up and carefully hid it underneath the pillow on his bed.

Gypsy sighed. "Preston, what's going to happen to you? You can't live in this lousy room for the next twenty years."

Hicks sat down again, on the floor, and tried to take his clothes off. This time he wasn't able to untie the string that was anchoring the pants of his pajamas. Outwitted by a bowknot, he looked at Gypsy listlessly and recited slowly, "Somebody took my cigarettes. I wish my wife would bring me cigarettes like she used to." He lowered his head.

Gypsy felt a terrible wave of pity for this poor, lonely wreck. "Come on," he offered suddenly, "do you want to watch some television? Let's go look at TV."

Preston raised his head and almost smiled. "Yeah," he said. "I like television." Gypsy helped him up off the floor and took him out to the empty solarium, where there was an old, donated television set that was perpetually and unheededly blaring.

He parked Preston in front of the television. A bald man who had a tic was on Channel 13, talking about Etruscan pottery. Preston was fascinated, and Gypsy left him sitting there. Then he went downstairs and bought Preston Hicks two cartons of cigarettes. While Gypsy was in the coffee shop buying cigarettes, one of the porters walked by the solarium, spied Preston, and made a special detour to go in and shut the television off. Preston remained where he was, staring at the blank screen.

Preston got worse and worse. During the daytime he wasn't that bad, but every night, in spite of pleas, threats, sedation, and being tied to his bed, he ended up wandering naked around the hospital.

"Irene," Gypsy said reluctantly one morning, "I think we have to do something about Hicks."

"I know," she admitted, "I know. What do you want to do?"

"Uh-uh. You're the resident. What do *you* want to do?"

She stalled for a while, lighting a cigarette. The cigarette triggered some obligatory coughing, which used up a little more time. Then Irene unhappily faced facts, looked Gypsy

[263]

in the eye, and said "Well, I guess we've got to send him to a state mental hospital."

"That's what I was afraid of," Gypsy said sadly. "I just hate to ship him off to one of those places, you know? He's probably going to spend the rest of his life there. And I kind of like him, Irene."

"So do I," Irene asserted quickly. "He's actually a harmless guy. But what else can we do with him? He has no clinical problems, and we're never going to be able to make him think any better, no matter how long we keep him here."

"It's a shame his goddam wife won't take care of him."

Irene grimaced. "That woman's a real prize. Did you talk to her?"

"Last week. You were right. She thinks the government should make her a woman of leisure—because Preston was in the Army. Aside from that, she doesn't give a shit about him."

"That's Mrs. Hicks. Well, look, if he's got to go to a state hospital, then he's got to go. That's all there is to it."

"Yeah," Gypsy said. "Damn."

"We have to get him certified by an attending before we can send him over," Irene mentioned.

"Certified? Jesus, certified for what?" Gypsy complained sarcastically. "Does he need references to get into a state mental hospital?"

"Cut it out, will you? I don't like doing this any more than you. The attending has to certify that the patient needs chronic care in a state facility."

"Okay," Gypsy said with very little enthusiasm in his voice. "We'll ask Sunshine after rounds tomorrow."

"Oh, I don't know about that," Sunshine responded dubiously when they asked him to certify Preston for the funny farm. Sunshine was an academician, which meant that he was very good at making long lists of obscure differential diagnoses, but that he was no good whatsoever at making up his mind about anything. "No," he said finally, looking undecided, "I don't think I can certify this patient Hicks."

"Well," Gypsy reminded him reasonably, "you're the attending, and it's your ward, and Hicks is a patient on the ward, and he needs to be certified. I'd say you have to sort of shit or get off the pot. But I'm only the intern, of course." Irene had a small coughing fit.

Sunshine got off the pot. His lugubrious face grew slightly longer, and he edged away from Gypsy and started to move toward the stairs. "Listen, why don't you try to work with this man? A lot of these people can be rehabilitated, you know. See what you can do. Anyway, I have to go to the men's room now." Sunshine vanished.

"That's a lie," Gypsy said to Irene. "He never goes to the bathroom. He just doesn't want to sign the paper."

"You know what? He forgot to tell us how to rehabilitate Preston."

"We could let him have cab fare to Queens," Gypsy suggested. "It's nice there in the spring."

"Stop that," Irene said. "We'll have to sedate him heavier at night, that's all. We certainly can't perform a brain transplant."

"No? Why not?"

Little Mr. Murphy hobbled up to them at this point, wearing his comic nightshirt. "Mr. Murphy," Irene admonished him, "you really should be staying in bed. And with your leg elevated, too. Otherwise it's not going to get better."

"Bed, crap. You gotta do something about that wild man, or I'm leaving. He's crazy, for Christ's sake. What kind of hospital is this?"

"Well, Mr. Hicks is sick, Mr. Murphy," Gypsy said, feeling asinine trying to defend whatever idiocy Preston had perpetrated. "He's not, uh, he's not responsible for some of the things he does."

"Who's responsible?" Murphy protested excitedly, hopping in vexation on his good leg with his nightshirt flapping. "Who's responsible? Me?"

"What happened this time?" Irene asked sympathetically. "Is Hicks talking about throwing you out the window again?"

"He keeps trying to get into my bed!" Murphy yelled. "The son of a bitch takes his clothes off in the middle of the night and tries to get into my bed."

"He's confused," Gypsy maintained apologetically.

"He's crazy!" Murphy shouted. "He's a crazy man!"

"Mr. Murphy, calm yourself, please," Irene said. "Go back to bed and keep your leg elevated. I promise, we'll do something about Hicks."

"That's what I said yesterday," Gypsy noted after Murphy had hopped away. "Do what?"

"We can't do anything with Hicks," Irene confessed. "The whole situation is impossible. We've got to have him certified; there's no other way. And look, make sure he's well sedated tonight, will you?" Gypsy made sure.

The next day they absolutely wouldn't take no for an answer, and they dragged Sunshine into Preston's room to certify Preston Hicks for the nut house. Preston was fast asleep, with his sheet twisted around his head and the covers wrapped around his feet. Everything in between, naturally, was naked.

"Preston, wake up," Gypsy said cheerfully, "this nice man wants to talk to you." Gypsy untangled the sheet from Preston's head. Preston generated a mighty snore and turned over, presenting his bare ass to them. He was dead to the world.

"Would you please cover this patient?" Sunshine requested prissily. "I'm an attending, you know." Gypsy tried

[266]

to unwind the covers from Preston's feet but they were wrapped too tightly. "Help me turn him over again, man," he said to Sunshine.

"Christ," Irene said. She stubbed out her cigarette and covered Preston below the neck with the sheet that Gypsy had removed from around his head. Gypsy stopped struggling with the covers and with Preston's feet, and smiled at her. "That was very good. Why didn't I think of it?"

"Don't ask," Irene told him. "Don't ask." She addressed herself to Sunshine. "Please, would you care to evaluate the patient for transfer now?"

"Ah, Mr. Hicks, I'd like to talk to you if you have a few minutes," Sunshine said. A muffled snore arose from Preston, whose face was still buried in the mattress. "Mr. Hicks?" Sunshine tried again. "Mr. Hicks, wake up, please." He shook the slumbering Preston by the shoulders, which caused Preston to fart resoundingly.

Irene pulled Gypsy aside. "My God," she said, "what did you do to him?"

"I sedated him last night."

"With what?"

"Oh, I gave him a little paraldehyde," Gypsy explained casually.

"That's all?" she asked suspiciously. "How much?"

"About fifty c.c.'s," Gypsy said sheepishly.

"Good God!" Irene exclaimed under her breath. "Are you insane? He's not going to wake up until midnight."

Gypsy shrugged his regrets. Sunshine had ceased poking at Preston; the morose attending came over to Irene and Gypsy. "No wonder you're having difficulty with this patient," he announced. "He's oversedated."

"Yeah, I know he's oversedated," Gypsy said, "but that's not his problem. I had to snow him so we could control him at night—because his head doesn't function any more. But we can't just keep him unconscious permanently. That's why he needs to be in a state hospital."

"Well, I can't possibly certify this patient for transfer. The man is much too heavily sedated for me to evaluate him." Sunshine sounded greatly relieved. He also left the room very fast.

"Our attending is losing his taste for patient contact," Irene observed wryly. She took a deep breath. "Okay, we'll try again. Take Hicks off everything tonight and we'll see what he looks like in the morning."

"I don't know about that, Irene—the unclouded vista of Preston's mind! Do you think Sunshine can stand the competition?"

"Oh, leave Sunshine alone. He's an old man."

"He should get his prostate taken out," Gypsy said reflectively, "so he can piss once in a while. I told you, all that urine backing up in there is what's making him such a sourpuss. Don't you think?"

"I think you should get Preston unsedated by tomorrow morning," Irene said humorlessly.

For the third time in three days, they cornered Sunshine after rounds. "Yes?" he asked innocently.

"We have a patient we wanted you to see," Gypsy said equally blandly. "Mr. Hicks."

"Oh, yes, Hicks," Sunshine recalled, putting on a small show for their benefit. "That's the patient who was oversedated the other day, right? How is he doing now?"

"Fine, just fine. He's walking around and breathing. That's all he knows how to do."

"Oh, it can't be that bad. You probably haven't spent enough time with him yet. You have to really work with these people."

"Uh-huh," Gypsy said. "Well, we were hoping *you* could

[268]

spend a little time with him and tell us what you think, if you don't mind."

Sunshine inspected his wristwatch. "Now, look, I have to leave soon," he said warningly. "I have a very busy schedule today."

"This won't take long, don't worry. Preston doesn't say much."

Sunshine got up unwillingly. "All right. But I won't be able to arrive at a decision anyway if the patient is still sedated."

"No problem," Gypsy assured him, smiling. "I stopped his medications. You're going to see Preston Hicks at his very best."

The three of them walked off toward Preston's room— Irene and Gypsy walking like people who were about to accomplish something, and Sunshine walking like a man going in to have his income-tax return audited. "Gypsy," Irene whispered nervously, "are you sure you cut everything he was on?"

Gypsy smiled again. "He hasn't even had an aspirin since yesterday. I just hope he didn't throw Murphy out the window yet."

Preston wasn't in his room.

Sunshine's face lit up with delight and sudden confidence. "Well, well," he said, "it seems that the patient's not here. That's a pity, of course, but unfortunately I'm very busy today. I'll simply have to see this patient some other time."

"Irene, hold him," Gypsy muttered. "Don't let him get away!" Gypsy ran out of the room and went on a wild search of the ward, and found Preston taking an early-morning bubble bath. Gypsy's smile reappeared and he relaxed. He returned to Preston's room, where Sunshine was protesting acrimoniously to Irene about how busy he was. "Success!" Gypsy announced. "I found Hicks. He's taking a bath, but he'd be happy to talk to us."

[269]

"Oh, no," Sunshine said hastily, "I'm not going near that bathroom. I'm not having anything to do with any more patients drowned in the bathtub."

"There's nothing to be concerned over; Preston isn't drowned. He's in the best of health, and nice and clean, too. Let's not keep the patient waiting, man."

Flanked by Irene and Gypsy, Sunshine walked into the bathroom to evaluate the mental status of Preston Hicks. Preston was seated in the bathtub, along with a few inches of water and a whole lot of bubbles. He appeared to be enjoying himself. The interview was quite brief.

"Sir," Sunshine began, "I'd like to ask you a few questions. They may seem rather silly to you, but I want you to answer them. All right?" Preston gave him a friendly look and splashed around a bit.

"Okay," Sunshine said, "now, what's your name, please?"

"Hicks."

"Uh-huh, right," Sunshine said approvingly. "Where are you?"

"I'm in the bathtub," Preston replied promptly.

"Well, yes, of course. I really didn't make myself clear that time. I meant, what kind of building is this? A school? Or a hospital?"

"A whorehouse," Preston answered after a moment's thought.

"Oh," Sunshine said. "Well, we'll skip that one. Who is the President of the United States?"

"Franklin Roosevelt."

"Now, you know that's not right, Mr. Hicks. Let's start from the beginning. Tell me what your name is again."

"Franklin Roosevelt," Preston repeated, soaping his armpit.

"Mr. Hicks, how can your name be Franklin Roosevelt?" Sunshine was getting a trifle impatient with Preston. "Concentrate, all right? I want you to tell me what year this is."

[270]

Preston pondered the question for a while. "Somebody took my cigarettes," he said finally. Then he pulled his penis up out of the bubbles and began to masturbate. That was too much for Sunshine. "This patient has to be institutionalized," he proclaimed quickly, pretending not to see what Preston was doing. "Why wasn't he brought to my attention before?"

"Because you wouldn't hold still long enough, is why," Gypsy answered truthfully. Sunshine, however, had already departed.

They packed up the bits and pieces of Preston's possessions after lunch and called the state hospital to arrange the transfer. Gypsy wrote "Property of Mr. Preston Hicks" on the two cartons of cigarettes and handed them to their owner. "Preston, you take care," Gypsy said. "I'll come and see you. I mean it."

When the attendants arrived, he walked outside with Preston and watched them put him in the hospital car. Gypsy waved until they'd gone. He felt very bad, and he didn't know why. He went back to the ward with his head down, thinking about Preston, and found Irene embroiled in an argument. She was being badgered on two sides by Sergeant Drobek and his grandson.

"There he is," Drobek said, pointing accusingly at Gypsy. "He told me yes!"

Sergeant Drobek was another hopeless old alcoholic. He had not had a job in thirty-nine years, and he could do almost nothing except drink liquor. He was a sergeant in the Reserves. He had an end-stage alcoholic cardiomyopathy and an unemployed grandson.

Irene looked very disgusted. "Gypsy, did you have something to do with this crazy idea?"

"Which crazy idea?" Gypsy asked carefully.

"Drobek wants to drive to North Carolina with his grandson. This afternoon."

[271]

"Oh. That idea."

"Oh what?" Irene said impatiently. "Did you tell him an idiot scheme like that was okay?"

Sergeant Drobek and his grandson were both looking at Gypsy imploringly. Gypsy shuffled his feet. "Well, yeah," he admitted finally. "I told him he could go if he wanted to."

Irene rolled her eyes and hauled Gypsy into the corner. "Are you mad? Do you know that his schmuck grandson bought five cases of beer for the trip?"

Gypsy smiled despite himself. "I figured they'd bring something along to drink."

"Gypsy, what's wrong with you?" She sounded fed up. "The man is a Class Three-C cardiac. My God, he's practically a Four-D! Don't you know how much salt there is in beer? He's in congestive failure half the time now, for Christ's sake. He's going to be in pulmonary edema before he gets to North Carolina!"

"Irene," Gypsy said quietly, "are you able to cure his cardiomyopathy?"

"Of course we're not able to cure him. We're not magicians. But at least we can keep him comfortable here."

Gypsy motioned her out to the corridor. "Be honest," he said gently, "do you think Drobek's comfortable laying around the damn hospital waiting to die? Let him go back to Carolina. If he doesn't make it . . . well, he'll be having a little fun at the end of his life. He wants to die going home, Irene—not in this lousy place. Let him go."

Irene avoided Gypsy's face for a long time. "I'm sorry," she said at last. "I can't. I don't know if you're right or if I'm right, but I just can't practice medicine that way."

Gypsy shook his head slowly. "Irene, explain something to me, then. What are we doing here? What are we doing for these people?"

Irene sighed deeply. "I wish you wouldn't ask me those

[272]

questions, Gypsy. I can't answer them for you either. I don't think anybody can."

They weren't admitting that night, but they both planned to stay around into the evening to finish some work on their charts. At a little after six o'clock Preston Hicks walked back onto the ward. He was still carrying the small paper bag that held his belongings, but the two cartons of cigarettes were gone. Gypsy took his arm and stopped him as he wandered past them. "Preston, what happened to you? What's going on?"

Preston gazed at Gypsy with the pathetic, empty stare of an old blind dog. He didn't say a thing. Gypsy found a note pinned to his pajama top. The note read:

> This individual has limited reality testing, but is otherwise intact. He does not qualify for institution-alization. Thank you.

Gypsy sat down and put his head in his hands. "My God," he said, "otherwise intact?" Then he got up again, and went over and took Preston Hicks by the shoulders. "Preston," he said to him softly, "Preston, do you know who I am?"

Preston just looked at the floor silently, and after a moment Gypsy let his arms drop.

"My name is Gypsy. Don't you remember? My name is Gypsy."

He might as well have been telling Preston he was John the Baptist. Gypsy gave up and drafted an aide to return Preston to his room, and then he resumed working on the chart he was attempting to complete. A few minutes later there was a commotion outside the nursing station. Another one of the aides was struggling with Preston. "Come on, you retard, don't you bother the doctors. You hear?"

[273]

"Let me in," Preston entreated. "I want to talk to my doctor."

Gypsy intervened patiently. "What's the matter now, Preston?"

"The man in my room . . . he's . . . he's sick."

"Oh," Gypsy said. "Well, don't worry about him. We're going to fix him all up; that's why he's in the hospital."

"No. No." Preston swiveled his head like a marionette and flapped his arms helplessly. "He's . . . sick . . . he's sick, sick."

The aide pushed Preston away. "Ahh, get out of here, you dummy."

"Poor Preston," Gypsy said under his breath. He went back to trying to decipher the chicken-scratchings on some ancient clinic note in the chart. He couldn't concentrate, though; something was wrong. He didn't know what precisely, but something was funny.

"Irene, you got a bad feeling about anything?"

She shook her head. "You're probably just upset because of Preston."

Gypsy bit his lip for a moment. "I'm going to go see what the hell Preston was talking about." He stood up.

"Oh, be serious, Gypsy; you know Hicks. He doesn't even understand what he's saying."

"No, I really think he was trying to tell me something then."

Irene shrugged. "You're only wasting your time. You'll never finish those charts at that rate."

"The charts won't go no place," Gypsy said. He walked out into the corridor, and then down to Preston's room. He went inside.

For a few seconds Gypsy thought the room was empty. Then he saw Murphy—crumpled in a heap on the floor. Gypsy ran across the room and turned him over. "Mr.

Murphy, what is it? Can you hear me?" Murphy's breathing was labored and shallow, and his eyes weren't focused. He still had a weak pulse.

Gypsy ran back out to the corridor and shouted for help, and quickly returned to Murphy's side. Irene ran into the room a minute later, followed by two of the nurses with the ward's crash cart. "What happened?" she asked, wrapping a blood-pressure cuff around Murphy's arm. She looked angry with herself. "Did he Code?"

Gypsy was starting an I.V. in Murphy's other arm. "I don't know; I found him lying here like this." He got into a vein, hooked the tubing up to the cannula, and hung a bottle of saline.

Irene jerked her stethoscope out of her ears and dropped the bulb of the blood-pressure cuff. "Damn, he's shocky. Get some Isuprel running, fast." She hurried out to the corridor and grabbed the page telephone, and began paging people. Then she came back and helped to untangle the wires on the EKG machine that a nurse had just rolled into the room. She ran off some of the leads and studied the tracing. "He's shifted his axis—he's got an S-One, Q-Three." She looked up. "My God, I think he's thrown an embolus."

Gypsy had started an Isuprel drip and was kneeling on the floor, listening to Murphy's heart. He got to his feet and twisted the stethoscope in his hands. "Jesus. It must have been a big one." Irene agreed, silently and ominously.

The cardiology Fellow arrived at that point, spoke to them briefly, and bent down to examine Murphy. Then an inhalation-therapy technician came into the room pushing an oxygen tank, and in a little while Murphy was also receiving oxygen. Irene took his blood pressure again, and shook her head. "It's not holding—his B.P.'s dropping."

Gypsy prepared for the worst and paged anesthesia and chest surgery. Back in the room, the cardiology Fellow was

[275]

inspecting the EKG. He looked over at Irene. "I think this man's had a massive pulmonary embolism," he said to her. "He's got a good source for it in that leg."

"That's what we figured, too," Irene answered. "Now what?"

The cardiology Fellow drummed his fingers together. "I don't know; he looks terrible. How old is the patient?"

"He's only forty-one."

Gypsy was waiting in the corridor; he was thinking how small and frail Murphy had seemed, lying there on the floor. After two or three minutes an anesthesiologist and a Fellow in cardiothoracic surgery came running out of the stairwell. Gypsy quickly explained the situation to them, and they both went into the room. Then Vittorio and Otto got off one of the elevators, wearing their coats, and walked over to Gypsy. "What's going on?" Vic asked. "We were just leaving and we heard them paging everybody for your ward."

"One of our people threw an embolus."

"Bad?"

Gypsy was very somber. "He's in shock—we can't get his blood pressure up." Otto took his coat off and went inside to help.

Vittorio removed his coat also. "Gypsy, maybe you should try to have him transferred to the Unit," he suggested. Gypsy didn't look hopeful, even of that. They walked into the room together. Murphy had been picked up and placed on a bed. There were more I.V. lines running by this time, and Irene and the cardiologist were injecting things into one of the I.V.'s. They were juggling different drugs, in an effort to get some improvement in blood pressure and tissue perfusion. Murphy's face was gray. Otto, the anesthesiologist, the cardiothoracic Fellow, and some nurses were working over him. Several more residents, apparently on the surgical house staff, had responded to the pages and crowded into the room, too, clustering about Murphy.

Gypsy went over to Irene. "You think we should call the Unit?" he asked her.

"He's really bad, Gypsy—I don't think he's going to last that long."

The cardiothoracic surgeon gestured to Irene. "Are you the resident up here?" She nodded at him. "This patient should go to surgery right now, as soon as he has a pulmonary angiogram. Is he anticoagulated already?" Irene nodded again. "Then he needs an embolectomy," the surgeon continued. "If he can make it to the O.R., maybe we can get it out. There's nothing else we can do for him."

Irene held a short conference with the rest of the senior house staff in the room, and then concurred. "Let me call my attending," the surgeon said.

Gypsy went up to the head of the bed to see if he could talk to Murphy. Murphy had come around slightly, which meant that at least he was supplying some oxygen to his brain. "What happened to me?" he asked Gypsy.

"Your blood pressure is a little low, that's all," Gypsy lied. "You'll be okay." Gypsy felt Murphy's extremities, and they were still cold and clammy—a sign that his pressure was not being adequately maintained.

Gypsy walked back to where Irene was adjusting an I.V. line and frowned worriedly. "He could go any minute, Irene."

"I know . . . Let's start on that angiogram. Vic, why don't you and Gypsy roll one of those stretchers in here and we'll take him right down to X-Ray."

Before they could do anything, the cardiothoracic Fellow stalked into the room, looking absolutely infuriated. "I don't believe this!" he shouted. "My attending's on his way here to operate, and we can't get an angiogram! How can we operate on the patient's embolism if we can't get an angiogram?" Everybody stared at him.

"What are you talking about, you can't get an angiogram?" Gypsy said.

"I just called X-Ray. I even had my attending call them! There's no Special Procedures technician in the hospital at night—he's got to come in from home. And he lives out in Port Jefferson, and he doesn't even have a car. He's got to take the goddam train!"

"Port Jefferson?" Gypsy repeated incredulously. "That's absurd—this guy might die before the damn technician ever shows up!"

"What can I do? They told me there's a goddam budget cut, and they had to lay people off. Bastards!"

A long silence hung in the air. Then Vittorio had an idea that was born utterly of desperation. "Well, why should we just stand here? Let's send him someplace else. There's other hospitals."

"You mean *move him?*" Irene asked, astonished. "In an ambulance? Like this?"

"Why not? Why should he die because there's a budget cut?"

"Vic's right, I think," Gypsy concluded a moment later. "We can bring him over to Cornell ourselves!"

"That's fine with me," the cardiothoracic surgeon said. "I don't care who the hell operates on him, as long as somebody does."

Irene groaned and shook her head uncertainly. "He won't make it, I don't think. He'll die in the middle of the street somewhere."

"He's going to die right here otherwise," Gypsy insisted heatedly. "What have we got to lose?"

"Oh, Christ," Irene labored with the Hobson's choice, "I don't know. It's . . . it's insane. I never heard of anything like this."

[278]

"I really don't think that the patient can be moved," the cardiologist objected to them. "He's not nearly stable enough. What's the point of cutting him open anyway?"

The surgeon raised his voice angrily once more. "The point is to save his life! All you damn internists are the same —the only thing you know how to do is sit there and discuss the diagnosis all night. You don't care if the patient drops dead, as long as his goddam electrolytes are in balance!"

Gypsy turned to Irene. "Look," he said with rising frustration, "you're the one that's responsible for Murphy. What are we going to do?"

Irene agonized over the decision. "Jesus . . . I just don't think he'll make it, Gypsy."

"Do you have a better idea? You want to stand around and watch him die?"

"Okay," Irene decided abruptly. "Maybe you're right. Let's try."

Gypsy, Vic, a number of the nurses, and a couple of the other residents got Murphy off the bed and onto a wheeled stretcher that they brought in. Irene and the cardiologist gathered together all the I.V. lines and bottles and hung them on three I.V. poles. Then they started to push the stretcher and everything else into the corridor. The inhalation-therapy technician blocked their path. "Wait a minute," he announced, "you can't take this oxygen tank outside the hospital. You've got to have a portable tank if you want to do that."

"For Christ's sake, get out of the way," Irene said to him.

"You don't understand—it's against the rules. You have to use a portable tank."

Gypsy was flabbergasted at what he was hearing now. "Do you know who my Chief of Service is?" he yelled at the technician. "I swear to God, if you don't stop this shit your ass is going to be fired by tomorrow morning. Move!" The technician stepped aside, reluctantly.

[279]

They ran the stretcher out of the room and down the corridor toward the elevators. All at once the ward's charge nurse appeared, as they passed the nursing station, and tried to intercept them. "Just a second, just a second . . . what kind of nonsense . . ."

"We're transferring Murphy," Gypsy explained impatiently and without slowing their speed at all as they rolled the stretcher past her.

The charge nurse ran after them. "You can't do that! I have to know about any transfer twenty-four hours in advance. Where's the consent form? You haven't even got a signed consent form!"

Gypsy glanced back over his shoulder. "Fuck you," he said as they reached the elevators. "And fuck the consent form, too." After some frantic button-punching, and then some pounding on the doors, they finally succeeded in attracting an elevator. The elevator operator and one of the evening-shift X-ray technicians were engrossed in the Knicks game on a portable radio.

"Don't you bang on them doors," the operator began to lecture them. "Who do you people think you are?" He looked at the stretcher they were pushing into his elevator. "Hold on there," he commanded, "where do you think you're going? This car is for ambulatory patients and wheelchairs. Stretchers gotta go on the other car."

Otto came around from the opposite side of the stretcher without a word, grabbed the elevator operator by the shirt, and threw him off the elevator. Then he yanked the doors closed, slammed the gate shut, and started the car down. "I'll break that guy's ass when we get back there," he muttered.

The X-ray technician spoke up from the rear of the elevator. "You headed for X-Ray?" he demanded. No one answered him.

[280]

Gypsy glared at him contemptuously. "Why don't you go listen to your fucking basketball game?"

"Yeah, well I'll tell you something, smart-ass," the technician replied. "That patient don't look like he can sit up by himself to me. Somebody's gonna have to hold him for every film, or we're not shooting no damn X-rays."

"It's a real pleasure working with you bastards," Gypsy said to him.

They were almost at the ground floor when Murphy Coded. The anesthesiologist, who was poised right next to him, began bagging him immediately; Otto shoved a bunch of people out of the way and climbed up on the stretcher itself to pump Murphy's chest. The elevator doors opened, somebody pulled the gate open, too, and the rest of them rushed the stretcher through the Emergency Room and out into the ambulance dock. There was an ambulance standing there being unloaded as they raced out; the flashing lights hadn't even been turned off yet. Vittorio and Gypsy started to wrestle the stretcher, with Otto on top of it, through the open doors of the ambulance.

"Hey," the ambulance driver shouted, coming back out of the E.R., "what's going on? What are you doing?"

"Quick," Gypsy instructed, "get up front—we've got to take this patient down to Cornell!"

"Oh, no; no way, man. We don't take nobody nowhere. We only bring patients in."

"What?"

"We ain't supposed to take no patients noplace. That's Transport Service."

"My God," Irene pleaded, "stop making a speech. The man is dying—drive the ambulance!" They all began screaming at him.

"What do you think this is, a taxicab or something?" the

[281]

driver answered. "You just climb in and tell me where you want to go? We got rules to follow here."

"Where's MacKinley?" Gypsy yelled. "Where's Mac-Kinley?" The ambulance driver ignored him and reached up and shut the doors on the ambulance. Otto had been shouting for someone to take over the pumping, and Vittorio now returned to the stretcher and began performing the cardiac massage. As soon as he was freed from that crucial job, Otto leaped down off the stretcher and ran over to the ambulance. He wrenched the doors open again. "Come on, let's get him up here!" he cried. "I'll drive the fucking ambulance myself!"

"You get the hell away from there," the ambulance driver threatened him, "or I'm gonna call the guards. You're breaking the rules, you son of a bitch!" He grabbed Otto's arm.

Otto spun around and knocked the ambulance driver's hand off his arm. Then he picked the driver up by his collar, raised him into the air, and hurled him at the ambulance. The driver's face smashed against one of the metal doors, and he slid down to the ground, leaving a bloody streak along the side of the ambulance.

"Jesus, we're losing this guy!" Vittorio suddenly shouted. "His pupils are up!"

They stopped trying to lift the stretcher into the ambulance, and as many people as were able to crowd around Murphy joined the interns already working frenziedly over him. More doctors and nurses came running out of the E.R. to help. Everyone was shouting and cursing.

"God help him," Gypsy breathed softly. The whole scene —garishly lit by the flashing red lights of the ambulance— seemed unreal. It looked like something out of Dante. Gypsy stared at the blood now dripping down the side of the ambulance. He stepped over the motionless driver, and then turned away from all of it and walked across the courtyard. He went through the ambulance entrance, past the driveway, and out into the street. He walked slowly along Lexington Avenue and kept on going as far as Seventy-first Street. Finally he got on a bus and rode the rest of the way home. As soon as he was inside the apartment, he put his pajamas on, went to bed, and stayed there.

His phone rang about ten o'clock the next morning. It was Irene.

"Hello, Irene. . . . I'm sorry I left you like that last night," he said quietly. "That was a rotten thing for me to do."

"Never mind, Gypsy, it's okay. We had plenty of help. There were more people there than we knew what to do with. How are you feeling?"

"I'm all right. Did Murphy die?"

There was a pause. "Yes."

"I figured."

"Gypsy, that couldn't be helped. Sometimes patients with thrombophlebitis throw an embolus. You know that. It just happens; it's no one's fault."

Gypsy didn't say anything. "Uh, look," Irene asked him, "are you coming to work today?"

He sighed. "I don't think so, Irene. I think maybe I've had it. I'm sorry."

"Okay, Gypsy. I tell you what, why don't you take the day off? I'll talk to you tomorrow. Go listen to some of that trashy music—go to a concert or something."

"Sure," Gypsy said. He hung up.

Gypsy stayed in bed the rest of the day; he didn't even feel like eating anything. Late in the afternoon, though, he got dressed and went outside. He walked over to the river, and watched it turn dark as the sun started to go down. The last things that remained bathed in sunlight were the spires at the top of the Fifty-ninth Street Bridge. Gypsy knew that he had a decision to make, and he just didn't want to make it. He walked home and went back to bed, feeling completely drained.

Early the following morning his telephone started ringing. Gypsy ignored it, but every ten minutes it rang again. He waited for one of the barrages to stop, and then took the receiver off the hook. He switched on his stereo—and listened to both sides of every Rolling Stones record he had. Loud. And came to a decision.

He began collecting his white uniforms. He made a big pile of them all in the middle of the floor and carried the pile out to the hallway. Then he stuffed his whites, one by one, into the incinerator. When the last bloodstained jacket had vanished, he returned to his apartment, lowered the stereo, and got back into bed.

At three o'clock, when his doorbell rang, Gypsy was still in bed. He bided his time, pretending he didn't hear the bell, but it continued to ring. Eventually he climbed out of bed and opened the door, and Vittorio walked in.

"Hello, Vic. How are you?"

"How am I? I'm fine." Vittorio glanced at Gypsy's pajamas. "What the hell are you doing in bed at this hour?"

Gypsy shrugged. "I like it there."

"Are you stoned?"

"No," Gypsy replied. "Are you?"

"We're not talking about me, God damn it. Irene said you didn't come to work again today."

Gypsy nodded.

"Well, what kind of behavior is that? What are you trying to do?"

"Vittorio, I retired from medicine this morning. I quit."

"Crap," Vittorio scoffed. "You don't have to quit; the year's almost over. Two more lousy months and we won't ever have to look at that dump again."

"Vic, did you accomplish anything worthwhile this year?"

"Nah. Who accomplishes anything during their internship? Do you know what I'm going to do?"

"No," Gypsy answered. "What?"

"Dermatology. I want to make some money before we get socialized. A few years of residency and I'm set. What are you going into when the year's over?"

"The year is over. For me, anyhow."

"Don't be ridiculous, Gypsy. Don't you want to be successful?"

"I guess so, yeah," Gypsy said distantly. "At least I'd like to be able to pay off my loans."

"Well, that won't be a problem at all, once you get a nice practice going. Besides, you can move to the suburbs somewhere—there's regular patients out there. Without lice or anything." Vic laughed. "These bums'll kill you here."

"Vic, Vic, this is killing me. Medicine; the hospital. I've got to quit."

Vittorio gave him a funny look. "My God, you're serious, aren't you?"

Gypsy nodded again.

"That's crazy," Vittorio told him. "That's just crazy. What about all the time you put in? All those years! Gypsy, you ought to think about this, before you do something stupid."

Gypsy shook his head. "I thought about it already. I'm through."

"I don't understand you," Vittorio said, exasperated. "I mean, you're not going to win the Nobel prize, but you like people. Some of those bums back there really love you."

"I know, Vic, I know. I can't help it; I just can't take this any more. I got no stomach for suffering, Vic. I never did."

"Well, Christ, what are you going to do, join a band? Sell cars?"

Gypsy was silent.

"Listen, for God's sake, do you realize what you're throwing away? You spent two-thirds of your life in school al-

[285]

ready so you could get this far. Gypsy, June thirtieth! A couple of more goddam months! All you have to do is last out the year."

"Vic, I don't want to last out the year. That's not why I went into medicine, to last things out."

"Jesus Christ!" Vittorio exclaimed in frustration. "Well, how about all the bums, then? Who's going to worry about them? The guys like me sure won't. If you don't want to make any money, you can go work in a clinic someplace."

"That's the only part of it I feel bad about," Gypsy said sadly. "I feel like I'm abandoning the patients."

"Right, definitely, you're abandoning the bums. You're screwing them and yourself."

"Vittorio . . . all I did this year was watch people die. Old people, young people, it didn't matter. If they didn't die of congestive heart failure, they died of emphysema. And if they didn't die of emphysema they died of meningitis. And if they didn't die of that they died of cancer. Or if they had a nice, benign disease like thrombophlebitis they got a pulmonary embolism and died. Or if there was nothing wrong with them at all they overdosed and died. And if they weren't able to kill themselves, then they went out and murdered some poor old lady who hadn't died of any of the other things yet. And you know what I did when I wasn't watching people die? I watched people get destroyed inside while I told them their kid was dead, and could I please have permission for an autopsy. I can't handle it, Vic. I tried all year."

Vittorio did not speak for several minutes. "Gypsy," he said finally, "this is a job, to make a living at. It's a decent, honorable profession, that's all. You have to learn to separate your feelings from your work. Your feelings are for when you go home—they aren't for the hospital. That's your trouble."

[286]

"No, Vic. It's the way I am. I want to stay that way, too. I don't want to learn to be any different. And if I don't get out of that place, I might learn. Your feelings, your feelings are why you're a human being."

Gypsy's face brightened then. He picked up his jeans and started to get dressed. "Vittorio, I've got a wonderful idea. I'm going down the block to buy some hamburgers, and after that I'm going straight over to Central Park to watch the seals."

"The what? The seals?"

"Sure. You want to come too?"

"Seals? I have to go back to work. What are you talking about, anyway?"

"This is better than work, Vic. I'll see you around."

Vittorio Mazzoli retraced his steps to California at the end of the year, to be a dermatology resident. Kid Otto became an orthopedic surgeon.

Gypsy listened to records and hung out in Central Park for three weeks. Then he showed up on Male Medicine in his jeans, said hello to Irene, and returned to his patients.